DEAD BAIT 4

EDITED BY
CAMERON PIERCE

SEVERED PRESS
HOBART TASMANIA

DEAD BAIT 4

Copyright © 2017 Severed Press

WWW.SEVEREDPRESS.COM

This novel is a work of fiction. Names,
characters, places and incidents are the product of
the author's imagination, or are used fictitiously.
Any resemblance to actual events, locales or persons,
living or dead, is purely coincidental.

ISBN: 978-1-925711-41-7

TABLE OF CONTENTS

THE THIEF WHO MARRIED THE SEA

CS Nelson

"Rules are there for a reason. Even if they don't make sense, even if you don't agree with none of them and they don't seem fair, they're there for a reason. So you just mind the rules and no one gets hurt."

Those words destroyed your world when you were twelve, when the man who raised you said them after taking away your four-pronged gig and telling you, "No fishing in November," without any further explanation. "Never more than five; never, ever no females," he said. Then, "Throw 'em back, boy." You wept and released your catch beneath the dark water. Those were the rules.

We don't flounder with four-pronged gigs.

We don't flounder in November.

We never take more than five and never, ever, under any circumstances, do we take females.

The blanched face, the white knuckles and busy hands; the rheumy eyes long yellowed from too much Wild Turkey and Lone Star beer. Fingers stained equally sallow from a never ending chain of Bugler cigarettes. This was the man who raised you, and this was the only time you saw him afraid. Of the water. Of what lurked beneath the murk of waves slapping the beach that night. The night you struck off on your own a week into November. When the sand beneath the waves is more flounder than ray, great beds of fish gazing up at the moon in clusters so close you can't help but stab at least twice your limit in a night.

Matagorda Island offers the best flounder fishing in the world, according to the Texas Parks and Wildlife Department handbook. The Texas Gulf, it says, supports a wide variety of flat fish, easily caught by three-pronged gigging trident or in angler fashion, making the southern flounder and less common gulf flounder a well sought after prize for avid fishermen. However, the TPWD handbook goes on to caution, "…there are in place stringent rules for the sports fisherman to adhere by." It then spells out those three rules that broke your heart when you were a child and later, would come to haunt you as an adult.

"It's not the flounder you need watch for, boy," he said, on a more relaxed evening, before the night you tried to steal from the Sea.

1

It was your first time out and the man who raised you, he was hell-bent and maybe a little beer-drunk, but vibrated with this energy you'd never felt before. You followed along in the dark, the cool gulf air blowing across your bare chest, salt and silt and sour hops on the breeze, peach fuzz singed from the Coleman lantern despite your homemade heat shield of foil and driftwood. He waded ten feet apart from you. Water, only up to his knees, licked at your waist and maybe it was just a little scary, but by night's end and moondown you'd have your first string of fish.

"It's not the flounder at all," he said again in that rumbly whisper, his fishing voice. "It's the stingarees you gotta mind, boy. They get you, and you wanna see a grown man cry?" He eyed you over his shoulder with a sly grin.

"Nosir."

"Hn. That's good. Me neither."

Then he laughed. So you laughed too, same as him, in that low and rumbly whisper.

"Sst!" He stopped dead still and motioned you with two fingers above his head, barely visible in the lantern's umbra, then waving the same hand in downward flutters to beckon you carefully through the dark water. "You wanna shuffle your feet slow, so as to not step on no rays, but you also wanna mind stirring up sand. It spooks the fish."

"Yessir."

You pulled up beside him and the look in his eyes scared you some. A predatory sharpness that had never been there in all of the years he'd raised you. But it was there in that moment.

He nodded ahead, just inside the gaslight nimbus. A sandy oval with two beads shining up at you rested right there in the swath of light, distorting in waves from the rolling tide. The water heaved and dipped, like a dark, breathing giant.

That brown oval of eyes and scale was the most beautiful thing you'd ever seen until the man who raised you thrust his gig upon it, piercing. Stabbing. Impaling. A violent cloud obscured all. He bent low and slipped his hand beneath the catch, trapping it onto his three prongs as he lifted the jerking fish topside.

"Go ahead, boy. String her up."

Through the gills and out the mouth. The next one was yours. By morning you would be beat tired and salt sticky, but your soul would be full from your first night out. Five big ones, each way over the regulation 14-inch maximum, the length of your middle fingertip to the crook of your elbow. Gutted and cleaned right there at the bank as the sun, too shy to yet rise, spread his day blood through the clouds in pinks and bruised purples.

Every night taking what the Sea granted. Every morning packing fish to sell before bedding down. You lived a life of happiness only the Sea could give.

***

"Boy, you got to watch the clouds some."

"Yessir."

"Fish cain't see you when the clouds are right, but by full moon," the man who raised you said, "they see us. Oh you betcha, they see us alright. And we see them."

"And then we lose 'em?" You asked this, then a spry fifteen years and doing well with just the two of you and the Sea. Never a day wasted in school; no time spent working anything other than the shore for the catch. Sleep till sundown and fish till rise.

The man who raised you, he got a look when you said that, though. Much opposite the look he gave when you first saw him gig a fish. No, this was a look you had never encountered, lest imagined in such a powerful and confident figure as the man. He was worried at your thinking.

"No, boy," he said softly. "You don't want them to see you because it ain't *right*."

Silence passed between you, heavy like a weighted net.

Then, "Boy, you must understand. What it is we do, with all this," he waved a hand across the dark water, "with the catch She gives us, it's a blessing to us but a sacrifice from Her."

"Yessir."

"Never take Her for granted. Never take more from Her than what She offers." The next part he said with a distant stare, a sad, lonesome look: "She's a harsh mistress."

You never asked what that meant.

***

"Sir, we understand this child has not yet registered with the Matagorda Independent School District?" The lady who asked was a busybody in a fancy pants suit. Coffee colored jacket and khaki slacks. She dressed like the kind of candy only adults eat on account it tastes like shit and is full of liquor. "I will be back tomorrow with the proper admin—and constable if need be—so we can get this young man in school. I'm afraid it's the law, sir."

3

"Law of the land, ma'am. Not the Sea."

"It's still the law." She turned a shade of cherry to top her nasty candy suit, then spun in a huff, mouthing off about how she would be back, and rest assured, and people like us need to realize where we live.

The man who raised you also taught you to be on the lookout for her ilk.

"They're everywhere, boy. Mind who you talk to and what you say."

"Yessir."

This said not long after that visit from the busybody woman, her still making her way across the long bridge to the shore. At night of course, in the month of October when the fish clustered in ripe beds. A few weeks before the man who raised you would fall upon a nest of stingarees.

"Mind who you talk to and what about, but also mind what folks see. Do you know what they see when they look at you?"

"Nosir."

"They see a young man who ain't never had traditional schooling."

"Yessir."

"But they also see a young man who holds hisself well. And one who can read and write and haggle with the rest."

"Yessir." Because he taught you these things in order to keep you out of their system and in the water where you belong.

"You're a good boy, boy."

"Yessir."

Your growing chest blossomed with pride at that. Rarely was a compliment forthcoming. This would be one of those rare—and last—occasions.

"Now mind that one there, boy. It's a good size to keep, but look at the underbelly. Feel it?"

You slumped some but ran your hand across the smooth slime of the underbelly, palpating until you hit the knobbies. A girl fish.

You looked up at him with pleading eyes, but despite the sympathy you found there, his own eyes testified to what you already knew.

"We gotta follow the rules. She's female. And your Mother takes care of her own."

"Yessir." You released and the great fluke swam away free, her three puncture wounds trailing momentary ribbons of blood barely visible by lantern.

"A good boy."

In that moment, a dark wave the likes you'd never seen before reared back to the west where the bridge touched the island to Matagorda County mainland. You stopped together to lean on your gigs and admire the

4

beauty, the rolling dark of Her great wall eclipsing the far city lights, faint luminescence of Her building foam; the rage of her final crash before settling to sleep. A car horn pierced the night briefly then sputtered to silence.

"Truly. A harsh mistress."

The man who raised you said nothing else about the rare incident and no more such waves were forthcoming, but you would always be reminded, with love, of his final act that night, cupping a handful of seawater to his mouth and kissing it before murmuring a warm "thank you," and letting it spill back to the murk.

The busybody woman who aimed to have you in public school never made it to the mainland.

***

The Atlantic stingray, according to the TPWD handbook, is the most common ray found along the shallows in and around Matagorda Island. However, it goes on to say, in recent years there have been rare occurrences of the alien, round-bodied Indo-Pacific stingaree which prefers the same hunting grounds as Atlantic breeds. The TPWD handbook cautions the angler and spear fisherman alike to shuffle their feet whilst wading in order to avoid stepping on the normally docile creatures, lest they incur a most painful sting from the razor sharp barb, a cartilaginous protrusion capable of delivering a highly toxic venom. In some circumstances, the barb may break off from the ray and continue to envenom the hapless fisherman even after the initial sting. According to the TPWD handbook, little is known of the uncommon stingaree, except despite being a smaller specimen when compared to the Atlantic stingray, much larger rays have been reported during the forbidden spawning period lasting between November and early December.

The man who raised you would live long enough to caution you about the rules before missing his own good guidance and snagging twice his limit, one a female, then falling to the bone sting of a lying ray whilst gigging solitary one October night. He would forget to tell you the why of the rules before crying as a grown man, before faltering in his step and falling into a much bigger stingaree, one who would pierce him just beneath the xyphoid process and dump squirt after deadly squirt of venom into his abdominal cavity, arresting his heart.

He suffered a moment of blindness in the face of bounty: He chose to steal from the Sea. Of course, the Wild Turkey and Lone Star and Buglers had some to do with it, but what good Texas doctor would ever admit to such unpatriotic heresy out loud?

"Harsh mistress, indeed," the man who raised you would have said.

So there you were, at sixteen with hair grown in funny places and hormones starting to swell with the moon cycle, on your own. Alone. Is it right to blame a man for not having a proper indoctrination into the world? Doesn't seem so. But you were a good boy. A careful boy. You heeded the man who raised you and all of his good wisdom, and you made your own way in the fish trade.

It wasn't until your twenty-fifth spawning season that the loneliness took its hold on you. You cried out to the Sea one evening, to the ocean who had blessed you with such rich harvest for so many years, the Mother who kept you company through all of those long nights.

"I need more." Your tears slipped into Her depths and the water receded until fields of sand and fish lay before you. In the distance, a great wall of water climbed high as it rushed toward the bridge, overtaking it and a single figure dangling from the railing. It receded back to you with a delicate package.

Lifeless, with dark hair spread around her like tendrils of creatures from deeper fathoms, a young woman floated upon the backfill of the second great wave of your lifetime. She crested and coursed directly toward you until she lay in your arms, black hair the color of deep night, skin fair as the moon. Her chest did not move and no air slipped past her full lips. You knew from the man who raised you about drowning, had witnessed him rescue a fallen child once. Back on shore, you locked your lips onto hers and breathed life into her flooded lungs.

She coughed and gagged a spout of swill, drawing ragged breath before crying out, then just crying, sobbing against your chest.

Her name was Naomi and she had come to die. Mother took her first. For you.

You shared everything you knew of the ocean with Naomi. She accepted you as her lover and took your knowledge of the world beyond anything the man who raised you had ever hinted at. You became one. In her alluring green eyes rolled waves of a different ocean. A place of warmth and beautiful mystery.

Months passed with a new magic for each. Winter was the best, with a day set aside for giving love, and a day set aside for giving thanks, and a day set aside for giving unconditionally. Summer became a season of laughter and frolic and play. Nights, you fished while Naomi sang from the shore. Early mornings were for love and entwined slumber.

Naomi accepted life with you, but time soon grew heavy upon her and she longed for more. Naomi wanted a child.

She asked of your mother and you had no answers.

"I come from the Sea."

It was not enough. She laughed and taunted you playfully. Inviting you into her.

You agreed, but only under the right conditions. It must be during the month of November.

"Okay," she said, large eyes betraying her excitement, her grin an open-mouthed and anxious one.

And it must be within the embrace of the water, at the warmest spot near the shoals.

"The fish? I love it." She snuggled close against your chest and stared up into your face, eyes capturing your soul. "We're gonna have a baby."

You agreed and took her to the warm spot, the only other night you had gone out during the forbidden month of November; the only time you had ever gone out without a gig or stringer. You both waded, hand in hand, naked into the Sea.

Naomi pulled you close in the moonlight. She climbed you, your manhood stiff and swollen, her naked breasts soft against you, and took you inside of her. The waters rose and a gale picked up, but there amidst the spawning flounder, you and Naomi created life within the womb of the Sea.

***

"When the flounder spawns, boy," the man who raised you said, "she lays her eggs."

"Yessir."

"But the ray? No, she don't lay no eggs. She gives live birth. Sometimes a dozen, but stingarees bring their young into the world same as us. From life to life. No egg to break."

"Yessir."

"Always remember that, boy. It's the difference between us and them."

You gave him a quizzical look, because you weren't exactly certain what he meant by that last.

"We're of the nature which comes from the womb. That's why She gives us the fish. We are over them as they are beneath us. One born of a womb, the other a shell. And the rays? Like us, they are the guardians of the Sea. Just as we are all Her children."

"Yessir."

This sat well with you. You never had reason to ask about a mother figure, for you knew all along who your Mother was.

***

The baby came during summer's end, just as the beaches emptied of the mainlanders and dirty trollers chased the currents to richer waters. Naomi followed you to the shoals once more, her big round belly glowing white and full in the night. Fish trailed her, as if she leaked cut bait, but you knew it was but your brothers and sisters of the Sea paying homage.

Naomi smiled, a smile holding back agony, and you squeezed her fingers to give reassurance.

"Oh, this is it." A sharp intake of breath told you the contraction was a big one. "Are you sure this is safe?"

Squeezing her hand again, you took her in your arms and balanced her at the surface.

Naomi screamed. A giant shape rose behind you, water falling from majestic wings, tail stirring the tide, but you dared not look. You calmly, with much composure, talked her through the birth, breathing with her, consoling her, soothing as she screamed and the great beast continued to loom.

When her final push came and your baby girl was born unto the Sea, you smiled down upon your beloved and kissed her once before your gig pierced her heart four times and she settled to the sand.

***

"We have these rules for a reason, sweetheart."

"Why, Daddy?"

"Because we do. We have to follow them or Mommy won't let us have fish anymore."

"Ohhh." Her beatific face squinches as she navigates the possibilities before settling on, "Then we'd have to eat mainlander food?"

"We would, sweetheart."

"Gross."

You laugh and she giggles, slipping her tiny hand into yours. The two of you wade out to the moon, gigs lazy, lanterns blazing at a field of flounder before you.

She never asks about Naomi and only knows that her Mother, your Mother, will always provide.

She is sixteen when the Sea finally calls you back to Her bosom. Unlike the man who raised you, you step willingly into the wings of the great stingaree, savoring the pierce of release as Her venom floods your abdominal cavity, Her syrupy embrace pulling you silently down, carrying you home.

8

THE MOST PAINFUL COMPANION

Meghan Arcuri

Do you really think a woman your age should be wearing a skirt like that?

I don't know how your husband puts up with all that nagging you do.

You probably shouldn't have said that to your son. He's so fragile, you know.

These are the words my mother says to me.

Okay. They're not the only words she says. And not all the time.

But it feels like that, even after thirty-five years.

I'm supposed to be over this stuff by now, too distracted by my own life to care. But parental guilt's not like that, is it? It burrows into your consciousness, spreads its seeds and grows, grows, grows.

Not that she did an entirely bad job. I'm still here, right? I did well in school, have good friends, a good family. The job? Well … I gave up my career in finance to be a stay-at-home mom. But people say raising kids is a full-time job and I've gotta say, I don't know if they're giving me a line of bullshit, but I totally agree.

So I don't have a medical degree like my perfect brother and his beautiful wife, as my mother always points out. But I do have my master's. Doesn't that count for something?

Not when you've relinquished that master's for diapers and doodling all day.

Maybe she's right.

Whatever.

"You're going on another vacation?"

Treading in the aquamarine water, I strap on my mask, last week's conversation with my mother echoing in my mind. The bright sun rises in the clear sky.

"Yes, Mom."

"Didn't you just get back from Florida?"

I strap on my flippers. The treading just got easier.

"If five months ago qualifies as 'just getting back,' then yes."

"Why do you have to get so defensive?"

I put the snorkel's mouthpiece in and bite down just a little too hard.

"I'm not getting defensive."
"It's in your tone ... anyway, where are you going?"
I take a deep breath.
"Hawaii."
"Hawaii?? Again? Must be nice."
I dive into the cool, refreshing water.
Yes. It's really nice.
I go down.
Down.
Down.
Down.
The water caresses my body, soothes it, hugs it like a second skin. Whatever's happened to me in my life, whatever issues I've dealt with, the water has always given me peace. I feel at home here. Almost more at home than I do anywhere else.
Whose fault is that?
Jesus.
At first I see nothing but lava rock covered in coral. After I move a little closer—and shake off my mother's words—the fish come into focus.
Mostly parrotfish at first, then one of my favorites swims by: *humuhumunukunukuapua'a.*
It's Hawaiian for "trigger fish with a blunt snout like a pig's."
It's a fairly accurate description and, honestly, if it were anywhere else in the world, I'd probably find it ugly. But this is Maui; everything's beautiful in Maui.
That's if you're lucky enough to be asked to go to Maui.
I grunt and shake my head. Why can I not escape her words? Snorkeling or a quick swim usually does the trick.
I come up for air.
Makena Landing is not far behind me, but what's in front of me takes my breath away every time I see it: West Maui rises to my right; the island of Lana'i is in front of me, distant and cloud-capped; and the red-spotted island of Kaho'olawe is to my left. All against the backdrop of the clear, blue sky. The sun hovers above, the palm trees and flora in my periphery dance in the wind. It is tribal, ancient-feeling. This vista transports me to the past, making me long for the time of outrigger canoes, grass skirts, and fresh lava from Haleakala.
I've never seen a volcano.
I inhale and submerge myself, heading toward my ultimate destination, Five Caves, with all of its colorful fish and green sea turtles.

The locals don't recommend snorkeling here, as it's a little too deep for the average snorkeler. I've been doing this for a while, though, so I'm not worried.

I swim through a school of yellow tang, the yellow almost too bright to be found in nature.

As I approach the first cave, something moves below me.

Was that a shimmer?

I swim toward it, but I only see water, cut by a ray of sunlight.

Pretty.

... for those of us that are lucky enough to see it. Don't you think I might like to snorkel in Hawaii? See that rainbow of fish *you always talk about? Share that experience with my grandson and my daughter and her husband? I don't move around as well as I used to, but that doesn't mean I wouldn't like to try. But you've already dismissed me as too old, too weak, too useless. I did everything for you. And this is how I'm thanked for all those meals I made and practices I drove you to? I thought my daughter would treat me better, but I guess I was wrong. You would think we would spend more time together what with you being a stay-at-home-mother. What is it, exactly, you do with all of your time, anyway?*

The water pushes me down, heavy on my limbs. My heart throbs. My lungs burn.

An amorphous, purple cloud floats beneath me, the purple so dark it's almost black. It swirls around and around and around. It's haunting, hypnotic. Is it moving toward me?

I kick, kick, kick.

Up.

Up.

Up.

I rip off the mask and gasp for air. I inhale some water and cough. When my throat clears, I float on my back and take a few deep breaths.

What the hell just happened?

Was that her voice? Mine? Sometimes I can't tell where her thoughts end and mine begin.

I put the mask over my eyes and stick my face back in: no dark cloud.

What was that thing? It looked like octopus ink. I've heard people talk about the octopuses around here, but I've never seen one.

Before I can figure it out, a head pops out of the water, about a foot away from mine.

A greenish-brownish head, with sweet black eyes and a wrinkly mouth.

A turtle. A huge one.

I don't know why I'm so surprised. This area is affectionately referred to as Turtle Town.

I fumble to put my mask back on as the majestic creature disappears under the surface.

I get my gear set and put my face in the water. Fortunately, the turtle is still close to me. I still see no sign of that inky patch, though. Or an octopus.

I follow the big guy for a while. He moves with a leisurely grace, so at ease and content in the water. And it is a *he*: male turtles have bigger tails. Apparently size does matter.

When he swims deeper, I try to follow him, but my lungs are too tired from my earlier episode.

I come up for air again.

"Hi, Mommy!!"

The voice is distant, but familiar.

I smile as my husband and son paddle over to me on their kayak.

Well, my husband is paddling. My son isn't even holding his paddle, smiling and waving at me instead.

I wave back.

"Hey, Zach! Hey, Derek."

"Did you see any turtles, Mommy?" Zach says.

"I just saw one."

His eyes grow wide. He starts to bounce. "Where? Where?"

I point to the spot where I was just swimming. "He was right over there a minute ago."

Zach leans over the side of the kayak, shielding his eyes from the sun.

"Where??"

The kayak rocks a bit.

"Careful, kiddo," Derek says, grabbing the sides.

"But I wanna see the turtle."

"He dove down pretty deep before I came up, buddy," I say.

A small whine.

"Did he go into one of the caves?" he says.

"Probably."

"Did you go into one of the caves?"

"I didn't make it this time."

Another whine. He likes to hear about my exploits. But not go on them himself.

"Really?" my husband says. "Everything okay, Kate?"

12

We discovered Five Caves the last time we were here. He knows how much I like it. How I like to challenge myself by trying to swim to each cave.

I hesitate but say nothing about the episode. My husband would be annoyed to know that one of my mother's guilt trips ruined a swim for me.

"Everything's great. You want to swim for a little bit with me, Zach?"

My son scans the water again, a worried look on his face.

"No."

I sigh. "Okay."

His face drops.

Okay. A two syllable—sometimes two-lettered—word. So small, so simple. But the tone can make it so powerful.

I could have ended it on an up, letting him know everything was all right. But I ended on the down, letting my disappointment—with a side of guilt—seep into it.

Why do I do this? Why don't I let it go? This is the small stuff, and I'm sweating it. Giving him guilt over a short swim in the ocean, just because I'm worried he doesn't like the water as much as I do. Just because he isn't a strong swimmer, and I don't want him to feel badly when he's with other kids who can do neat tricks. Why do I always have to turn everything into a teaching moment? Because it always seems like the only thing I'm succeeding at is making him feel bad.

I'm such a jerk.

"I'm sorry, Mommy." His eyes are big, his face is sad.

I grab his leg and squeeze. I give him the warmest smile I can muster. "No worries, buddy. Maybe I can hop a ride with you guys."

His face brightens. "You can sit here!"

He moves from the front seat to the spot in the middle that's not quite a seat, but is perfect for a six-year-old heinie.

"Thanks, baby."

I climb onto the kayak and put my gear in a net bag.

"Here, Mommy." He hands me the paddle.

I kiss his sweet face. "Thanks, bud."

We paddle back to shore.

***

The next morning, I return to Five Caves. Before I reach the caves, I dive down a few times to see who else is awake. Maybe I'll see that octopus.

The sunny skies give the water a sparkling clarity. The coral is lumpy and bumpy and dotted with red, spiky sea urchins. I don't know what they're called—something to do with a pencil.

The fish nibble at their breakfast, different types sticking together but often intermingling with other breeds.

Their movement is simple but enchanting. Effortless. As we are not too far from shore, the tide pulls us back and forth, back and forth. This never seems to bother the fish. As they nibble, the tide pulls them away from their food, then pushes them back, pulls and pushes, over and over. Eventually they're attracted to a new spot, a new nibble, all the while the water pushing and pulling. And the fish go with it. They don't struggle. They don't care about the interruption. They simply accept their fate, moving with the water instead of against it.

I wish I could be more like that.

But for now, I enjoy watching them.

Of course, it'd be more fun if my son would come with me.

Maybe if he wasn't so afraid of the water, he would.

I dismiss her words and come up for air, Five Caves a few yards away.

My mask is fogging up, so I take it off and spit in it, spreading the saliva around with my finger. Derek was so grossed out the first time I did that, but in the absence of dishwashing soap, saliva helps keep the fogginess away.

I put the mask back on and dive toward the caves.

I dolphin kick my way down.

Down.

Down.

Down.

One of the mouths of the caves is in front of me. I wonder if any turtles are hiding in here today.

Another shimmer beneath me.

I assume it's a ray of sun, like yesterday, but as I swim toward it, a bead of my saliva drips down the inside of my mask. Gross. But I'm not going back up to rinse it. I want to see the turtles.

It'd be nice if Zach could swim well enough to see the turtles. Maybe you should spend more time with him, teaching him how to swim, making him less afraid. He says you always disappear when Derek is home. Getting some of that precious me time, I guess. Don't you think your husband and son might like it when you're all together? If you got a real job, you'd probably appreciate your family more. You'd value your time with Zach. Because if you haven't noticed, he loves being with you. Playing and reading with you. He even sings with you because he knows it

14

makes you happy. He just wants to make you happy, but every time I'm there, you always seem to be yelling and criticizing.

My limbs are leaden; my muscles ache. Her words—my words?—weigh heavily on me. The water weighs heavily on me. My heart pounds, my lungs beg for air. But I do not move.

Once again, a cloud swirls underneath me, thicker and darker than before. Closer to me than last time. I try to find the octopus, but I see nothing but the dark fog. A smoky arm extends toward me.

Then a turtle swims through the cloud, and it dissipates. As he glides in front of me, I snap out of my trance. He swims to the surface. I follow him.

Up.

Up.

Up.

I reach the top, shoving the mask to my forehead. Tears mix with the water streaming down my cheeks. I struggle to keep my face above the surface, my jagged breaths tempting the water to enter my open mouth. I flutter kick, harder and harder, relieved my limbs have returned to normal.

I've swum competitively since I was six. I've been snorkeling since I was ten. Nothing like this has ever happened to me before: the inky cloud, the voices ... none of it.

Is it the water?

Is it me? Am I going crazy?

My foot nudges something. I jerk back.

God, I hope it's not an octopus.

A turtle pokes its head out for a quick breath then submerges again.

I don't even feel like following it this time.

I feel like having a mai tai.

***

The waiter places mai tais in front of Derek and me, and a virgin lava flow in front of Zach.

I waste no time in taking a sip, the tangy sweetness cascading down my throat.

"Been a long morning already, eh?" the waiter says.

His deep, sun-tanned skin, dark, dark hair, and tribal tattoos running up and down his arms make him seem like a native Hawaiian. That and his accent: lilting and easy, it sounds like a variant of California surfer dude.

"My mommy likes snorkeling."

"What's up, little cousin?" He holds his fist out to my son, who immediately bumps it. To me, the waiter says, "Where'd you go?"

"Five Caves."

"Oh, yah." He nods his head slowly, his expression more serious. "Five Graves."

Wait. Did he just say *graves*, with a G?

"I thought it was *caves*, with a C, as in Charlie," I say.

"Oh, sure. It is. But it's also called Five Graves, with a G, as in don't go there."

Is he serious? First of all "Don't go there" technically starts with a D. Second of all … graves? Don't go?

"Really?" Derek says, his expression half smile, half *is this guy for real?*

The waiter laughs.

"I'm just kiddin', brah. You can totally go there."

"But is it really called Five Graves?" I say.

"Yah. But that's just because there are, literally, five graves on the way to the water. Haven't you seen them?"

"No. I usually swim out from a little beach near Makena Landing. Are they near there?"

"Yeah. But if you're swimming out from the beach, you might miss them."

"Who's buried there?" my husband says.

"Not sure. Just some ancients, I think. Local legend says they sometimes haunt the caves. Prey on people's weaknesses, or something,"

"Haunted?" Zach says. "Like ghosts?" His eyes are huge.

"Oh, no worries, my man," the waiter says, smiling and ruffling Zach's hair. "People say stuff like that to mess with the tourists. There's no such thing as ghosts. And even if there were, the *honu*—the turtles— are big and tough. They'd keep them away."

"But there aren't any ghosts, right?"

"No ghosts, buddy."

"Phew!" Zach relaxes into his seat and takes a big sip of his lava flow.

"You want something to eat with that?" the waiter says, pulling out his notepad.

We order our food.

I hope Zach doesn't get nightmares tonight.

***

16

On the way back to the resort, my phone vibrates. It's a text from my mother.

The beginning of it reads, "It's dad. Your mother …"

My father? The king of the Luddites?

I unlock the phone to finish reading the message.

"… is in the hospital. Call me."

My mother is prone to huge bouts of hypochondria, so we've been down this road before. My dad, although he'd never say it, knows how ridiculous she is about this stuff. But he's never used her phone to text me before. Not to mention the time difference. They're in Connecticut; it's only about seven in the morning in Connecticut. Is it worse than usual?

Shit.

"Something wrong?" my husband says.

"I don't know." I tell him about the text as I call my dad.

He answers on the fourth ring, awkward and grumbling.

"… damned phone. Hello? Katie? Is that you?"

"Yes, Dad. Yes. It's me. What's the matter with mom now?" I don't know why I add the word *now* to my question. It changes the tenor of the whole thing. And it's kind of mean, isn't it? I guess I'm hoping it's just another one of her over-exaggerated sinus infections.

"Katie." His tone in that one word tells me it's not. "She fell. Head first, down the stairs. I saw the whole thing, Kate. The whole, damn thing, and I couldn't do anything about it."

His voice wavers. It's low, weak. Nothing like the voice of the man I usually speak with.

My heart thuds in my chest.

"Is she okay?"

"No, sweetie. No. She's in a coma."

The shock of his statement arrests all of my senses. In that second, nothing seems real. The only thing I can say is, "What?"

"She's in a coma. They did a scan on her brain, and they see a lot of blood. They don't think she has much longer."

My hands shake. My stomach churns.

"Pull over," I say to Derek.

"What?"

"Pull. Over."

He finds a spot and stops the car.

"What's the matter, Mommy?"

I take off my seatbelt, open my door, and retch everywhere.

"Oh, my god, Kate," Derek says.

"Mommy?!"

I find a tissue in my purse and wipe my mouth. Derek rubs my back, worry all over his face. I hold up a finger to him and put the phone back to my ear.

"Katie? Kate? Are you okay?"

"Sorry, Dad. I'm here. How much longer do they think she has?"

"They don't know. But I really think you should come home as fast as you can."

I nod my head. Up and down, up and down, up and down.

"Katie?"

"Yeah. Yes, Dad. We're heading back to the resort now. We'll book our tickets as fast as we can. Are you okay?"

It's a stupid question, but I want him to know I'm thinking of him, too.

"I'll be better when you get here."

"Okay. I'll call when I have all the information."

"Love you, sweetie."

"Love you, too."

I hang up the phone and put it in my bag. I inhale. My stomach is still not right, but I think I'm past vomiting.

Then I tell my husband everything. I hate that my son has to hear it all, too. I usually shield him from the uglier aspects of the world, but I can't avoid this one.

He starts to cry.

I don't. I sit and I stare out the side window. The palm trees and vibrant flowers zip by. My stomach gurgles, chiding me for drinking that mai tai.

My son is still crying. Derek tries to soothe and calm, but I offer Zach no comfort.

I think I'm in too much shock.

My mother and I always butt heads. We are the classic oil and water. She says something, pushes my buttons, and when I react to it—as I always do—she plays innocent. For the longest time, I'd wondered if it were just me. Early on in our relationship, however, my husband saw it and said, no, indeed, it wasn't. And even though he, and my friends, and my therapist have told me how crazy she is, how tough she is on me— which had felt so good, so affirming at the time—now I'm wondering if any of it was really that bad.

I mean, I never wished her dead. Other than that one time in third grade. But I immediately regretted it and felt guilty about it for a week and never let the thought enter my mind again.

I would never wish this fate on anyone.

Would I?

"You should have some water," Derek says.

I nod. Up and down, up and down, up and down. I reach into my bag and grab my water bottle. I try to open it, but it's not working.

My husband puts his hand on my arm. "Kate. That's your glasses case."

I drop the case into my bag and find my water bottle.

Definitely in shock.

***

We spend the rest of the afternoon trying to get a flight back to the East Coast. This is the only bad thing about Hawaii: it's so far away from everything.

The resort, the airline, everyone is sympathetic, but the earliest we can get out of here is tomorrow afternoon.

No one is pleased: not me, not my dad, not my husband or son. I feel horrible that we have to cut our vacation short. They had been looking forward to this for months, and now we have to leave a week early. As always, though, Derek is a trooper. He does not complain and spends his time hugging me, dealing with Zach, and helping me pack the suitcases.

We try to enjoy our last night on Maui, but the mood is, understandably, sour. Zach is worried, so we distract him by eating outdoors and stopping at the shave ice place for dessert. We let him play on the iPad for the rest of the night.

Not a stellar parenting moment, but I think even the mommy bloggers would cut me some slack.

I try to fall asleep, but my brain swims with thoughts of her and my dad.

How the hell does something like this happen?

***

The shrill ringing jolts me awake.

Had I really been sleeping? What time is it?

The clock on the ringing phone says two a.m.

It's my mom's number, which means it's my dad.

Oh, god.

"Katie?"

His voice is low, raspy.

"Hi, Dad."

Hurry up and tell me why you're calling. Spit it out. Hurry, hurry, hurry.

"She's gone."

I sag back into my pillows. "What?"

Derek rolls over and turns on the light.

I say nothing and hand him the phone. He talks but I have no idea what he's saying. The only other thing I hear is the blood rushing through my ears. I see nothing. I feel nothing.

What?

***

I swim along the shoreline, taking long, slow strokes. I have my mask and snorkel on, my flippers helping to propel me along.

I feel weird being out here with so much going on, but I didn't sleep much after last night's phone call, and Derek thought the swim would do me some good. Wake me up. Clear my head.

But the water does not caress, does not soothe as it usually does. I am numb. The usual sights and sounds—even the taste of salt water on my tongue—barely register.

Maybe I should turn around.

How can you be out here, gallivanting, while your mother is dead?

I come up for air. I am just over Five Caves.

I take a long, slow breath and dive down. Right into a school of butterfly fish, their yellow, black, and white stripes reminding me of a bumblebee. They scatter, making way for me.

As they disappear, I see no more movement: no other fish, no turtles. Just coral and open water.

Then a shimmer appears before me. It's not a ray of sunlight or drip of saliva. It is a weird patch of water, lighter-colored than the water surrounding it, oblong, and about my height. I reach to touch it, but it moves away from me, sinking toward the bottom. It turns darker. I follow it.

Down.

Down.

Down.

Snorkeling when you should be mourning your mother. You are one cold bitch, aren't you. And what about your father? Your husband? Your son? You've abandoned the three men in your life and for what? To soothe your soul? You've been reading too many self-help books, you fucking hippie. You should have been checking in with your father more frequently: offered more help, talked to the doctor, called your cousins. Was this afternoon's flight really the best you could do? The earliest you could get home? Sometimes you're so lazy. Did you really decide to be lazy with your ailing mother and struggling father? And what about your son? You couldn't even bother trying to console him when he learned his grandmother was in a coma. Just left it up to your husband. He picks up a lot of your slack. Earns all the money for the house *and* does the bulk of the playing with Zach. It's a wonder he even stays with you. All you do is complain, and whine, and criticize. Just like your mother. You always said you'd never be like her, now here you are. No? You disagree? Why don't you ask your son about all the guilt you give him? The same way she gave it to you.

The purple cloud is below me, swirling and spiraling. A dark arm reaches and reaches. It coils around my toes. A sharp, icy pain seizes my foot, working its way up my leg. I try to pull away, but my limbs have stopped working. My heart thuds, my lungs are on fire.

I look for the turtle. Is that him up there? Even if I wanted to move to find out, I don't know if I could.

Maybe you shouldn't move. Your husband, your son … they'd be better off without your harping, anyway. And you've always felt at home down here. Maybe you should just stay.

Maybe I should.

FISH LAUNCHER

MP Johnson

There are two things I know about my man for certain and for all time: He cannot keep his hands off my ass and he hates fishing. So we are going fishing. Because I want to go fishing, and my ass is coming with me.

Patrick and I hitch the trailer to our sweet wood-paneled station wagon and cruise a few hours to my favorite spot in northern Minnesota. I'm not going to tell you where specifically, but it's up by Grand Marais. It's nothing special anyway, nothing you'd want to seek out. Just one of those little pocket lakes buried up there in the woods. Traffic is light and the fish bite, but mainly I like to go there because it's where my dad took me when I was a little boy.

Patrick grouses all the way. When his arms aren't crossed, he's worrying his forearm hair like it's a field that's ready for harvest. He's got a lot of it. He's got a lot of forearm. He's one of those weightlifter guys. If you get him started, he'll talk your ear off about drop sets and split stance squats. But not fishing.

We stop at the Ugly Baby bait shop, even though it's a bit out of the way and I don't actually need any bait. I've got a hot pink tackle box filled to bursting and I'm going to be sticking with spinners today, but my dad always said, "Son, it's sacrilegious to go onto a lake without a pot of worms." Plus I need snacks.

Inside, the proprietor locks eyes on Patrick and hobbles over. I'm invisible to this man, this high-cholesterol Northern Minnesota M-A-N. I'm not threatened though. He has no designs on Patrick. This is strictly a "Hey, you're a man, let's talk about man stuff" interaction. He has deemed me unworthy, but Patrick fits the bill. I get it. Patrick's butch. I'm femme. A friend once dressed me up as Cher and I looked so good I have a framed picture of myself on my desk at work.

"What you fellas fishing for today?" the proprietor asks Patrick.

Patrick responds with one word, which he forms carefully. He shapes it like a stop sign to ensure it's not mistaken for a joke. "Fish," he says.

The proprietor pauses. "Well, they're biting."

He walks back behind the counter. He still doesn't see me. I couldn't possibly hold down a conversation about fishing, not with all this gel in my hair, not with my perfect eyebrows, not with my cutoffs and skinny legs for days. Goodness no. You need to have a bushy beard to talk fishing. Your skin has to be sun-wrinkled, like Patrick's. You have to be wearing work boots.

I've gotten this all my life, and not only from straight people. Half the time, it's queers stuck in our own stereotypes. Whenever I tell someone how much I love fishing, I get weird looks. Nobody expects it from a twink like me. I show them my lures, and then they think they understand. They're like, "They're so pretty!" and I'm like, "Ummm, yeah, I guess, but this one catches crappie and this is good for smallmouth and this is for walleye." Then eyes glaze over and the convo is basically done until they can break in and tell me how cute my shoes are.

I punch my fist into a trough of potato chip bags just to make the foil packages crinkle loud. I swish my hand around and create a hell of a racket. When I finally pull one out, both Patrick and the proprietor are looking at me like, huh?

"Can I get a pot of worms too, pretty please?"

At the lake, we manage to get the fourteen-foot boat into the water with minimal grunts from Patrick. His shirt is already soaked in sweat and I tell him to take it off, which is the first thing he agrees to do without groaning.

He gets into the boat and gives me his hand. I take it and pretend to stumble in so he can catch me against his hairy chest. So much hair. I swear he has hair growing out of the very tips of his nipples. If we had a baby, it would not get milk. It would suck the hair out of Patrick's teets like spaghetti. His chest hair is not quite long enough for me to twirl around my fingers, but that doesn't stop me from trying.

The metal benches in the boat have been collecting the heat from the sun all day. Patrick puts down a foam pad with some sports team logo and guides me onto it, careful not to sear my precious ass on the aluminum beneath. Then he places a foam pad for himself and plunks down across from me to start rowing.

This is the part of fishing he enjoys. We don't have a motor, because he likes the workout of rowing, and I certainly don't mind watching the striations in his shoulder muscles go wild as he whisks us out onto the lake.

We're fishing for crappie today, so we look for a messy spot. My dad always said they like to hide near fallen trees and brush. We find just such a place and I make Patrick drop the anchor. Grunt. Groan. Grunt. Splash. Sink.

When the anchor is set, he stops grousing and sidles up next to me. He puts his arm around me, and presses the side of his face against mine. Nothing makes me lose it more than having his beard against my cheek. Despite its masculine appearance, it's cotton candy soft. My lips go into it and find his.

I pull out of the kiss before I get revved up past the point of no return. Patrick gets his massive arms around me and I have to fight to break free. I'm not only fighting him. I'm fighting myself. I want to do this. I will do this. But not yet.

"You know the rule," I say. "No makeouts until we catch our first fish."

Patrick makes a lemon-drop face and unleashes a solid groan, a real thick one. It makes the water around the boat ripple. But he obeys the rule. He moves back over to his bench and crosses his arms.

Before I can ready my pole – my fishing pole – a fish thumps down in the boat, flopping in the space between Patrick's feet and mine.

Patrick looks at me expectantly.

"That doesn't count," I say.

Patrick grunts and kicks the crappie gently with the tip of his boot. It flips over and I cover my mouth with my hands. It's a disaster. Scales have been scraped away. Needle-like bones protrude at random angles. An eyeball slides out of its socket like butter across a griddle. It would be choking on air, if it weren't already choking on its own insides threaded through its gills.

I snatch it up by its tail and throw it into the water.

"Where did that come from?" I ask.

Patrick squints at the shore near our messy spot.

"Probably some redneck kids," I mutter. Then I scream into the trees, "You mutants are exactly why I'm pro-choice!"

I don't hear a reaction or see any movement. Part of me wants to go ashore and find the pieces of shit, but I'm not sure what I'd do with them. Yell at them some more? Chase them? Make Patrick put them in a headlock? Better to ignore them.

Patrick agrees. He's got the anchor up and is rowing to find a new spot before I can even unclench my fists.

"My dad started taking me here when I was five. I've been coming here almost twenty years. I have rarely even seen other people, let alone had something like this happen. This is my lake! Those troglodytes!"

Patrick shrugs and keeps rowing.

"They'll probably grow up to be serial killers," I say. Another fish zips past my face and splashes into the lake on the other side of the boat. "What the fuck?"

With those bulging muscles of his, Patrick is a fast rower. We're in the middle of the lake now. If that fish was thrown from shore, it was by an Olympic-level fish-hurler. I scan around to see where else it might have come from. The sun is bright and reflecting off the water so I have to squint hard, but I don't see any other boats nearby. Is someone swimming and tossing fish at us?

Another one flies our way. I duck and cover. Patrick bats it away so hard it leaves shiny scales and guts on his hand. He points in the direction the fish came from.

In the distance, I see something floating on the surface of the water.

"What is that? A log?"

"Logs don't launch fish at people," Patrick replies.

"Good point. Can you row us in closer?"

He nods and does.

As his rippling muscles pull us toward the object, I realize it's no log. It has a skull, bleached white by the sun and slick with lake slime. This is not like any animal skull I've seen. I haven't spent a lot of time with animal skulls, but I grew up in Minnesota. I've seen deer skulls, cow skulls. This is more like something from a tucked-away corner of a museum, with a big question mark on the placard beside it.

My knees start shaking as I realize the skull is staring back at me. There are eyes in its sockets still. They're pocked and shot with green veins. Its barbed mouth is wide and unmoving, a perfect circle. Its body, what I can see of it, does look log-like.

And it's not just floating. It's bobbing up and down. It disappears under the surface of the lake for a moment and when it comes up again it shoots another fish carcass out of its cavernous maw. The bass comes out with a spray of water and catches ever so slightly on the barbs that line the thing's mouth. It's enough to cause the fish to unravel as it flies through the air. When it gets here it's nothing more than a thumping heart and a twist of white intestines that splatter against the boat's hull.

"Let's get the fuck out of here," I say, even though Patrick is already splashing the oars in to row us to shore as quickly as possible.

I try to keep my eyes on the creature, but it bobs under again. At first, I assume to collect more ammo to launch at us. When it doesn't re-emerge, I feel a tinge of hope in my heart that the thing has gone away, but there's a tension in my bones that knows that would be too easy. I visor my hand to my forehead to block the sun so I can catch sight of it

25

again. I desperately don't want to catch sight of it, but it might be com-coming closer. I can't let it surprise us.

Sure enough, I see a long shadow beneath the surface. It doesn't move like a fish. It's rigid, completely unbending. It comes at the boat, but dips at the last moment. I feel it scrape aluminum underfoot. "It's chasing us," I say.

Grunting, Patrick takes one of the oars from its lock and stands. Holding it like a baseball player stepping to home plate, he moves to the edge of the boat. He gazes into the murk. The long shadow – it must be ten feet – circles us. Patrick slaps at it. The attack does little more than get us wet. The cool drops mingle with my sweat and remind me how hot it is. We're baking here. I suddenly want air conditioning. I want Minneapolis. I want off this lake and out of the woods.

"I'm so scared, baby," I say.

He looks at me with furrowed brow and chastises. "It's just a fish."

But I know fish, and that thing is no fish.

Like a battering ram, the creature bursts out of the water. The monstrous skull hits Patrick square on the chest and propels him overboard. They both disappear into the lake, leaving nothing behind except a few air bubbles and a tint of crimson from where the barbs of the thing's launch-hole bit into Patrick.

I stare into the water after them, freaking out, flapping my arms. They're flapping out of fear, of course. At first. But they keep flapping as I dive in. And they keep flapping, in the cold water, harder and harder, pulling me down into the murk. As daylight disappears behind me, all I can think about is Patrick's beard against my cheek and how I won't let that feeling be taken away from me.

I can barely see in front of me, but I go deeper.

The blackness of the water gives way to white. Suddenly, I am eye-to-eye with this skull-faced creature. I react fast, but not fast enough to prevent it from striking me under the chin, slamming my jaw shut so hard my ears ring. My exclamation of pain comes out in bubbles, the last of my held breath, and my last hope for finding my man.

The creature disappears into the darkness.

I stop moving and begin to let myself float back to the surface. Am I going to let Patrick go? Just like that? Over a little bump on the chin?

I clench my abs and find a pocket of air tucked away in my lungs somewhere, enough to hold me over while I go a bit deeper. I'm not just flapping now. I'm sweeping the lake further behind me with each stroke of my arms. I can feel its cold weight on me as my empty lungs begin to spasm.

26

I keep going until I see a hand. I grab it. Even though I can't see the rest of the body, I know it's Patrick. I've held that hand so many times over the last four years, I know exactly what it feels like to have his weight-room calluses pressed into my lotioned palms. When I squeeze, I feel a squeeze back. It's light, but it's there.

I turn around and kick so hard I almost collide with the creature as it shoots past my head. Again and again, it crisscrosses the waters between me and a lungful of fresh Minnesota air, not making contact, just taunting. Nonetheless, I do not detour. I take the shortest path to the brightness above.

As I'm reaching for the surface with one hand, my other holding tight to Patrick, the creature jolts past my ribcage, ripping me open with its mouth barbs. I'm in a cloud of red and the lake suddenly gets a lot colder. But the pain seems far away, farther than the air above, so I ignore it and keep kicking.

When I finally splash through, I suck in a deep breath and feel like I've overdosed on oxygen. Lightning bolts go off behind my eyes, and when they're gone they're replaced with storm clouds. Black clouds. I'm going to pass out. I can't though. I don't have that luxury. I have to take care of my man.

I get his head up into the air. His eyes are rolled back. He's leaving me.

I spin around. Shore is far. At least a hundred feet. And the creature is circling us. The top of its skull cuts the surface like a shark's fin. It's not going to let me get to dry land, but I need to get air into Patrick's lungs now.

I don't know shit about CPR, but I have to try. I kick as hard as I can to keep both of our heads above water. I latch one hand to the waist of Patrick's jeans and pinch his nose with the other as I lock my lips around his and blow. I turn him around quick and give him a series of squeezes. Then I blow into him again. I don't know how many times I repeat, but I don't stop until he coughs up water and I can hear him breathing. He doesn't really regain consciousness, just kind of lolls around, but he's alive, and that is everything.

I notice how scraped up he is. A piece of his cheek is missing. I can see bone. I need to get him ashore. Fuck a monster. I'm going to save my man.

I let the creature take another couple of laps around me. Let it play. Let it think I've given up. Then, when it thinks it has me and its circles go too wide, I kick so hard my thighs burn immediately. I kick so hard I'm soaring above the water, even with Patrick in tow. My heart beats against every one of my ribs.

I don't make it fifteen feet. The creature is in front of me, coming straight at me, readying another battering ram maneuver. I splash and shift and almost dodge it. Almost. It digs its barbs into that same spot along my side, opening me up more. I don't touch it, but I can feel the cold water getting into it. There's a hole in me.

But I also have a window, and I don't miss it. I adjust my grip on Patrick and start kicking toward shore again. I get another five feet. Ten feet. Fifteen feet. My head's filled with competing cheer squadrons. One screams, "You're gonna make it!" The other yells, "You're gonna die!" I ignore both and just swim.

Out of the side of my eye, I see the creature skimming the surface beside me. My gasp causes me to suck in a lungful of water. I choke and cough, but I keep going, even as the creature jumps completely out of the water and then dives in skull-first, piercing the lake like an arrow. It's going deep.

I try not to think about what it intends to do next. What will that help? What good will it do me to know it's going to shoot up from the bottom of the lake and punch me right in the stomach, destroying me? All I can do is swim until it feels like my one shoulder is going to tear from its socket and my legs are rubber.

To my surprise, the creature doesn't hit me from beneath. I hear it break the surface of the water behind me. Why is it taunting me like this? What is it doing? I don't have time to look back. I'm so close.

Now there is splashing all around me. Little explosions of water shoot up from the lake. I stop and tread water. It takes me a moment to figure out that the creature is launching fish again. Its aim is worthless though. Dozens of them plop down in front of me, disappearing into the murk.

"Do you think I'm scared of fish? I came here for the fucking fish!"

Then one of the fish bobs to the surface, blue and bloated. It's not a fish at all. It has toes. A foot. A human foot. The skin is ragged and one of the nails has been ripped out of place and is impaled like a shard of glass in the tender spot between little toes. Suddenly I can't breath again. It's like I'm under the lake, with no air in my lungs. The creature is eating my man right out of my arms and I didn't even notice.

More parts appear. Feet. Hands. Indecipherable chunks of meat in various states of decay. A face stares at me with empty sockets full of seaweed and a nose that has peeled away in so many layers it looks like a flower that forgot how to blossom. I'm almost relieved. These are not parts of Patrick.

Whose parts are these?

I do not even push them out of my way. I swim through them, toward the shore. They rub against me. Their icy touch is all the motivation I need to ignore the fatigue creeping into me, the fear waiting to take me over.

Patrick is coughing now and breathing hard. He's coming to, just as I'm able to touch my feet against the bottom. I get him upright in front of me and guide him in. The water might as well be cement. It does not want to let us go, but I push forward until it is only up to my waist. When it is ankle-deep, I shove Patrick as hard and as far as I can. He stumbles out and falls face-first onto a patch of grass.

I hear the skull-faced creature rushing through the lake behind me.

One. Two. Three. Four. I count Patrick's limbs as I feel barbs sink deep into my lower back. The impact pushes me forward. Something snaps in my spine before I abruptly change directions. There's so much blood. I'm being pulled back into the cold darkness of the lake. I'm moving fast and I have no air.

But it's okay. My man is safe.

THE BLACKEST EYES

Adam Cesare

The shark was a loaner.

Loaner with an "a".

Come to think of it, the shark was a loner, too.

Phil had read the shark's Wikipedia page. Multiple pages actually, because first he'd looked up hammerhead sharks, in general, but it turned out that there were many different species of hammerhead.

Most of those other species, like the scalloped hammerhead, traveled in schools. Those were the kind you most commonly saw in aquariums, but the shark living in VCX FX's warehouse was a lone wolf.

Their shark was a great hammerhead.

No. She didn't do tricks or anything—she wasn't *Some* Shark, *Charlotte's Web* style—she was a member of the species sphyrna mokarran, a great hammerhead. Like how the 'great' in 'great white shark' wasn't an indicator of quality, just a name.

Phil Court had been resistant to housing the creature in his workshop, but the artists who worked under him had been strongly in favor of the animal's proposed three week residency.

"We'll be able to watch it for reference any time we want," they'd claimed.

Phil hadn't poured a mold or soldered any circuitry in ten years, these days he was more of a figurehead for the company. He was the liaison between VCX and the studios, he offered his input on their various projects but it was the staff who did the work.

But even with his hands-off approach, he recognized that their argument was sound. You can watch YouTube videos all you want, but to capture the *soul* of the shark and transmute it into foam latex and animatronic puppetry: it would be better to work with a live subject.

Yes, the argument was sound, but in the time it had taken for the aquarium to drop off the temporary tank, treat the water, and introduce the shark most of the work on VCX's shark models had been completed.

After they were finished with their initial work, all Phil's employees wanted was to get up close to the damn thing's tank and take selfies with it.

This was a big budget picture and if the studio was willing to partner with the Anaheim Oceanic Conservancy (itself a public relations outcropping of the Ocean Planet theme park chain) and they wanted the sharks in *Deep Hammer* to be photo realistic animatronics. Who was Phil to stop them from spending their money?

VCX did a lot of television work, way more than enough to keep the warehouse lights on. These days the only time they were hired for creature fx for feature films was lower-budgeted gigs where the director was trying to capture a "throwback" vibe. Phil found it refreshing to be working on a hundred million dollar picture again, and oh so rare that a hundred million dollar picture would want to use some of that money on practical FX.

And that was not to say that there weren't going to be computer animated sharks in *Deep Hammer*, there would probably be CGI in great abundance, but for inserts and close-ups their puppets would be needed. And their puppets would be *fucking great*.

"Right, Rosie?" Phil asked, extending a finger to tap on the Plexiglas of the tank. The shark's temporary home was a combination of tarp and lightweight synthetic glass that could be collapsed for transport on a flatbed.

The shark didn't react to his tapping, she just kept swimming. The rectangle of the tank was maybe ten by twelve, the depth another seven feet. It was not much room for a shark that was nearly as tall as Phil if you stood her up on her fins.

Rosie had settled into a lightly psychotic pattern of swimming clockwise for a few minutes or so before switching to counterclockwise for a similar round.

Was this tank that much bigger than the one she had at Ocean Planet? Phil didn't know, Mary and him had never had kids so he'd never had a reason to go.

It was easy to look at Rosie, lonely and swimming in circles, and get ready to sign up for PETA and start protesting Ocean Planet. While Phil had been searching for info about hammerheads, he'd stumbled upon some videos of shark fin fisherman, huge nets filled with sharks who then had their fins sliced off and their finless bodies tossed back into the ocean to die, providing chum for even more sharks to be caught up in the nets.

Maybe a depressing life in captivity was a better fate than that.

Phil tried to imagine Rosie, no fins and releasing clouds of blood as she sank to the bottom of the tank. He was probably part of the problem, helping a multi-national corporation make a movie about killer hammerhead sharks wasn't going to endear the creatures to anyone.

"I'm sorry," he said, walking away from the tank and shutting the lights out on the warehouse.

***

"Well, what we're doing now is testing the salinity. There's pumps and a filtration system, but that doesn't monitor everything. Salt water tanks are very temperamental, there's a lot of material in the air in your workshop, and we want Rosie to be safe," the girl said.

She was standing atop a ladder and leaning over the tank.

Rosie didn't seem to care that there was a nubile young woman practically dunking herself into the tank. The shark was more concerned with lazily scooping up the frozen fish that were beginning to sink to the bottom of the enclosure.

Less than half of the artists looking up from their workstations seemed like they were listening to what Gloria had to say. Most were admiring how her ass looked in her Ocean Planet-issued cargo shorts.

"And we appreciate it, Gloria," Phil said. "In only a few days Rosie's become a regular mascot for the guys, we're quite fond of her..." he said, not catching himself say "guys" before it was too late. VCX was a progressive employer, these days, and Phil kept two female artists on staff.

"But," he began.

Gloria dismounted the ladder and turned to him. With one hand she shook out the litmus strip she'd dipped in Rosie's water, the way people used to shake out Polaroid pictures. Was Gloria even old enough to remember Polaroids?

"But wouldn't it be easier to train one of our people to do this?" he continued. "The four-oh-five must be murder on you driving up every day."

Phil certainly enjoyed watching Gloria, a caretaker at Ocean Planet, stop by to check on Rosie, but it seemed like overkill for them to pay an employee to drive, daily, from Anaheim to Burbank to feed and check the water.

"I don't mind, really," Gloria said. Phil noticed she dropped her voice down to a more conversational tone and volume. "What I'd be doing at work isn't much more interesting than sitting in traffic. There's a whole team of us dedicated to working the touch-tank. Starfish, nurse sharks, stuff that it's safe to pet. Any day I don't have to explain what a stingray is to six hundred children, individually, is a good day. "

Behind her, Rosie had made quick work of the frozen fish and squid chunks she'd been fed. With no more to the show, Phil's employees focused back to their work tables, heads down.

The novelty of working in a place where every surface was covered with disemboweled corpses, severed werewolf heads, and mechanical spiders had worn off years ago. For Phil this was just another day in the office.

Phil and Gloria's conversation had moved from public to intimate in a matter of seconds.

"I kind of assumed that you spent your days helping walruses brush their teeth or riding on the backs of killer whales. You know, the exciting stuff," Phil said. He felt his face redden and wished they weren't having this conversation where his staff could so easily overhear their boss trying his best to flirt.

It had been three months since Mary had moved out and she only last week finalized the divorce. But no one at VCX knew that. For all they knew the boss was perving on the new fish. Pun intended.

"No. I wish I was anywhere near an orca. That's what they don't tell all those little girls who try and follow through on their childhood dreams of majoring in marine biology: at my level, I'm one stop removed from selling churros. And the pay grade is the same. Having to take care of Rosie," she said, turning to watch the animal. "Gives me a purpose."

"That's," Phil didn't know what to say. "That's saying a lot."

"Well, that and I'm getting paid to drive the van up here and that gives me time to listen to my podcasts."

"Ah, well...that's nice to."

"In fact," she said, and reached into her back pocket. "If Rosie's ever in trouble or you notice something odd about her behavior, it'd probably be best to call me directly instead of whatever number my bosses gave you."

With that, Gloria asked Phil if he had a pen. He said he didn't and she pointed to the side of his head: "A pencil would be okay, too."

Phil removed the pencil from behind his ear, somewhere he'd been keeping one for close to two decades. He gave her an awkward 'silly me' chuckle and she wrote her cell number on the paper backing of a promotional Ocean World sticker.

"What do you mean by 'something odd about her behavior'?" Phil asked, suddenly concerned that he was missing something crucial as he watched the shark. Was it possible for Rosie to die if he was not paying close enough attention to her?

Gloria smiled and stood on her tip toes to get quiet enough that Phil's staff couldn't hear. It was a nice gesture but their closeness probably looked worse than anything she was going to say.

"It was just an excuse to pass you my number, dummy," she whispered in his ear.

***

This week, the second of Rosie's three week residency, Phil had been staying at work later and later.

There wasn't much going on at home. The movers were there during the day. Most nights Phil would come home and be surprised to find Mary had made a claim on another piece of furniture. The living room no longer had any couches or chairs and the only thing left in the kitchen was the water bubbler that she'd always hated ("It makes our home look like an office breakroom!").

So he'd find reasons to be the last one out of the warehouse's door at night. To fill time he'd respond to emails that at any other point in his career he would have let languish in his inbox. Many of them were requests for work that read like fan letters, written by independent filmmakers who were making movies on consumer camcorders in Tacoma.

Sorry, Jimmy, and good luck with your film, but VCX currently has its schedule filled through the next three years. Keep fighting the good fight! —Phil Court

When even the tertiary-ily productive tasks were done for the day, Phil would walk from his suspended-crow's nest of an office down to the warehouse floor. Once there, he would spend an hour or so watching Rosie swim circles in her tank.

The path she took through the water—he'd tracked it as exactly five circles clockwise and then five counter clockwise—hadn't changed, but there was something about her demeanor that struck Phil as sluggish.

It could have been that he was reaching for a reason not to go home, but what else was he going to do with his time? He scoured his office for spare change and used the company vending machine to buy a selection of snacks.

Apparently Cheetos held no appeal for Rosie. The cheese puffs weren't able to reach the bottom of the tank until the cornstarch dissolved and made a portion of Rosie's water cloudy.

He considered tossing a few peanut M&Ms over the lip of the tank, but he guessed there was no way Rosie would be interested in chocolate. Especially chocolate with a candy shell blocking it from (what

34

Wikipedia purported to be) her acute sense of smell. And chocolate was poisonous to dogs. What would it do to a great hammerhead shark?

Phil could have sworn that the vending guy used to stock the machine with beef jerky, that would have been a much better fit for Rosie's carnivorous palate. But alas...it must not have sold well among the staff.

"Sorry girl, that's all I've got," he said into the blue. In the quiet of the empty warehouse he could hear the water sloshing against the side of the tank, occasionally Rosie would get high enough in one of her circles that her dorsal fin would crest over the waterline.

Rosie didn't respond to his voice in any way, but she did keep one eye on him, as she did for every lap.

He wondered how she saw the world. There was the barest sliver of white on the outside of her black, black eyes. And with her eyes so far from each other, one on each side of her oblong face, it was amazing she could see anything in front of her to eat it.

He'd like to see the world like that, sometime.

Split in two. That's how he imagined it, a different world for each side of her face.

Taking the Ocean World sticker out of his back pocket, Phil noticed Gloria's pencil marks were beginning to fade. Another day in his pocket and they'd be completely illegible.

It was just an excuse to pass you my number, dummy.

He punched the number into his cell but just to save it into his contacts.

He didn't call Gloria, not that night.

***

"Isn't she beautiful?" Gloria said, the earnestness in her voice almost too pure not to be the result of the two bottles of wine they'd shared at the restaurant.

She *was* beautiful. They both were. Although their beauty was nothing alike. Gloria was young and happy, the kind of beauty that Phil mentally associated with summer. Gloria was sunshine cutting through the jeweled amber of a glass of unsweetened ice tea.

Rosie, though. Rosie's beauty was strong and sleek. Although she was grey with a white belly, she reminded him of a sable horse in full gallop, running at night. In captivity, hers was the beauty of a melancholy poem. She was blue from the reflected light of her tank but also the other kind of blue. The blue of sadness.

Phil didn't say anything like that, though. Nothing as faux poetic. He just said: "She sure is."

It was hard to tell if he was slurring or not. He certainly wouldn't have been able to drive them back from the restaurant. So they left his car and her van parked and had taken an Uber home.

At least he *thought* he had requested the Uber take them home, but he must have mistakenly put in the address for the VCX warehouse, because that's where their driver, a Ukrainian named Fedir, had dropped them off. And he hadn't seemed happy about it either.

"Here? You sure?" Fedir asked, rolling down his window to look around the empty industrial park.

"Yup. Here's good," Gloria said. "I've got to make sure that this guy's hammerhead is healthy." She hooked a thumb at Phil and they both laughed hysterically at the double-entendre. The driver did not.

They'd poured themselves out of the back doors of the Uber, found each other for support once the driver pulled away, and made their way into the warehouse with considerably less difficulty than Phil had some mornings when he was stone sober.

"So beautiful," Phil said, coming up behind Gloria and snaking his hands around her waist. He immediately regretted initiating contact this way. She'd brushed his hand a few times during dinner and they'd shared a chaste, friendly hug outside the restaurant, but hugging her from behind felt far too intimate, it was the way you saw teenagers spoon while waiting in line for the movies.

Gloria didn't seem to pull away, but she did stiffen against his touch.

"Not where she can watch us," she said. It was hard to tell if she was kidding.

Phil sniffed her neck, then turned to look at the warehouse. He walked away, leaving Gloria with both hands pressed against Rosie's tank. Her young face was splashed with blue.

When they'd come in, he'd only hit one switch for the warehouse's rows of overhead lights. The single switched caused a third of the high-up florescent bulbs to ignite.

It was good mood lighting but the gloom didn't do much to help him choose a worktable where he and Gloria could bed down.

Did he clear off the table with the foam rubber shark attack victim or the one with the animatronic chickens VCX was making for a fast food commercial?

"I just can't get over it," Gloria said, still fixated on the shark, not at the sexual encounter Phil was hoping was in the near future.

While she had her attention elsewhere he palmed the Cialis he'd stashed in his jacket pocket. What had seemed like wishful thinking earlier in the night may have just turned into a life saver.

"Can't get over what?" Phil asked, beginning to move the wire skeletons of the chickens off the table but keeping the layer of downy feathers that had been spread atop the workstation.

"How good Rosie has been to us. When we've been nothing but shitty to her."

Okay. That came out odder than most drunk talk Phil was used to hearing.

"How so?" he asked, satisfied with how the table had been cleared and moving back to where Gloria was watching the shark.

"We catch her, we put her in a cage that's a million times smaller than what she needs. And still, she survives. She not only survives, she..."

Her words trailed off and Phil began to look around for a bucket. *She's going to puke.* It had become apparent that this night would not end the way he wanted.

Gloria didn't puke. Instead she began to make a high, keening noise through clenched teeth.

Phil laughed, at first thinking the noise was some kind of Ocean World inside joke, a dolphin call that trainers used.

But then, with both hands planted firmly against the synthetic glass of the tank, Gloria reeled her head back and smashed her nose into the side of Rosie's enclosure.

"What are you doing?" Phil yelled, still a few drunken steps away from being able to stop her from lowering her face into the unbreakable Plexiglas a second time.

There was a crack that coincided with the second impact and Gloria began to speak again.

"I just want her to know!" She yelled into the side of the tank. As she spoke Phil could see dark spittle hit the side of the tank. Backlit black against the blue, he could see that there were flecks of broken teeth mixed in with the blood.

"I want to be a part of her!"

Phil tried grabbing Gloria's arms and pressing them flat against her side, but she fought, elbowing him in the stomach and knocking the wind from his lungs. How did she get so strong? Was this a seizure?

Had Gloria been hiding some kind of mental illness from him? Well, not hiding, that wasn't something you probably got into on the first date.

Free from his grip, Gloria dove down to the nearest work table and came back with something metallic, it was hard to see in the darkness.

"Stop it!" Phil said to her, but he could see from the look in her eyes that she was somewhere beyond his words.

She doubled back to where he was crouched and he could see her face more clearly.

Her nose, which moments ago had been perfectly symmetrical, was now favoring the left side, split at the end in a mess of blood. Her front teeth were gone.

She smiled a broken smile and he put his hands up. In that moment he was sure she was going to attack him with what he could see now were fabric sheers, large scissors that the artists used to cut the excess latex or "flash" off of molds.

But she ignored Phil. She was returning to the tank to get access to the ladder.

Her feet were two rungs up before Phil realized he had to stop her, that whatever psychotic break she'd had involved offering herself up to Rosie. Like a native-girl virgin being pitched into a volcano.

"No," he screamed out, reaching the base of the ladder at the same time Gloria was reaching the top. She had her hands over the tank, pinky and ring finger of her right hand wedged between the blades of the fabric sheers.

"Take of me," she said, her voice a whisper but perfectly clear in the dark of the warehouse.

With no better plan, Phil grabbed both sides of the ladder and pulled the whole thing away from the tank. The idea was to send Gloria over his head and onto the feathered worktable, where she would land safely and he could hopefully disarm her before she could do any more damage to herself.

But Phil had seen too many Buster Keaton movies. That shit never works in real life.

Gloria missed the table by a good four feet, missed it with everything except for her head.

Her head caught the corner of the workspace with a wet smack and sent a cloud of feathers flying into the air.

"Gloria?" Phil asked into the darkness. There was no response. The only sounds in his ears were the rush of his own blood and the gentle slosh of the water in Rosie's tank.

Pushing the ladder off of himself, he turned onto his belly and looked up. Gloria had managed to kick off one shoe, a tasteful but not too dressy pump, and her knees were splayed in an unladylike fashion.

She'd managed to sever both fingers before he could stop her, but that was the least of her problems. Her neck could have been used as a t-square, it was so nearly at a right angle.

38

"Jesus," Phil said, even though he wasn't religious.

***

It had seemed like such a good idea once he'd committed to the decision to start.

It was his only option, really, since they'd both left their cars downtown and he wasn't going to call Fedir back to see if his new Ukrainian friend would help him dispose of a body.

Cutting Gloria apart hadn't been difficult. No, it was disturbingly easy once he found the right tool for the job (the electric Sawzall the artists used to cut fiberglass), but it made such a mess.

Such a mess that he'd be unable to clean up in time. The first of his employees would be arriving to work in a matter of hours. He doubted he had enough time or up-to-date contact information to call and tell them they had a day off.

But they'd come looking for him anyway. Surely Gloria told someone where she was going? And he'd gone too far now to tell the truth about how it was an accident.

Take of me.

He'd searched, but he couldn't find the fingers anywhere. She must have cut them off over the tank and Rosie had taken care of them.

It's what she wanted, anyway. She made that pretty clear.

It was insane, but Phil returned the ladder to its upright position, grabbed a length of Gloria's forearm, and climbed to look over the edge, stopping at the second to last rung.

His fingers were thick with blood and it had begun to cool and go sticky already, in the thirty or forty minutes since Gloria's death.

From this vantage, Rosie was a black shadow in the pool.

She didn't act any different as the droplets of blood fell from Phil's hand onto the surface of the carefully-monitored salt water.

Rosie's swimming did not deviate from her normal circles, but Phil did catch a flash of white at the edge of one of her eyes.

I know you're watching, girl, he thought and let the piece of flesh and bone drop into the water.

Nothing. It were as if he'd dropped in a Cheeto. Rosie didn't touch the half-foot square of Gloria meat, not even a test bite. She barely seemed to notice the cloud of blood that got into her path.

As the arm sank, it bumped Rosie on the nose, but the shark just glided onward.

"It's too cold." Phil said, not thinking but *knowing*.

Having their workshop located in California was an absolute must, that's where the industry is, but it also meant that their rent and air conditioning bills were astronomical. Phil could try turning the air down, but he'd only manage to leave more physical evidence in the process. Forget fingerprints: he was practically dripping with Gloria's bodily fluids.

Standing at the top of the tank, he watched Rosie swim, spotting the slight movement of her eyes and understanding that she was watching him as well.

Somehow he'd gotten to the top step of the ladder, the one that had "No Standing" pressed into the plastic.

He looked back down at the VCX warehouse, at all the pretend atrocities he'd helped create. And the one real one.

"I'm warm," he said to himself and to Rosie.

Phil Court understood what those black eyes were asking and he jumped in.

THE APPETITE OF OLD SIMBA

Dyer Wilk

They sailed the acid sea from San Francisco to Maro Reef, a garbage-stench wind blowing across their bow.

Aaron stood on deck, letting it all soak in as he watched the men work the nets and listened to the sounds of the water. It had been like this for nearly two weeks now, living as a bystander in a world he didn't belong to, standing aside as men sweated and cursed and told jokes he only half-understood, understanding that he would have to pick the right moment to ask questions.

The article was half-finished, or maybe it was complete shit and he'd scrap most of it. He couldn't be sure yet. He'd started it nearly six months ago, writing on other ships like this one, crewed by more men who sweated and cursed and told jokes he only half-understood, captained by Americans and Canadians and Japanese, all with the same leathery years-in-the-sun complexion and a propensity for silence.

Later was Captain Markovic's favorite word. It explained things quickly without actually explaining them, implying that after days of asking questions Aaron would still have to wait for an interview, one that would be brief at best. The agreement had been very specific: Aaron could stay aboard and write about whatever he wanted as long as it didn't interfere with the fishing, and the fishing always came first.

He hadn't actually *seen* many fish though. In two weeks, the nets had caught mostly trash, which the men angrily tossed over the side. Aaron recognized much of it. Sneakers and toothbrushes and ancient cellphone cases, plastic bags and soda bottles. Every corner of the Pacific was filled with it, innumerable pieces of man-made crap swimming on currents that had once held marine life.

"We've had worse years than this," one of the men told him a week after he boarded. "Once went a whole year without catching anything. Not even jellies."

The hauls on the other ships hadn't been much different. He'd seen islands of garbage caught in the swirling gyre, some larger than the ships themselves, serving host to gray-backed terns and sea lions. The men told stories of seeing trash islands the size of aircraft carriers, dotted with makeshift houses that sheltered small communities of sun-crazed squat-squatters, content to go wherever the sea took them, drinking water purified by solar-powered stills and shooting albatross from the sky with crossbows to cook in fires fueled by driftwood. Aaron was skeptical of course. He'd heard his share of tall tales. But then, it was tall tales that had brought him here in the first place.

It had been accepted long ago that the seas were mostly dead and devoid of fish. But it was the other things, the things not easily explained, that made men like him leave dry land. It was the stories of the odd and unbelievable shapes beneath the waves, lying in wait for unsuspecting ships to pass.

Aaron had pitched the article to his editor as part ecological study, part exploration of maritime folklore. The fishing industry had been on its way out since the late 2020s and no one was interested in a profile on sailors who were too stubborn to accept that fish had been driven to the brink of extinction. It was too depressing and it was hardly a mystery. People knew the reasons. Greed, pollution, shifts in the food chain. But the tall tales held some mystique. Even if people thought it was bullshit, they'd still be interested. It was just the way people were. They didn't believe, but they *wanted* to. And so did Aaron.

The trawler slowly moved along the outer edge of the reef, keeping a wide berth. Aaron had asked where they were headed, but the men wouldn't give him more than noncommittal grumbles about good fishing along the northern rim. He tried to press them for more than that, but they were tight-lipped. It was part of the centuries old sailor's code. Never divulge your secrets to the competition. He wasn't planning to come out here and steal their fish of course, but Captain Markovic had been very clear that the article had to be vague on latitude and longitude.

He passed the time by pacing the deck, listening and watching and waiting. Overhead, sea birds glided on the salt air, occasionally darting down to land on the radio antenna. Men smoked cigarettes and played cards on a wooden crate, talking of home and girlfriends and wives and children they only saw two months out of the year. It was peaceful out here. Even if they rarely caught anything, the sea was more of a home to them than dry land.

"Hey, Oliveira."

Aaron turned around to see the first mate, Dimitriou, standing behind him. The man was big and knotted from years of hauling in heavy lines, his right bicep bearing a small tattoo that Aaron had seen on some of the other crewmen. At first glance it resembled a crucifix, but the general shape was made out of fish, and in the center (where a crucified Jesus would have been) there was a jellyfish, its tentacles coiled around the crosspieces. Aaron tried not to stare. Some of the men didn't like it. But Dimitriou was one of the friendlier ones, his expression holding an almost perpetual softness.

"What's up?" Aaron asked.

"The Captain wants to see you."

"Did he say what it's about?"

Dimitriou shrugged his massive shoulders. "He just said to get Oliveira."

Aaron smiled and pulled his laptop bag up onto his shoulder. "Thanks. Tell him I'll be right there."

Dimitriou walked back to the bridge slowly, making no effort to exert himself in the midday-heat. Aaron hurried below deck and went to his cabin to grab his flash recorder. He had a feeling Markovic was about to give him the big (or small) interview and he wanted to be ready.

Topside, he nearly ran into a skinny deckhand named Crudele, receiving a "fuck you" and a scowl as he made his way to the bridge. He quickly ascended the stairs and ducked through the open door.

The bridge was shaded and cool, filled with crisscrossing currents of air driven by fans bolted to the wall. Captain Markovic stood at the radar console, holding a cup of coffee.

"You wanted to see me, Captain?"

Markovic turned to look at him, managing a smile that was closer to a sneer. "Come on over here, Oliveira. Today's a good day to talk."

Aaron pulled out the flash recorder and aimed the microphone toward Markovic, consciously trying to angle it low enough to keep from being intrusive.

"So where would you like to start? With your first command?"

Markovic looked unimpressed. "You know people don't really give a shit about that."

"Sure, they do. It's good background."

"*Right*. How about we just cut to the part where you ask me what you really wanted to ask?"

Aaron nodded slowly. Markovic was more shrewd than he'd realized.

"Tell me about the Gyre Giant."

Markovic laughed. "Is *that* what people are calling it?"

"Well, that's just one of the names I've heard. But I was going to use that one for the article."

The Captain shook his head, a deep crease forming between his eyebrows. "Sounds too cheesy. Nobody's gonna read that."

"Okay. Which name should I use? The Deep One? The Kraken? Tidal Tim? The Undertower? Everyone I've talked to calls it something different."

"Sure. And they make *it* sound like a profession wrestler."

"I guess so. But...well, what do *you* call it?"

Markovic shrugged. "Usually I don't call it anything. You fall in love with someone, you don't even think about their name half the time. You just see them. You feel them. Same when something scares you."

"*Does* it scare you?"

Markovic let out a rasping cough that told of years of cigarettes. "No. He doesn't scare me. Actually, I love him a little bit. I admire him. He's just doing what nature intended."

"So, let me get this straight. You believe it's a he. And he's just...what? Something you don't mind having around?"

"Oh no. Sometimes I hate the bastard. He's eating most of our fish. But like I said, that's just who he is. And I don't know if he's a he or she or both. I just think of him as a he."

"And can you describe him?"

Markovic held up a hand. "Now hold on. Don't get ahead of yourself. You haven't even told me what you've heard."

"Well, I'm more interested in what *you've* heard, Captain."

A sly grin spread across Markovic's leathery face. "Humor me, Oliveira."

Aaron let out a deep breath and turned to look out through the windows at the flat gray-blue stretch of water ahead of them.

"People talk about there being some kind of monster out there. Something that sinks ships and kills sailors and eats sharks whole. That kind of thing."

"And you think it's bullshit."

"It's my job to be skeptical."

"So why come out here then? You could Google sea monsters and write the article at home."

"It's not the same."

"No, but there's no point in hitching a ride on a ship if you know it's all just made up."

"I guess I wanted to look someone in the face as they talked about it, to see if they believed it."

"And do they? The others you've talked to, I mean."

"Some of them do, I think. I know the Captains usually do."

"But you think there's a difference between what they think they saw and what they really saw."

"Yeah. I do."

"Too many hours at sea. Cabin fever. The mind playing tricks."

"Something like that."

"Hell, I don't blame you. You spend enough time out here, you think some strange things. Being alone does that. But then, sometimes you just see something and you know it's real."

"But how could you be sure?"

"Oh, you doubt yourself sometimes. You think there's no way you saw it because something like that can't exist. You think it's those stories you heard getting to you. Not enough sleep maybe. But sometimes you just know. You see it and it's not a glimpse. Something you could write off as your eyes playing tricks on you. No, you get a good look. A long look. And the longer you look, the more sure you are. It's real and you're seeing it and it doesn't matter that it's unbelievable. You *know* it exists."

Aaron double checked the flash recorder to make sure it was still running. He wanted to quote that word for word, use it in the first paragraph of the article.

"What else can you tell me about him?" he asked.

"We call him Old Simba."

"Simba? Isn't that from a cartoon?"

Markovic shook his head. "I'm not sure. That's just what people called him when I first heard about him."

"Yeah. It is. Some kind of musical. I don't know. It came out maybe 60, 70 years ago. Simba was a lion."

"Oh, right. Yeah, I think I remember that."

"Why would they name him after a lion though?"

"No idea. It's probably just one of those things. Someone started calling him that and the name just stuck."

"So he doesn't look like a lion at all, I take it."

"No."

"But you *did* get a good enough look to tell me."

"Oh yeah. More than once. Me and Old Simba are practically friends at this point."

"When was the first time you saw him?"

Markovic looked out at the water, taking a moment to find words to match his thoughts.

"I guess it must have been about thirty years ago. My first voyage. I was maybe 18, 19. It was a swordfishing boat. We were a couple hundred miles south of Tahiti. Calm seas. Good visibility. I was up on deck, baiting hooks. And...I don't really know how anyone could have missed it. We weren't going more than ten knots, but the boat just stopped dead. I got thrown down onto the deck. Felt this sharp pain, looked up and saw the hook I'd been holding stuck in my palm.

Someone tried to help me up and then someone else started shouting that we had men in water. I got up and saw them over the port side. Guy named Siddons and...I can't remember the other one's name. Young kid. Younger than me. Maybe 16. Then I saw this cargo container floating just above water, one corner stabbed into the hull.

"Siddons and the kid were treading water trying to climb back up on deck. The first mate and the Captain came down from the bridge to help out. We lowered a rope into the water. Siddons was climbing up first. The kid was behind him. And then he wasn't. He didn't sink. Not the way people do. I mean, he was pulled down. Above the water, then *poof.* Underwater. Siddons let go of the rope and tried to get to him, but then he saw it. We all did. Just under the water, almost as big as the ship. It happened quick though. He tried to swim back, grabbed onto the rope, but he wasn't strong enough to hold on. The rope was ripped right out of his hands. Then he was gone. And that's when the Captain told me about Old Simba."

For a moment, Aaron felt something close to fear, imagining it just as Markovic had described it, his mind filling in the gaps, allowing his disbelief to be suspended just long enough to believe it and scare himself for actually believing.

But it wasn't true. Of course it wasn't. Two men are killed by an undertow or a shark, and a young sailor (with help from a few imaginative shipmates) tells himself it was an actual sea monster out of a Jules Verne novel.

"You don't believe me," Markovic said.

Aaron stopped recording. "It's not that I don't want to. It's just...I don't know. It's a hard thing to believe. There are other possible explanations."

"If you saw him, you would though."

"Maybe. But I'd still have to rule everything else out. And I'm guessing sea monsters don't just appear whenever you want them to."

"Oh no, Mr. Oliveira. Old Simba is very reliable. I can promise you we'll see him soon."

"But how can you know that?"

Markovic nodded toward the water. "He likes to hang out around the north rim. Don't ask me why. But whenever we head up that way, it's not too long before we see him."

"I thought the fishing was good up there."

"The fishing is shit, there and everywhere else. Old Simba takes the lion's share. He's got a real appetite."

"So why not kill him?"

Markovic laughed. "I'm no Ahab. Besides, don't think people haven't tried. He's been around at least forty years and he's still going strong."

Aaron started to record again. He was missing good stuff.

"So you're telling me, he can't be killed."

"No idea. I'm just saying no one's succeeded."

"You realize that sounds pretty far-fetched, right? Not only a sea monster, but one that nobody else but a few fishermen believe in."

"I don't expect anyone to believe it, that's why the only websites that mention it also claim gray aliens are fallen angels and Hurricane Stella was man-made in order to destroy Miami to prevent them from winning their bid to host the 2052 Summer Olympics. But you wanted proof. So I'm going to show you."

***

An odd hush had fallen over the crew.

For the last two hours, Aaron had been sitting in a shaded corner, watching the men work on deck, their laughter and conversations gradually tapering off into nothing but the occasional grumble of acknowledgement as they reeled in the nets and secured them. He wondered if they believed it, too. If the sea monster stories were some great superstition that haunted them whenever they approached this spot in the vast emptiness of the ocean.

Occasionally, Crudele walked by and stopped to look at him, as if sizing him up and calculating the perfect moment to pounce on him and start hitting.

"Can I help you?" Aaron asked.

Crudele stared in silence for a moment and then ran a hand over his forehead to wipe away the sweat. As he lowered it again, Aaron saw a tattoo poking out from under his sleeve. Another cross.

Slowly, the sun arced across the blue dome sky and moved westward toward the horizon. Aaron got up and walked to the bow, finding a good spot to watch the sunset and take a few photos. As the light faded and the sky darkened, he spotted what looked like ships a few miles out, a convoy of some sort.

He tried to get a picture, but a combination of extreme zoom and the moving sea caused each shot to blur heavily.

He slipped the camera back into his shoulder bag and started to pace the deck impatiently. All the waiting was starting to seem pointless. He'd spoken to the captain more than five hours ago and still there was nothing. No big revelation that was supposed to make him a true believer in a myth that was most likely bullshit.

He went aft and found Dimitriou smoking by the hatch leading to the cargo hold.

"Can I ask you something?" Aaron said.

"Sure, Mr. Oliveira. Of course."

"I talked to the Captain earlier. He said we're heading to the north rim so he could show me something."

"Oh yeah. We'll be there soon. He really wants you to see."

"So you've seen it, too. Or *him*, I guess."

"All of us have seen him. You will, too. I promise. I know it sounds like it's made up, but it isn't. First time I heard about it, I thought they were playing a joke. Hazing the new guy. But no. They showed me. It's all true."

Aaron searched Dimitriou's face for some hint of a lie, but he couldn't find any. The man struck him as slightly dumb, but not dishonest. It was something about the innocence in his face, as if he *couldn't* lie and being asked to would hurt him deeply.

"Let me ask you something else then," Aaron said. "What's with the tattoo?"

Dimitriou looked down at his bicep, as if he'd forgotten what it looked like. "This?"

"Yeah."

"Oh, nobody told you yet?"

"No."

"Well, it's – "

"Hey!" a voice shouted from behind them.

Aaron turned back to see Crudele standing on the stairs, his mouth stretched into an angry frown.

"Captain wants you on the bridge."

Dimitriou started to get up.

"Not you, dumb ass. Oliveira."

Aaron shook his head and followed Crudele up the steps. At the door to the bridge, the fisherman refused to completely step out of the way, looking Aaron in the eye as he tried to squeeze past.

"Soon," he said.

"Excuse me?"

Crudele turned away and walked down the steps. Aaron frowned, still wondering what he'd done to piss the guy off so much.

Markovic stood on the bridge, his wrinkled features illuminated from beneath by the green glow of the radar screen. There was a bottle of bourbon sitting on top of the console, along with two glasses.

"You wanted to see me, Captain?"

"Here," Marvokic said, holding out a glass. "Have a drink."

"I'm not much of a drinker."

"Humor me."

Aaron took the glass and sipped it. The bourbon burned all the way down and tingled in his stomach.

"Ten years old," Markovic said. "The good stuff."

"I guess so."

"Sorry. I meant to call you up here earlier. I should have told you that it would be awhile. We have to keep it under fifteen knots out here because of the debris, especially at night. You rupture the hull or get steel cables caught up in the propellor and there's not a lot you can do."

"You think it'll be tomorrow?"

Markovic shook his head and took a drink. "No. It'll just be a few minutes. It's right over there."

Aaron looked out and saw the convoy of ships, each lit up now, their flickering reflections mirrored by the water.

"What is that?"

"Some friends of ours. I radioed ahead. It's safer if we stay in a group."

"Safer?"

Markovic smiled. "I told you what he can do. Do you want to see him or not?"

"Yeah."

"Then relax. Have another drink. You're gonna need to be calm for this."

Before Aaron could protest, Markovic filled his glass halfway to the top. He hesitated before taking a sip and then forced himself to swallow, fighting to hold back a cough.

"See?" Markovic said. "A couple more of those and it's smooth sailing."

Aaron cleared his throat, squinting tears out of his eyes. "I'm fine for now. Thanks."

Markovic tipped his glass back. He was still working on the first one, in no hurry.

"Let me ask you something, Oliveira. Sorry if it's a little personal."

"What is it?"

Markovic looked at him for a moment, studying him from up and down. "Do you believe in God?"

"Um...I'm not sure. I was raised Catholic, but we didn't really go to church much."

Markovic took a drink. "My old man didn't believe in church. Believed in God though. He always told me I'd meet him one day."

"I don't think I've met him yet then."

"That's the reporter talking again though. You need proof. So how do you prove that to a Catholic? Does it have to be angels and Jesus flying down from heaven on a cloud?"

"I'm not sure it works like that."

"Oh, I know it doesn't."

"So you believe in God?"

"Oh yeah. For a long time I didn't, but then I met Him, and there really wasn't any doubting it."

For almost ten minutes neither of them spoke. Aaron sipped his bourbon, watching as the convoy of ships came into full view. They were anchored end to end in a wide circle, with one spot left open for the trawler to squeeze in. The man working the wheel knew exactly what to do, positioning the ship without so much as a word from the Captain.

As the ship moved into the gap, Aaron saw the dock. It was a wide ring of metal platforms set atop orange pontoons, lined with chain guardrails and metal posts topped with spotlights.

"What is that?" Aaron asked.

Markovic filled his glass. "We built it about six years ago. Don't worry, it's very safe. Anchored to part of the reef at the bottom. Finish your drink and we'll go down and take a closer look."

Aaron did his best to choke down the last of the bourbon, but he felt slightly sick now. Markovic clapped him on the shoulder and pushed him toward the door.

"Come on, I'll introduce you to everyone."

They went down the steps, Aaron's head starting to spin. He'd had too much. Or he wasn't handling what little he had very well. Markovic saw what was happening and took him by the arm, steadying him as they crossed the deck and went down the gangway onto the dock.

Along the circle stood a dozen crews, at least a hundred fishermen in all, bathed in cold electric light. Beyond the edge, the water glowed yellow-green, lit from below.

"You're going to like this," Markovic said.

"Wait. Wait. You still didn't...still didn't tell me why you built it."

Markovic stepped over to the railing and looked into the water. "You have to understand, we were different people back then. We thought we could capture him and kill him. This was a trap. Not that it worked. Old Simba saw right through it. Almost pulled it down into the ocean, he was so mad. But we made our peace. We have an understanding now."

"An understanding?"

Markovic nodded at the water. "Take a look and see for yourself."

Aaron stepped to the railing, struggling to keep his balance. His head was throbbing now. He looked down into the water. In the cast of the lights, it was clear at least fifty feet down, the yellow-green giving way to darkness at the bottom.

"Do you see?" Markovic asked.

Aaron shook his head. "No."

"Keep looking."

Aaron looked. He wasn't sure what he was supposed to be seeing. It was just shadows. Nothingness. Empty –

No.

There *was* something.

It moved slowly in the darkness, coming closer. A hint of red.

"You see?" Markovic said. "He's very dependable."

"H-how?"

"You said you'd have to discount the other possibilities. What do think *that* is?"

Aaron watched it rise from the depths, it's body growing until it was almost as wide as the circle itself, its translucent, dome shaped membrane glowing in the light, flexing and contracting as if it was breathing the ocean in.

"Oh my God."

"That's exactly what He is," Markovic said. "He *is* God."

"*What?*"

"He gives and He takes, Mr. Oliveira. It's true, He mostly takes. But we can't blame Him for that. He's given us so much."

Aaron backed away from the railing, almost tripping over his own feet. The inside of his skull was tumbling.

"What the hell are you talking about?"

"You wanted to see Him. Here He is."

"Yeah, I see. But that's not...I'm not even sure what it is."

Aaron turned away from Markovic and saw Crudele standing on the gangway, blocking his path. The look on his face was unmistakable, a knowledge of what was about to happen. As he turned back, he saw the same look on a hundred other faces watching him, a sense of unwavering purpose. He saw it on Dimitrou's face as the big man reached down and grabbed him, lifting him off the deck and carrying him toward the railing.

"Stop!" he screamed. "Wait! Wait! *Why*...Why are you doing this?"

"I'm really sorry, Mr. Oliveira," Dimitriou said, without a hint of malice in his voice. "It's gotta be this way."

51

"No. Please. Stop. Stop it. Captain. Captain, for God's sake, listen to me. You don't have to do this!"

Markovic leaned against a light post, staring out at the water. "There's no other way. Sometimes we have to feed him. But he's very fair. We give him something to eat and he lets us take all the fish we want for a little while."

As he stepped away from the post, Aaron noticed the tattoo partially hidden beneath his sleeve for the first time. It was identical to the others, a fish cross with a Christlike jellyfish at the center.

He understood now.

Markovic looked at him apologetically. "Believe me, Mr. Oliveira. This is an honor. Each one of us will have our turn in time. And we'll give ourselves willingly. But tonight it has to be you."

"Please. Don't."

"God bless and keep you."

"NO."

Dimitriou's strong arms lifted him high into the air as if he weighted nothing at all. Aaron saw the night sky and the moon and the ships at the far end of the circle. And then he felt himself falling freely, the world turning over until he saw the water beneath him.

Cold saturated his skin from head to toe, a low drone filling his ears as his body became fully submerged. He flailed his arms and legs trying to find the surface, but down and up were the same. The entire world was yellow and green, dancing with small bubbles. Something moved before him, a thin hairlike strand that curved and swayed. Another appeared. And then another. Until there were dozens, moving toward him in slow motion.

Aaron pumped his arms and legs, trying to move away from them. But it was useless. His body was stiff, unable to function. The bourbon or the drug that had been slipped into it had done its work.

He hovered in the still water, feeling it gently pulse, watching as the tendrils glided and wrapped themselves around him. There was a sharp sting as they tore into his flesh, but the pain was almost pleasurable. It filled his mind with exquisite fear, paralyzing him as he was slowly dragged upward toward the underside of the jellyfish's quivering membrane, the hundreds of flagella radiating from beneath it as dense and delicate as the hairs on a lion's mane. They caressed him gently, pulling him inward and swallowing him whole.

Old Simba was hungry.

THE BLACK WATERS OF BABYLON

Brendan Vidito

When Philip Vorstadt arrived at the Seaside Rehabilitation Center, his body was broken, his mind on the brink of collapse.

The facility jutted from a rock cliff, its outermost wall suspended over the waves rolling and thundering below. Its sterile concrete exterior was splashed and bleached by sea spray, the windows girding its length tinted black and opaque. The main body of the facility was capped by a secondary structure that rose more than fifty feet into the air, a massive stone finger pointing at the sky. It appeared to serve no practical purpose and stood out in stark contrast against the heavy black clouds marshaled across the horizon.

A flight of stairs carved out of the rock ascended to Chinese-style double doors inlaid with brass gilding and painted a dark emerald green. Two men wearing hybrid outfits—part formal suit, part workman's uniform—of the same hue as the door behind them, stood guard. Their faces were entirely covered by helmets equipped with dark, reflective glasses and some kind of tubing that extended from the mouth area to the back of the head. They stood completely still, hands folded over their abdomens.

Vorstadt had not taken the stairs because of his confinement to a wheelchair, but instead rode an elevator encased in glass up to the main entrance. When he reached the top, he turned his head slowly to one side, grimacing at the pain sizzling like an old dynamite fuse down his neck and back, and stared out at the landscape fronting the rehab center.

Emptiness. Nothing but emptiness for miles and miles to the ends of the earth. At some point, the rocky terrain gave way to cracked soil studded with cottongrass, but otherwise Vorstadt perceived no other signs of life. Not a single seabird glided below the belly of the clouds, nor could a lone patient or doctor be seen taking a stroll to break the day's tedium. The facility and its environs were a drab purgatorial waiting room, a middle ground between shattered hopes and new beginnings.

Vorstadt had exhausted all other options, and only this desolate sanctuary remained. Doctors hundreds of miles away in the "other world," as Vorstadt had already come to know the place of his birth and residence, deemed his injuries irreparable. They had conducted various treatments and surgeries without any success. All Vorstadt was left with was a patchwork of thick, knotted scars and a debilitating twitch in his left eye as a result of post-surgical nerve damage. Granted, his injuries were extensive, but taking into account the recent advances in medical science and technology, Vorstadt thought it absurd that absolutely nothing could be done to improve his condition. As it was, his entire body was racked by perpetual agony. He could barely eat or drink on his own, let alone attend to his own toilet, and his speech—though he was rarely inclined to speak—tumbled past his broken teeth like hard chunks of vomit. The resulting sound was wet and nearly incomprehensible.

It all came down to this. The rehab center would either provide him with the healing he so desperately needed, or he would kill himself. He had even planned the method of his destruction. Seeing that he couldn't properly grasp a weapon between his fingers, he managed to convince his partner, Darren, who was skilled in computers and robotics, to engineer an execution device. Darren flat out refused to kill Vorstadt with his own hands, and so rigged the shotgun he would have otherwise employed in the assisted suicide to a simple contraption that responded to Vorstadt's voice command. The intention was for Vorstadt to position his face directly in front of the barrel and speak the word "flower," which he could pronounce with little difficulty. The computer wired to the contraption would then prompt a makeshift finger curled around the trigger to retract and discharge the shotgun, scattering Vorstadt's thoughts and memories in a spray of bloody bone. It was an elaborate and admittedly silly way to go, but prior to his infirmity, Vorstadt was something of a showman, easily able to capture the headlines as he ran his business with dramatic flair. So, to those who knew him best, his chosen method of destruction was very much within character.

"How are we feeling, Mr. Vorstadt?" asked the nurse who had been charged with pushing his wheelchair since he arrived at the center.

She was short statured and sturdily built, the sleeves of her olive uniform hemmed to reveal the lumps of muscle on her arms. Heir hair was dyed pale purple and combed flat toward the crown of her head. A pale curlicue of discolored skin in the shape of a snake—likely a manifestation of vitiligo—sketched itself around her left eye and across her forehead. When she smiled, Vorstadt had noticed that many of her teeth were capped with gunmetal fillings.

In response to her question, Vorstadt returned a clumsy nod. He was feeling fine. Not very optimistic or nervous, just fine. He had long since tempered his expectations, even though the rehab center came highly recommended in the more affluent circles he frequented. Many of his colleagues and acquaintances had paid ridiculous sums of money to treat their gout, back pain or arthritis. One guy even claimed to have been cured of his erectile dysfunction. However, had these been the only anecdotes associated with the facility, Vorstadt would have dismissed the place entirely, but there was another story, one that wasn't as publicly flaunted as the others, that capture Vorstadt's attention.

Her name was Mia. Six months ago, shortly before Vorstadt sustained his own injuries, Mia's now ex-husband had beaten her to the point where she was no longer able to walk. Vorstadt had seen her condition in the aftermath of the assault, a dispirited wreck, and it had hit him like a fist to the abdomen. Which made it all the more shocking when he saw her again after she had returned from the facility, her scars healed, her gait more graceful than ever. Vorstadt could only conceive of the change in the most cliché of terms: it was nothing short of a miracle.

And yet even having seen what the facility could do, Vorstadt was still cautious to hope. Whenever he closed his eyes, he saw the barrel of the shotgun pointed at him, seductive as a lover's bedroom gaze.

The doors to the facility opened from inside with a whir of mechanical gears. Out stepped a tall woman in a sleek black suit with a jacket so long it trailed at her heels like a cape. She was shaved bald, accentuating the startling beauty of her slanted chestnut eyes. Approaching Vorstadt she bowed low and said, "It is a pleasure to meet you, Mr. Vorstadt. I am Director Maikawa, the heart that pumps blood through this facility."

Vorstadt nodded again, his preferred form of expression.

"If you will join me," Maikawa said, gesturing to the innards of the rehab center. "We shall begin your treatment right away."

The nurse pushed Vorstadt over the threshold, the slight rise of the transition strip jostling his body from one arm of the chair to the other. He vaguely felt a line of drool escape his mouth, but could do nothing about it. Vorstadt was used to such indignities, so to avoid frustration he focused on his surroundings instead. The first thing he noticed about the facility was the smell. It was a rotten odor, sickly sweet, like spoiled fruit with a fishy undertone. Mixed with this was the lulling perfume of lavender and other olfactory notes native to a bathhouse.

Aesthetically, the facility was a neutered bore: whitewash walls, echoing ivory floors, grey tone artwork. And to top it off, the place seemed empty. Vorstadt didn't see anyone else on his way down the central hall, past rows of steel doors and open rooms neatly arranged with Oriental furniture. It was as though he were the only patient on hand, or else the others were deliberately kept from his view to maintain the illusion that he was receiving the facility's utmost care and attention.

"We studied your infirmities at length," Maikawa said, breaking the almost hypnotic tedium of their echoing footsteps, "and believe that you will only benefit from our most intensive treatment. Tell me, Mr. Vorstadt, have you ever undergone hydrotherapy?"

"N-no," he managed to say.

"As its name suggests, it is a form of alternative medicine that uses water to treat various physical ailments. Outside this facility, it is used in a rather *benign* fashion," she lingered on the word, savored it, "usually through pool exercise or floating therapy. Here, we do things a little differently."

They reached the end of the hallway, where a set of glass doors led into darkness. Vorstadt could hear a faint wind howling behind them, strangely amplified as though the sound were conveyed through a tunnel. He realized then they must have been standing where the massive stone pillar rose out of the middle of the facility. The pillar was undoubtedly open to the sky, which explained the mournful bellow of the wind. What purpose could it serve, he wondered. He was confident he would soon find out.

Maikawa turned to face him. "Through these doors is the pride of our facility, the Rod of Babylon. It extends seventy-five feet into the air, and tunnels through the rock beneath us, to the cold, black waters below. It is there we intend to heal you."

She held out her hand toward him in a demonstrative gesture. Vorstadt followed the movement with his eyes and noticed, for the first time, the perfect grid of puncture wounds on her palm. Each hole was red with coagulated blood, the skin around them white as a fish's belly. When she noticed his gaze, Maikawa smiled modestly and slowly drew her fingers into a fist.

The sight left Vorstadt with a queasy feeling in the pit of his stomach. It didn't appear to be any injury he was familiar with; it was too perfect, too clean. And not to mention a trypophobe's worst nightmare. Before he could consider the matter further, he was struck by a blast of sea wind.

Director Maikawa had opened the glass doors and was now inviting Vorstadt inside. The nurse pushed him forward and the overhead lights sputtered into activity. The sudden brightness stung Vorstadt's eyes. They were gathered in a small antechamber lined with steel and reinforced with concrete. A series of vents along the far wall admitted the outside air. Every surface shined and gave back a distorted reflection. The place was bare except for a solitary locker in the corner and a canvas harness attached to some kind of pulley mechanism facing yet another door.

"Nurse, if you will please remove Mr. Vorstadt's clothing."

The nurse engaged the wheelchair's manual brake, walked around to face Vorstadt, who nodded his consent, and proceeded to undress him. He hated every moment of it. She was much gentler than his homecare nurse, he would give her that, but the whole process was no less undignified or embarrassing. He hated how she needed to guide his limbs into a more comfortable position as soon as she removed them from a shirtsleeve or pant leg; hated the feeling of her breath fanning his skin as she toiled at the task; hated the way his naked body looked under fluorescent lights, all pallor and sagging, atrophied muscles. He fixed her with his gaze and mumbled, "This had better goddamn work."

"We will do our best, Mr. Vorstadt," she answered with a gunmetal smile.

She wheeled his bare, pathetic form toward the harness and strapped him in, the coarse canvas looping around his biceps, thighs, chest, and buttocks to ensure maximum support. Vorstadt now realized that the harness could be raised or lowered, presumably down the shaft on the opposite side of the door, with the help of the pulley system. For the second time today, a queasy pang lanced through the pit of his stomach.

The nurse produced a keycard from her pocket and swiped it through a reader on the door. It beeped, disengaging the lock, and the nurse moved to open it. Vorstadt was assaulted once more by a surge of briny air, only this time it was strong enough to make him flinch. The spray dappled his face and sent gooseflesh skittering down his spine. When the initial blast of air had subsided and Vorstadt was able to open his eyes fully, he saw framed in the doorway a darkness so thick, it was more an absence of matter than light.

Wasn't the Rod of Babylon open to the sky? How else could the breeze find its way into the antechamber? And more importantly, wouldn't the drab daylight filter down? Why, or more precisely, how could this utter blackness be possible?

A headache started to pulse at the base of his skull. He averted his gaze, looking up at Maikawa, who said, "You will be lowered into the pool beneath the facility. Treatment will take anywhere between four and eight hours. When enough time has elapsed we will examine your condition and proceed with additional treatment if needed. Please be aware that that once you have been lowered into the pool, you will have no way of communicating with us. Treatment cannot be interrupted if you expect to see results. Do you understand?"

Vorstadt's mind was a maelstrom of conflicting emotions—confusion, fear, doubt and wonder—all vying for dominance, but none of them winning, and so he was left in a state of total bewilderment. All he could muster was a weak nod.

"Very well," Maikawa said.

A quick glance at the nurse and Vorstadt was lifted out of his chair and into the nurse's arms. She carried him to the threshold and lowered him into a sitting position, with his legs dangling over the edge of the abyss. Looking down, Vorstadt saw that the darkness cut his legs off at the knees. He blinked the illusion away.

"We will see you in a few hours. Godspeed, Mr. Vorstadt," said Maikawa.

From behind him came the grinding of old machinery. Then the nurse nudged him over the precipice, into the devouring dark.

***

He didn't know how long he was suspended, weightless, in that void; time was useless here, an artifact of the lighted world Vorstadt feared he would never see again. His ears were filled with the mournful cries of the wind. Sea spray kissed his naked flesh and set him shivering. He smelled the sea, the rotting stench of exposed algae, and the occasional whiff of fish guts.

Vorstadt closed his eyes and thought about Darren. He remembered his lover's reaction upon stepping into the critical care unit. If only his mind hadn't chosen consciousness at that precise moment. Never before had he seen a face transform so dramatically. The sheer horror and heartbreak that pulled Darren's formerly slack features apart was so surreal as to resemble a cheap prosthetic effect. Vorstadt would never have thought, never dreamed, that Darren's facial muscles were capable of such a sickening distortion. Unable to move due to being so tightly bandaged, Vorstadt could do nothing but stare, realizing in that moment that his pain was not exclusively his own. Darren, whom he loved more than anything, shared it too. Which meant that his sojourn at the clinic wasn't a selfish pursuit. Darren would be undergoing the same treatment by proxy.

The image of the execution device returned again to Vorstadt's mind. It occurred to him that should the treatment fail and the shotgun empty its load into his skull, he would be confronted one last time by Darren's horrified expression before plunging into death: his own brief moment of hell.

Cold, black water engulfed his toes. Vorstadt jerked violently, the movement sending a cataclysm of pain through his entire body. The water crept up his legs, washed over his thighs and swallowed his midsection. The pulley mechanism halted just as the sea lapped against his chin. Vorstadt let out a deep, startled breath. It was lost in the roar of the wind.

The long wait began.

He kept his eyes closed, cleared his mind, and tried his best to relax. Eventually the wind receded to white noise and he lost all sensation below the neckline. He was a disembodied head floating in space.

Doubt frequently tried to force itself into his mind—how can this possibly work? It's a scam. There's no hope you—but Vorstadt was easily able to push it back. He entered into a state of deep relaxation, becoming one with the water, a liquid being who swayed to the rhythm of the ocean. It entered into his awareness in the same way a truth is known in a dream that he was suspended over a trench several miles deep. The emptiness impressed itself on his brain, provoking feelings of reverence and wonder. He remained in this state of sublime gnosis for what seemed like hours then, over the noise of the wind, began to hear a faint music from somewhere below.

It was unlike any music he had heard before, and could only be distinguished as such because it had a melody. Slowly it grew louder and more distinct as whatever made it approached the surface. At first Vorstadt thought he was imagining the whole thing, but when something heavy brushed against his leg and the music swelled to a crescendo, he realized it was all too real. Whatever it was moved with fluid grace, its fleshy net-like body fanning his calves. Long strands of hair coiled around his toes.

He kicked in vain, his nerves flaring with agony, but the thing maintained its orbit around him. The music was almost deafening now. He lifted his head to the invisible sky and screamed. At that moment a stinger pierced the sole of his foot and flooded his bloodstream with warmth. His scream subsided into a drooling moan. Abruptly the music stopped and the wind resumed its howling dominance.

***

Winter receded into spring and then early summer. Vorstadt took advantage of the weather and decided to take lunch outside the office. The sidewalk was beautifully firm under his feet. He stuffed his hands deep into his pockets and walked fast, feeling the sultry breeze palm and caress his face.

At the café, he ordered a sandwich and coffee. As he extended a handful of coins across the counter, he noticed the cashier staring at the patch of discolored skin across his knuckles. It looked like an early manifestation of vitiligo. He smiled at her, completed the transaction and stepped out into the street.

His phone buzzed. It was Darren.

"Will you be home tonight?"

"Yeah. Why? Do you have something in mind?"

"Not exactly," he said. "I just want to see you. Ever since you recovered you can't seem to sit down for longer than five minutes. You're always busy doing something."

"I'll be there. In fact, if you want—"

A sharp, searing pain tore across his thigh and then the sidewalk was rushing up to meet him. He managed to break his fall with an outstretched hand, and as soon as he recovered, moved into a sitting position with his knees drawn up to his chest. A bicycle lay on its side several feet away, the rider in the process of getting to his feet.

"I'm so sorry, man," the cyclist was saying. "Are you okay?"

Vorstadt glanced down at the tear in his dress pants, the ragged edges dark with blood.

"I'll be fine," he said and allowed the biker to help him to his feet.

***

In the office bathroom, Vorstadt locked himself in a stall, unhooked his belt, and carefully shimmied out of his pants. The cut was at least an inch deep, but it had already stopped bleeding. He sat on the lid of the toilet seat and, using the pointer finger of both hands, pried open the laceration to examine it more closely. His mouth went dry.

Instead of muscle, fat and bone, the inside of his thigh was filled with rows of short, nubby teeth. When he prodded one of them with his finger, it retreated deeper into his body like a startled worm. In its place came a gush of yellowish brown fluid reeking of dead fish, and a black fingerling that landed on the bathroom tile and started thrashing around. Its skin was featureless and slick, lamplight eyes glowed with bioluminescence above a set of human-like teeth. Vorstadt calmly crushed it under his heel. He wasn't alarmed. This was the price of his treatment, the only way he could have avoided the kiss of the shotgun.

He opened the cut wider, hissing through gnashed teeth. A fish's eye became visible at the bottom of the wound and rolled to look at him. The pupil was large and inquisitive. He stared back, impassive, then yanked his hands away as the wound clamped shut like a mouth. The skin knitted itself back together, leaving behind a strip of bleached, colorless skin.

Vorstadt stood up and pulled up his pants, making a mental note to have them mended if possible. He turned and stared into the toilet bowl, its waters calm and sending back a mirror's clear reflection. Movement deep inside his thigh made his leg twitch. They were getting restless. Soon the full price of his miracle would have to be paid. The flood was coming.

WET TEXAS

Max Booth III

"Where does all the rain go?" a guest wanted to know, struggling to keep his balance in the lobby as he prevented the night clerk, Jose, from returning to his movie in the back office. The guy's breath hit Jose as soon as he entered the hotel. Some kind of liquor combination the man must have invented tonight in the spur of the moment. Exotic, repulsive, nauseating. Somehow the smell broke through Jose's clogged nostrils, penetrated his already raw lungs. Struggling not to wheeze and cough, he nodded along to the guest's ramblings. "The rain, it must go somewhere, anywhere."

"I think it just soaks into the earth." Jose had never studied rain, had never paid attention in science class, but hell, even a night auditor could answer some questions, and this was a question that seemed fairly simple. The rain didn't go back up into the sky, after all. Reality wasn't a video that could just rewind at a moment's notice. Then he glanced down at his hand, at the strange webs of skin that'd grown between his fingers over the last few days, and debated the accuracy of how he'd define reality.

"What, you're saying the Earth is a sponge, is that it?" The guest's face grimaced, all screwed up, too complicated of a concept to comprehend. "What are humans then, huh? You saying I'm a sponge, too?"

"Man, I don't know."

"What about now?" The guest gestured outside, at the rain that fell in sheets rather than drops. "It's too much rain. Where does it all go? The sewer? The sewer ain't infinite. The—what, the ocean? Ocean ain't infinite, either! This fuckin' planet ain't infinite, but this rain sure is, this rain is fuckin' forever. So where. Does. It. Go?"

Jose didn't have an answer, didn't care enough to stress his brain, couldn't stop thinking how in twenty minutes he'd need to start preparing the hotel's breakfast, and he still had a good half hour remaining of his movie, couldn't stop thinking about how his lungs were on fire and all he wanted to do was go home and sleep for eternity, stop thinking about the skin growth on his fingers and embrace the dream-void.

"I feel it already." The guest raised his arms up, as if preaching. "We're all gonna drown, that's how it's gonna end. It's just gonna keep on raining until this whole fuckin' planet overflows like a plastic cup under a beer keg. And what then? Huh? What then?"

"I...I don't know."

"Nothing, that's what. Absolutely fuckin' nothing."

The hotel's power blinked off and on, as if to serve as an exclamation mark to the guest's statement. The guest grinned, nodded at Jose, then turned around and stumbled down the hallway toward the elevator. Jose thought about warning him against it, seeing how the power couldn't make up its mind, but decided fuck it, he'd already wasted enough time for one night. He had a movie to finish, breakfast to cook, reports to go through. In a few hours, he'd have two nights off. Someone else could worry about the rain.

And sure enough, it was still raining after he clocked out and drove home, still raining as he slept all day, still raining when he woke up later that night to the sound of his phone ringing. How the fuck hadn't it slowed down yet? It'd been days since it first started. Texas rain typically didn't last long—it hit in sporadic blasts, like machine gun fire—but no, if anything, it'd started coming down harder.

Jose should have known better than to answer the phone. He saw the caller ID. He knew what Javier was going to say. He should've just ignored it, turned it on silent, gone back to sleep. But of course he answered. He always answered.

"I can't come in." No 'Hello?', no 'This is Jose, how can I help you?'. Straight to the chase. He wasn't fucking coming in. It was his night off. It was the only thing he ever looked forward to and he wasn't going to throw it away.

Javier didn't seem to understand. "Trenton called off. There's nobody else."

"There's you."

"I don't know how to run the audit."

"What kind of manager doesn't know how to run the audit?"

"Please, Jose, I don't know what else to do. Everybody's too sick. This bug going around is awful. Taylor's still at the hotel and she's blowing up my phone about abandoning the front desk if someone doesn't come soon."

"It's my night off."

"You can have tomorrow off."

"I already *have* tomorrow off."

"You can have the night after that, too."

"And what's stopping Trenton from calling off again?"

"Well, I'll tell him he's fired if he does."

"Yeah, right. You're gonna fire the owner's son? Fat chance."

"Look, I don't know, okay? I need you down there."

"And if I refuse?"

"Then I guess you're the one who's fired."

"That's the way it's going to be?"

"That's the way it's going to be."

"Then I guess I'm out of a job. Peace."

Jose hung up and tossed his cell phone on the bed. He turned on his Playstation, played for twenty seconds, thought about how much he preferred having electricity and water over being homeless, thought about all the bums outside drowning in the Texas rain, then paused the game and called Javier.

"Okay, I'll come in."

"I love you."

"Whatever."

Besides, it wasn't like he could play video games tonight, anyway. His fingers felt too weird, made him lose focus. Tomorrow, after work, he'd need to get this checked out. Assuming the rain had stopped by then. He thought about googling "webbed fingers" but couldn't muster the courage to face what was almost certainly warnings of cancer. Instead he tried to call the hotel to let Taylor know he was on his way, but no one picked up. Maybe she'd already said fuck it and left. He wouldn't blame her. One look outside his apartment and his body tensed, nearly paralyzed. Absolute darkness interrupted briefly by sparse lightning bolts. Cracks of thunder drowned out the rain slapping against his living room window. Somewhere in the distance—sirens. And lots of 'em.

He owned an umbrella, but he never figured out how to open it. He gave it another try now, praying to god it'd suddenly decide to play ball. Instead it just stared at him and laughed and asked, "What kind of man can't open an umbrella?"

Jose threw it across the room. "Fuck you, too."

Once he was dressed, he locked the front door and booked it across a soggy front yard toward his parking space. He practically dived behind the wheel, already soaked. Pneumonia whispered its inevitable arrival and he tried to shake it off. Even on full blast, the windshield wipers did little to clear his vision. He glanced in the rearview mirror and noticed two vertical columns of tiny holes spread across both sides of his neck. He squeezed his eyes shut until his brain hurt, then looked again. Still there. Maybe not holes. Some kind of intense acne. Something to further investigate in the hotel bathroom once he made it to work. He attempted to touch one of them and flinched at the anticipation of pain, but none came. He probed a finger into one of the holes and felt a dull numbness. Jesus Christ, he was in no condition to work. He was clearly dying from some fucked-up disease. He should be driving to a hospital, not a hotel.

His tires fought to maintain traction as they spun out of the parking lot. He gripped the steering wheel with his webbed fingers until his knuckles whitened and muttered the word, "Fuck," over and over, turning it into a mantra, linguistic fuel to guide him onward.

The roads were empty save for his own piece of shit car. And for good reason. He refused to even slow down at stop signs lest the water's current drag him into a ditch. The flood wasn't yet deep enough to prevent him from moving, but another couple hours and he'd be doomed. He should have packed better before leaving, in case he found himself trapped at the hotel for a few days. It didn't seem likely, but Jose didn't exactly have the best luck. Sometimes he had to listen to his gut, and his gut told him there would be no relief come 7:00 A.M. Housekeeping wouldn't show up. The breakfast lady would be MIA. Even Javier wouldn't answer the phone. His gut told him that he was driving into a certain shit-show, that this rain, this flooding, it was only the beginning of an impossible headache.

His leg started vibrating, a sensation he figured belonged to the car bouncing over puddles and tree debris. Except then his leg started singing, too. One hand on the wheel, he dug out his phone from his pocket and answered it. A photo of the hotel glared at him from the caller ID.

"Yeah?" Jose shouted. Needed to shout because he couldn't hear, couldn't concentrate, the rain was so goddamn loud who could even think?

"You almost here?" Taylor sounded desperate and he knew why. If he didn't make it soon, she'd be stuck.

"Maybe five minutes away. Ten at the most. I'm trying, but it's terrible out here."

"I don't know what to do. Javier won't answer the phone."

"I'll be there soon."

"A guest is sick."

"What?"

"A guest, he's sick or something, I don't know. I tried calling nine-one-one, but it's just a busy signal."

"How is he sick?"

"He won't stop puking. He came in from outside, drenched, and just fell down in the lobby, screaming and puking."

"Gross."

"I think it's blood."

"Excuse me?"

"He's puking blood."

"What is he doing now?"

"I don't know. He's just lying on the floor, shaking and moaning."

"Have you...have you tried to help him?"

"Do I look like a fucking doctor, Jose?"

"No, it's just—"

"Every two seconds, another guest comes up and complains about the rain. Says they paid good money to stay here and they can't even leave. Everybody wants refunds. Javier isn't answering. It's almost midnight. I shouldn't even fucking be here."

"I'm almost there."

"Well, the keys are on the front desk. I'm fucking done. I'm sorry, but I can't do this."

"Taylor, please, listen, I'm—OH SHIT!"

Jose dropped the phone and grabbed the wheel with both hands, attempting to keep the car straight as a gush of water smashed into the side of the car. Rain and thunder drowned out his screams as the road disappeared and a tree swallowed the car's engine. Jose shot forward and headbutted the wheel, bounced back against the driver's seat and just sat there for a moment, confused and aching. Behind him, glass cracked, slowly at first, then all at once as rainwater exploded through and made itself at home. Frantic, Jose unbuckled his seatbelt and tried to push open the door, but it held shut, barricaded by the rising water. Where the fuck was he—in a lake? Trees weren't in lakes. No, this was just the side of the road, or what had once been a road, now it was something new, its own lake, its own monstrosity, newly born and hungry, starving, eager to grow up and be strong. He rolled down the window as his legs soaked in rising water and climbed out of the car moments before it disappeared in the murky depths of the flood.

Half-swimming, half-running, he escaped the flooded ditch and climbed back up on the road, where the current was still strong, but not deep enough to devour him whole. He ran without thinking, struggling to lift his legs as the road continued to be assaulted. He tried to continue his mantra of "fuck" but every time he opened his mouth he risked assassinating his lungs. Instead he reserved the song for inside his head.

fuck fuck fuck fuck fuck fuck fuck fuck fuck fuck

He moved without sight, relying on memory of his surroundings. The water continued rising as the rain fell harder. Gunshots from the sky, puncturing the earth and infecting it with its misery. Like running through quicksand or upstairs in a dream, his legs turned to rubber and even tiptoeing forward proved excruciating. Lips opened to release a scream but instead released a stream of bloody bile. The water smelled, not like chlorine but like a junkyard, a rotting corpse, an orgy of maggots. All the dirt in town reanimating with the rain, standing up and shambling, on the hunt for prey. An orchestra of sewer-stank decomposition violated his senses and wiped his innards dry of its half-digested contents. He struggled forward, swimming in his own mess, not giving a shit, determined to reach the hotel before it was too late.

If he lived to tell this story, the first thing everybody would ask is: Why didn't you just stay home? You knew how bad the weather was, knew roads were flooding, and you still went to work.

And Jose would tell them all the same answer, that he went to work because the next time Texas flooded, at least he'd still have a place to live, that he wouldn't be face-down under some bridge. People in horror movies never had jobs. Jose wasn't living a movie. He was just trying to survive.

Cramps shot through his legs. Something bit him, nibbled on his calves. He looked down but failed to penetrate the water's filthy layers. Some kind of fish, maybe, brought in from the lake. He tried to kick as he moved, but the water barely allowed him to step forward. He reached down into the darkness and swiped around his leg, fingertips brushing against something thick and prickly, something made of scales. He grabbed at it and pulled, except the creature didn't budge because it wasn't a creature at all. He was holding his own leg.

what the fuck what the fuck what the fuck

He vomited again, not just from his mouth but also from the tiny holes in his neck.

The holes that he refused to admit looked like gills. Gills like from a fish. Gills like from the goddamn Creature from the Black Lagoon.

Blood and vomit poured out of his orifices like a broken dam and he collapsed to his knees, into the dirty water, letting the current drag him off the road and into the ditch, into the trees, into oblivion. He closed his eyes and waited for death to take him, but the rain wanted him more, claimed him, promised to take good care of him, whispered its eternal love with wet kisses and gentle caresses.

Then it spat him out.

Jose sat up, emerged from the flood in the hotel parking lot. The rain had brought him here, somehow had known his destination, traded thoughts with his subconscious. He stuck his tongue out and expressed his gratitude with quick licks of the falling droplets. He didn't understand what was happening but he knew, somehow, the rain was responsible. The rain had birthed something inside of him, and it was hatching. His body was changing, his thoughts mutating into foreign concepts. He no longer feared the rain. He loved the rain. He did not understand this feeling, this desire to live forever in this dirty, disgusting, beautiful flood, but he could not deny it.

It was real and he could not run away from it.

Instead of standing, Jose crawled through the water. The automatic sliding front doors of the hotel were stuck open, the electricity in the building long dead. The lobby was dark and quiet save for the sound of water splashing as he crawled. He passed bodies floating facedown in the lobby. Guests who would never check out, trapped in this hotel until something came to eat them up. Jose tried to ignore his stomach grumbling, but it wasn't an easy feat. Up ahead, a body convulsed against the lobby wall in a sitting position. He recognized the woman from another life. He was supposed to relieve her tonight.

"Taylor?" The word left his mouth in a guttural voice alien from his usual tone, yet it felt right, like a baseball glove broken in from a previous generation.

She lifted her head and revealed a face mutated into something disgusting, something beautiful. Wide gills expanded from her cheeks. The skin on her face had been replaced by a layer of green scales. Jose wondered if his face looked the same. Judging by the way she stared at him, he didn't have to guess.

She opened her mouth to speak and blood poured down her chin. "What's going on? Why...why is this happening?"

"The rain." Jose moved closer, laid his head on her lap, content. "The rain, the rain."

"But...but how?"

"Showing us...showing us the truth."

"I don't understand."

"WHERE DOES THE RAIN GO?" a voice screamed behind them, and shot up, saw a man sitting on the front desk, naked and covered in scales, covered in blood.

The guest, the drunkard who'd harassed him the previous night. Jose couldn't fucking believe it.

"It must go somewhere, right?" he cried, rocking back and forth. "It must go somewhere!"

Nausea overwhelmed Jose and he collapsed back in Taylor's lap. She caressed his head, dug her nails into his cheeks.

On the front desk, the guest screamed, "*WHERE DOES THE RAIN GO WHERE DOES THE RAIN GO WHERE DOES THE RAIN GO WHERE DOES THE RAIN GO,*" and he didn't stop, not even as the bodies facedown in the water started to moan, not even as the water in the lobby rose and swallowed them whole.

FOR THE SEAFOOD LOVER IN YOU

Joshua Chaplinsky

300 million years ago, family cymothoidae ruled the shallow seas of the carboniferous. Long after their oniscidean cousins took to dry land, they continued to resist evolution's pull, resulting in their relegation to the bathypelagic depths as a relict population. Hypotheses abound concerning these and other "alien" inhabitants of the ocean floor, but there is little evidence of their origin being panspermian in nature.

In March of 1969, two entrepreneurs pooled their resources and opened a seafood restaurant in Lakelove, Florida. Two years later, a multinational corporation acquired the establishment and implemented a campaign of rapid expansion, one which would continue unabated for the better part of the next forty years. Despite multiple class-action lawsuits due to food poisoning and parasitic infection, as well as unsubstantiated rumors of fatality, the popularity of the restaurant remains at an all-time high.

Chitin split with a satisfying crack, sending a spray of lobstery water into Rayburn's good eye, the one he had jokingly referred to as his "seein' eye." Jolene emitted a panicked yelp and reached for her napkin, dabbed it at his face in an attempt to undo the damage. She couldn't help sneaking a look at the deflated orb next to the healthy one as she did. As offputting as the eye was, she had a good feeling about Rayburn. After a string of disappointing dates, he was her first potential keeper.

"Think you made it worse." Rayburn gently brushed her hand away, grin-squinting across the table. "There was more juice on that napkin than in the whole damn claw."

Jolene looked from his face to her napkin and back.

"I'll grab the waitress."

She went to raise her hand. Rayburn intercepted it, brought it back to the table and gave it a lingering pat.

"Really, it's fine."

Her concern transformed into a smile. A smile she proceeded to stuff with a hot Cheddar Cove biscuit. Rayburn smiled right back at her. In his experience, a well-fed woman was more inclined to spread her legs. He dipped his spoon into his lobster bisque, transferred its contents to his mouth with a slurp. Orange-pink droplets clung to his mustache.

"Here, let me get that."

She was a quick draw with the napkin. Rayburn pulled back, out of reach. Dragged a sleeve across his upper lip.

"Sorry," Jolene said. "It's the mother in me."

Rayburn stiffened, arm suspended mid-air.

"Your profile didn't say anything about kids."

"Not yet. But someday." She said it with the perfect combination of hope and wistfulness. Rayburn responded by letting his good eye wander across the nautical themed decor of the restaurant. Jolene could tell she was losing him. She mustered up as much sexy as she could.

"You sure you don't want a bite of mine?" She motioned to her plate with a miniature fork. The beady eyes and furry mandibles canceled out any effect the clumsy innuendo might have had.

"I don't dine on bottom feeding shit-eaters." Rayburn maintained wary eye contact with the creature as he said it. "Too many parasites."

Jolene frowned. Looked at his bowl of soup.

"What do you think's in that lobster bisque? Fried chicken?"

Rayburn scoffed.

"Everyone knows that bisque lobster ain't *real* lobster."

"It's not?" Jolene raised a skeptical eyebrow, defiant in its arch.

"Nope. Made out of something called *poh*-lahk. Like those folks they make all the jokes about? Much safer than shellfish."

Jolene stuck a walking leg in her mouth and sucked at a stubborn morsel of meat. She didn't care for racial humor. But like her momma always told her, if you wanted to catch yourself a Florida man, you had to make some concessions. She pushed the comment out of her mind as Rayburn dipped his spoon back into his bowl. Brought the utensil up to his lips.

Slurped.

Chewed.

Roared.

"God *dammit*!" He clamped a hand over his mouth. Jolene's eyes went wide as his spoon clattered to the table.

"What's wrong?"

"Sink I vit mah kung."

"What?"

"MAH KUNG."

It took a few seconds before it clicked.

"Oooh, your *tongue*. Let me see."

71

Jolene leaned across the table. Rayburn tilted his head back and opened his mouth.

"Aaaaaah…"

Jolene grimaced. It was like that old joke—*Do you like see-food?* Vinyl squeaked as she sat back in her seat. Her dream date was going south fast.

"Looks like you bit yourself but good."

Rayburn hunched over, drooling blood and bisque into his napkin. He forced a cough to shake loose any solid bits still in his mouth, then used a finger to inspect the contents.

"Wah ta huck es sat?"

He held out the napkin for Jolene to see.

"Oh god." Her cheeks ballooned. It was her turn to clamp hand to mouth.

"Wah?"

"I think it's a piece of your tongue."

They contemplated the lump of meat. It looked like a chewed up eraser. The kind you stick on the end of a pencil that doesn't have one.

"I think we should get the check," Jolene said.

"Huck dat. Ah nah thaying ha dis meal. Wayther!"

Rayburn raised the bloody napkin in the air.

The waiter, who quickly realized he was in over his pay-grade, deferred to the manager, who in turn ushered Rayburn and Jolene through the kitchen and into his office—which just so happened to be in the alley behind the restaurant. That's where Rayburn pled his case, in front of Jolene and God—and two men in hip-waders unloading 50 gallon drums of biscuit mix off an unmarked truck. The men paid the argument little mind, engrossed in the business of batter conveyance.

It took quite a bit of gesticulating and some translation on Jolene's part, but they managed to get 20% off the bill. Pretty good, all things considered, although Rayburn contested it was insufficient compensation for losing of a quarter inch of "pussy-licker." Jolene didn't appreciate his crassness, but decided to overlook it on account of the circumstances.

They walked across the parking lot arm in arm, Rayburn pressing a napkin against his tongue. Jolene made a mental checklist of pros and cons, comparing the night's events to previous dates, thinking how things couldn't get any worse, when all of a sudden they were awash in headlights. A voice cut across the parking lot.

"Rayburn Buckwalder, is that you?"

Rayburn stopped dead in his tracks.

"Huck."

"What is it?" Jolene dug her nails into his arm.

"Mah hucking wythe."

Jolene's stomach dropped.

A bottle blond emerged from the car and strode towards them, eyes green with jealousy.

"You sonofabitch. I didn't want to believe it when Katie-Anne called me..."

Rayburn swallowed with an audible gulp.

"How could you go to Crimson Crustacean without me?"

Jolene looked confused. Rayburn just stood there. Ten more steps and the blond would be on them. Nine, eight, seven...

Her ankle turned on six, sending her face-first into the pavement. Rayburn and Jolene winced in unison.

"I'm okay!" The blond bounced back like a Bumble. Rayburn shook his head in embarrassment.

"Ah you dunk?"

"Maybe." The blond jabbed a finger at Rayburn's chest. "But not on lobster." She turned to face Jolene, put out a hand." I'm Sandy, by the way. Rayburn's Mrs."

"Jolene," Jolene said in a soft voice, taking Sandy's hand. Sandy looked her up and down.

"She's cute," she said to her husband.

"Taught you wah at yah thister's baby thower."

"She called it off." Sandy brushed specks of errant gravel off her blouse.

"Taught it wath a supithe?"

"Not the shower, dumbass—*the baby*."

"Oh."

Rayburn went silent. Jolene looked out across the parking lot, trying to give them some semblance of privacy. She didn't believe in abortion under any circumstances, but this was none of her business. She noticed the two men from the biscuit truck had finished loading and were watching them.

"Why do you have a napkin in your mouth?" Sandy asked.

"He bit his tongue," Jolene said over her shoulder, still watching the men watching them. They weren't being very subtle about it.

"Oh, you poor thing." Sandy hooked her arm around Rayburn's. "Let's get you home."

"What about me?" Jolene said, turning her attention back to the couple.

"We'll drop you off."

"Wat abaht yah cah?" Rayburn said.

Sandy waved him off with a limp, bangled wrist.

"I can't drive, I'm drunk."

Rayburn squinted at the high beams of his wife's car.

***

Before Jolene knew it, she found herself in Rayburn's pickup, squished between him and his wife, speeding down the interstate.

"You sure you didn't burn it?" Sandy said.

Rayburn nodded. Sandy turned to Jolene.

"He probably just burned it. *Wait until it cools*, I always tell him, but no—"

"Ith not a thucking burn!"

Sandy rolled her eyes for Jolene's benefit. Looked back at her husband.

"I'll be the judge of that. Let me see."

"Ahm diving."

"You telling me you can't drive and use your tongue at the same time? Remember who bailed you out when Sheriff Johnson pulled you over for having Misty Evans' legs wrapped around your face."

Rayburn glared at his wife.

"Come on, then. Stick it out."

Rayburn dutifully obeyed. Sandy leaned across Jolene to see. Recoiled.

"Ugh, that smells awful. Turn on the light, I can't see a goddamn thing."

Rayburn flicked on the interior light. Stuck out his tongue.

Sandy and Jolene screamed in unison. Almost as if they'd been screaming the entire ride. Limbs flailed as they attempted to put some distance between themselves and Rayburn.

"Wah da thuck?!?!"

Headlights blinded them as the truck swerved into oncoming traffic. Rayburn yanked the wheel in the opposite direction. The pickup fishtailed all over the road.

"There's something in your mouth!" Sandy pointed an accusing finger.

"Dere's nuthig in mah mowth."

"It looked at me!"

Tires screeched and horns blared as the other vehicles attempted to avoid a collision.

"Your tongue—it has a face!"

Rayburn stomped on the brakes, bringing the pickup skidding to a halt mid-road. A cacophony of irate beeping threatened to deafen them.

He stuck out his tongue and looked in the rearview. His shriek drowned out even the horns.

Jolene clamped her hands over her ears and wondered if she should mention they'd passed her exit.

***

Rayburn burst through the apartment door, Sandy trailing behind him. He made a bee-line for the bathroom.

"Ray, I really think we should call an ambulance."

"I thold you, NO DOCTUTHS." He slammed the door behind him.

Sandy hovered outside the bathroom, hugging herself and pouting. Jolene poked her head through the still-open front door.

"He hates doctors." Sandy bent at the knees and mimed herself two-handing something large in front of her pelvis. Then she made a motion like she was wielding a giant pair of scissors. Jolene's face went blank.

"An accident." She said it in a whisper. "Blinded by forceps at birth."

"Oh."

"Say, that gives me an idea."

Sandy ran towards the kitchen.

Meanwhile, in the bathroom, Rayburn paced the floor in front of the mirror, mouth shut tight. His nostrils flared as he breathed heavily through his nose. A solitary sheet of paper fluttered on the toilet roll.

He stopped and faced the mirror. Gripping the countertop he glared at his looking-glass self. He imagined every doctor he'd never been to, standing before him with every tongue depressor ever made. He opened his mouth, stuck out his tongue, said *ah*.

That *ah* morphed into an open-throated scream

Nestled in the half-eaten pulp of his tongue lay a white, segmented body with beady black eyes. The thing observed him via the mirror as he screamed, its front appendages—the only pair not sunk into his flesh—folded together like a malevolent cartoon billionaire.

Rayburn panicked, both hands clawing at the creature to no avail. It only caused the thing to dig in deeper. The throbbing in his tongue intensified.

He fell back against the wall, chest heaving. Every exhalation accompanied by an ovine bleat. Bloody spittle collected in the corners of his mouth.

That's when Sandy burst through the door, brandishing a pair of metal salad tongs.

75

Rayburn flashed back to a moment he couldn't possibly remember—a man in green scrubs coming at him in the safety of his mother's womb.

"No! Thay away!" Rayburn back-peddled, tripping and falling into the tub, taking the shower curtain down with him, Marion Crane style.

"Hold still," Sandy said. "It's just me."

Rayburn whimpered as he presented his tongue. Sandy gripped it with the tongs, not able to see where the muscle ended and the creature began.

"Ready?" she said, more to herself than Rayburn. She didn't wait for a response. She pulled with all her might.

There was a sound like the tearing of fabric and the tension gave. Sandy fell backwards, tongs flying out of her hands. Rayburn screamed with renewed vigor, swinging his head back and forth as his tongue lolled a good six inches from his mouth, disconnected at the root. All the while the parasite held on tight.

Sandy started to cry. Jolene, who had finally worked up the nerve to poke her head into the bathroom, promptly fainted at what she saw.

***

Jolene awoke propped up on the living room couch, a whimpering Sandy curled up beside her. She instinctively put out a hand and stroked Sandy's hair.

Rayburn lay on the living room floor, dried blood encrusting his face. Somehow his tongue had found its way back into his mouth. His eyes twitched back and forth, tracing the cracks in the ceiling.

"What... was that thing?" Jolene said.

Sandy didn't respond, didn't even look at her, only held her smartphone out at arm's length. Jolene took in what appeared to be a flat, albino insect, attempted to pronounce the word in italics beneath it.

"See-moth... See-mothoa—"

"*Cymothoa exigua.*" Sandy said the words like she'd been repeating them over and over in her head. "It's an isopod. A parasite that... eats fish tongues."

Jolene shuddered, pushed the phone away.

"Shouldn't we take him to the hospital?"

Sandy shook her head.

"He'd never forgive me."

"I'm pretty sure the situation warrants it."

Sandy waved the phone in Jolene's direction again.

"Says here, the only damage the parasite causes is to the host's tongue."

76

Jolene leaned forward to get as good a look at Rayburn as she could without abandoning the safety of the couch.

"Can he talk?"

Rayburn startled them both by responding.

"Yeth."

"Baby!" Sandy rushed to his side. "Talk to me, baby. Say something!"

"I justh dead."

Sandy clutched at his hands, trying to hold both at once.

"This is all my fault. What should I do? Does it hurt?"

"Wather."

"Sure thing, baby. I'll get you some water. Just a second."

Jolene watched as Sandy ran to the kitchen, heard her fill a glass from the tap. A moment later she returned and held it up to Rayburn's lips.

"Thalt... wather."

"Oh. Okay." It was an odd request, but Sandy didn't argue. Jolene watched her run back to the kitchen. The tinkling of spoon against glass sounded and Sandy returned with a tornado of cloudy liquid.

"Juth paw it on my tung."

Sandy did as requested. The water pooled around the thing embedded in Rayburn's tongue. It responded by rubbing its forelegs together. Sandy tried not to look.

"Thath bether," Rayburn said, forcing the rest of the liquid to spill out of his mouth. Sandy used the hem of his t-shirt to wipe his chin. He smiled in appreciation.

"Thandy?"

"Yes, Ray?"

"Ahm thorry ah wen tah Kimsom Custation without you."

Tears welled up in Sandy's eyes.

"It's okay, baby. I know you were bringing home dessert."

Jolene pretended not to hear that part.

Rayburn propped himself up on his elbows, gazed into Sandy's eyes.

"Cud you do me won maw favah?"

Sandy gripped his hand tighter than before. "Anything, baby."

Rayburn leaned in towards her.

"Kith me."

"I'm sorry, what?"

Sandy stopped him with a hand to the chest.

"I thaid, kith me."

Sandy paused. Looked to Jolene, who shook her head *no*.

"I... what about... that thing?"

"Pleath..."

Sandy was torn. Her heart said *yes* with every beat, but her eyes screamed *hell-to-the-no*. Still, she puckered up nice and tight and pressed her lips against his cheek in a quick, perfunctory kiss.

"A reah won. Pleath..."

Rayburn's body went limp, as if the evacuating word took his life with it. Heavy lids threatened to close for a final time.

"Okay baby. Whatever you want. Just stay with me."

Sandy opened her mouth, tilting her head this way and that, attempting to find the right angle. Rayburn parted his lips. Sandy shut her eyes.

And then they were kissing.

Sandy held her breath, did her best to keep her tongue on her side of the kiss. But before long she could feel a tentative probing, the pin-point prick of tiny limbs meant for piercing flesh. She tried to pull away, but Rayburn grabbed her face with his hands, pressing into her. Sandy gave little moans that wouldn't be out of place during a dental exam. Her moans became muffled protests as she began to beat the side of his head with her fists. Then she was hyperventilating, pulling air in through her nose and screaming it down Rayburn's throat. Blood pooled in her sinuses, red bubbles frothing from her nostrils. Then her eyes rolled up into the back of her head and her whole body shook, as if she was having a grand mal seizure.

And then it was over. Rayburn went limp and fell back on the ground, dead. Sandy fell back as well, gasping for air. When she finally caught her breath she sat up, her mouth a crimson mess. She looked over at Rayburn. His mangled tongue once again lolled from his mouth. The parasite was gone.

"Sandy?"

She turned to the couch, where Jolene had tried to make herself as small as possible.

"Are you alright?"

Sandy paused, like a slow internet connection waiting for a URL to load. Nothing but a blank page, then all of a sudden—

"I'm bether than alright." She smoothed down the front of her blouse. "Thith body's quite the upgrade, don't you think?"

Jolene mumbled a string of nonsense before spitting out an actual word.

"Upgrade?"

"Old Ray really apprethiated thith body. I couldn't help but get a little second-hand intoxication there. It's a byproduct of mind-linking with such emotional creatures."

Sandy's speech handled the uninvited guest much better than Rayburn's had. The more she spoke, the more normal it sounded. She stood to her feet, wiped the blood from her mouth.

"In fact, I couldn't help absorbing a bit of his attraction to you as well."

She advanced on Jolene, step by shaky step. Jolene attempted to disappear into the corner of the couch altogether.

"And wouldn't you know it, I'm getting a little bit of that from Sandy here as well." She ran a pink press-on nail down Jolene's cheek, prompting the flesh to twitch. "They had such plans for you."

She pressed her tongue between her teeth, exposing the parasite like a puppet against a stained enamel backdrop. The pus-colored creature was visible for only a second, but Jolene could swear the thin black line of its mouth curved up at the ends to form a smile.

She would have screamed had the front door not slammed open to reveal two men wearing hip-waders. She recognized them from the restaurant. She also recognized the fishy smell that accompanied them.

"Looks like our ride's here," Sandy said. "Jolene, meet Billy and Charles."

Despite the terror welling up inside her, Jolene remembered her manners and gave a slight wave. Sandy jerked her head in the direction of Rayburn.

"Body's over there."

Billy and Charles shuffled over to the body, the sound of water sloshing inside their rubber pants. They grabbed Rayburn from either end and two-manned him out the door. As they passed, Jolene could swear she saw their flesh rippling, as if something pushed against it from the inside.

"Where are they taking him?"

Sandy put an arm around Jolene and flashed a smile. Jolene shuddered at the thought of the thing behind her teeth.

"You'll see."

***

They rode sandwiched between Billy and Charles in the cab of the unmarked biscuit truck. The whole time Jolene couldn't help but picture Rayburn being unceremoniously tossed into the back, atop what looked like a pile of similarly rag-dolled bodies.

"He said it was safe," Jolene said to herself as the lights of suburbia receded.

"What was safe?"

"The bisque. Rayburn said it was safe to eat because of the *poh-locks*."

"It's pronounced *pollock*," Sandy said. "And while it's true most bisque recipes call for the Alaska pollock as a lobster substitute, the Crimson Crustacean chain of restaurants has always utilized a cheaper mixture of langostino and crab."

Jolene had never heard of langostino, but she knew what crab meant.

"Shellfish," she said.

"The irony of the situation," Sandy continued, "is I wasn't even part of Rayburn's meal tonight. Even in our post-larval stage, a member of my species is far too large to go undetected in human foodstuffs. No, I was with him for much longer than that. In fact, my brothers and I were just eggs when he first ingested us.

"After we hatched, we awaited our sexual transformation while we dined on masticated nutrients in his stomach. One by one my brothers changed sex and were mated with. Lucky for me, I was the last of my siblings to mature. After protandry had taken place and I became fully female, no males remained with which to mate, so I traveled to the head of the host to take my rightful seat at the tongue. Unfortunately I had to make a last minute switch since my current host..." she glanced down at Sandy's body "...damaged the organ so badly. No matter. Things are going exactly as they should. Even now my siblings wait to lead their children to the sea, where their growth will continue unfettered by the constraints of the human body."

Billy and Charles grunted in assent. Jolene had no idea which drove the truck and which rode shotgun. She only knew she didn't want to dwell on the mechanics of this creature's reproductive process, let alone witness it.

The truck slowed and turned down a private beach road. There wasn't a lot of public property in the area, so the farther they drove, the less chance there was of intervention. Why hadn't the Sandy-thing killed her? Jolene resisted the urge to run down a mental list of fates worse than death. The truck's abrupt halt brought her back to reality.

"We're here," Sandy said with a smile.

Billy and Charles exited the vehicle. Jolene sat in silence and listened as they pulled open the roll door on the back of the truck. A shifting of dead weight followed as the two men grabbed ahold of Rayburn's body. Jolene watched as they transferred the body down to the beach and laid it on the damp sand, mere feet from the lapping waves. They repeated this action at least half a dozen times before Jolene lost count. Pretty soon lifeless human figures lined the shore.

"You're lucky," Sandy said, twirling a lock of Jolene's hair around her finger. "Very few have witnessed what you are about to see." She got out of the vehicle and extended a hand. "Come with me."

Jolene allowed herself to be led from the truck. She then followed as Sandy walked towards the beach under the power of the parasite, stripping off articles of clothing as she went.

Jolene looked from Sandy's tan skin to where the bodies were laid out. Beyond them moonlight glinted off the pale rocks of the shallows. She sidestepped Sandy's blouse and squinted her eyes. The rocks seemed to be gliding towards the shore. Sandy's bra dropped to the sand. She paused to step out of her jeans. Jolene stopped as well, maintained the distance between them. Sandy resumed walking, but Jolene's legs froze.

Those weren't rocks. They were those *things*. BIG ones.

All along the beach, the giant isopods emerged, their compound eyes shining in the night. They reminded Jolene of the pill bugs she used to play with in her mother's garden, except these were at least two feet long. Their antennae extended that length by at least another foot. A shiver of revulsion ran along Jolene's spine.

"Don't be afraid," she heard Sandy say. The woman was now completely nude, ankle deep in the water. "They are only here to witness the birth. The Day of Reclamation is not yet upon us."

Jolene refused to move any closer. She watched as Sandy threw back her head and opened her mouth. Billy and Charles did the same. What could only be described as a chittering emanated from them. A powerful sound, considering the size of the creatures that produced it. One by one by their larger brethren joined them, which produced a much stronger, deeper sound. Like a chorus of cicadas a thousand fold. The water around them churned with the vibration.

Jolene clamped her hands over her ears and dropped to her knees. The rumble threatened to liquefy her insides. It blurred her vision like a shimmer of heat. The flesh of the corpses seemed to ripple. They shook from the vibration in the ground.

No. Something moved inside them.

Flesh bubbled as if filled with pockets of air. It pushed outward, stretching thin before pulling back. Eventually it gave, rupturing in tiny red bursts as thousands of juvenile isopods broke free from their incubation. As the number of tears increased, the surface area of the flesh diminished, holes joining together to form bigger holes. Skin went slack and began sloughing off as the creatures escaped the body and made for the water.

The three hosts closed their mouths and the chorus ceased. That's when Jolene realized she was screaming. She continued to scream as the giant isopods and the newly released juveniles receded into the ocean. She didn't stop until the last of the bubbles floated to the surface and the water went still. Only then did she uncover shaky hands from ringing ears. Sandy turned to her, her face glowing.

"Did you see?"

Jolene gave a shell-shocked nod.

"One day you too will take part in the ceremony. Then you will know the joy of bringing life into this world."

A twinge of nausea tickled Jolene's stomach.

"What do you mean?"

Sandy gave her a patronizing look.

"Why do you think I let you live?"

"But... I didn't have the bisque."

"I told you, honey. Rayburn wasn't impregnated tonight. Besides, the rate of bisque consumption doesn't provide a high enough number of potential incubators. The biscuits on the other hand... everyone loves Cheddar Cove biscuits."

Jolene jammed her fingers down her throat and retched. It tasted of lobster and bile. She gagged once, twice more, but nothing came up except a string of drool.

"It's too late for that. They're already latching onto your insides. You could get your stomach pumped and it wouldn't make any difference. Our offspring are a lot hardier than yours. They don't allow themselves to be plucked from the womb before it's time."

The Sandy-thing turned back and began walking into the water.

"Billy and Charles will see you home. They'll make sure you don't do anything drastic."

Jolene turned to the two men in hip-waders. They stood there watching her, like they had in the parking lot of Crimson Crustacean. What she had previously identified as their lack of subtlety she now recognized as a lack of humanity. When she turned back to the ocean Sandy had disappeared below the surface.

She stared at the spot as the tide danced around the corpses. The water had already washed away most of the offal, leaving what looked like flesh-colored balloons someone had stuck a pin into. She placed a trembling hand against her stomach. She thought she detected a ripple of movement, but it could have just been her nerves. She closed her eyes and blocked out the carnage on the beach. Not taking into account her ultimate fate, the idea of being full of life did not displease her.

THE DUNPEAL TRAWLER

S.T. Cartledge

Graham hauled his fish to market. He was there before dawn with the frost clinging to his rain jacket as the fog rolled in from the ocean's edge, grey water slapping on rocks. It would be hours before the first customers came through, but already he had worked up a sweat dragging crates and stacking fish. He couldn't feel the cold. He couldn't sleep, but he didn't want to wake Laura with his restlessness.

He passed an anchovy beneath the table to Hastur, his twelve-year-old Russian Blue. She took it gently from his fingers and pulled the meat precisely from its bones. Graham bent down and stroked her soft cheek, then continued laying out his fish for sale.

He sat with Hastur in his lap and watched the ripples in the dark ocean as a familiar ship rolled through the mist. It pulled up to port with its beautiful dark wood shining wet, and the silver lettering of its name floating there like a ghost: The Night Watchman.

It came here first some months ago, a trawler drifted in from foreign waters, its fishermen already calling Dunpeal home before they'd even docked. Graham watched them then as he watched them now, and he knew them only as bad omens for him. The fishermen of the Night Watchman were tall and silent, hairless and pale. Cloaked and perfumed in a musk which smelled like bleach and industrial glue, they always set sail near midnight and came back before dawn. They disappeared into town before the light could touch them.

The Night Watchmen had reserved a shaded corner of the markets as their own, with a right-angle forming out of the buildings they were backed up against and with a balcony set out directly above them. They had their own awning set up with thick canvas hanging down the side, cutting out all sunlight. If you didn't see them rolling up each week with their outnumbered barrels of fish, they blended into the walls so well you wouldn't think they were there at all.

They walked dead silent past Graham's stall, and he caught a good glimpse of their catch. The same damn fish they'd been catching for months, a silver-white creature that Graham had never seen in these oceans, looked like some deep-dwelling beast with giant yellow-white eyes like old cue balls. Fins tinged a burgundy red. Their flesh was blacker than anything he had seen before. And the teeth on those things...

His eyes tracked the men closely, took note of the way they walked, the slow trudge through the morning dark. He knew intimately their mannerisms, the way they talked with heads leaned in close and muttering quiet. Of what he heard, there were no loose words he could identify the language. It made no sense to him.

They sped up once they noticed Graham watching, but it didn't matter to him. He was always watching, always taking mental notes of their manner, their movement, their habits, their morning's catch. This morning was a repeat of all the others. Graham's stall was another disappointment at the markets. More time spent ruminating the mystery of these people.

Hastur hissed at the Night Watchmen as they shuffled back with the crates which held their fish no more. Graham stroked her coat and watched the men return the crates to their trawler. He wondered how they could have been here for mere months and yet they had miraculous fishing secrets that neither Graham, nor the other locals knew.

***

In the evening he went to bed with Laura, and again he couldn't sleep. His mind was troubled so much with the Night Watchmen that he hadn't truly slept in weeks. He didn't really want to sleep. He made like his restlessness was an excuse to move from the bedroom to the lounge, and from there he slipped real quiet into the cloudless Dunpeal night.

He walked with Hastur to the docks, where his skeleton crew were waiting for him. He boarded his boat, the Yellow Maiden, joining William and Phillip as they watched the Night Watchman pull out into open waters.

The Yellow Maiden was small, yet strong. It was quick and its motors were reasonably quiet. She moved slick and graceful through the dark water. She shone no lights as she followed the Night Watchman. Graham steered her, restless in his sleep-deprived state. The answers to his constant questions were out here in these waters, where this boat went, he would find the mystery fish and bring the secret to light. His body shivered with excitement. He could feel with each passing moment, the boat cutting through the water, there would be the truth and there would be the promise of many solid nights of sleep ahead.

If only he could find it.

From the dark water, in the clear, cloudless night, there came a thick cloud of fog rolling in, falling around the Night Watchman, and falling around the Yellow Maiden too. There were rocks rising up here with no lighthouse warning of them. William called out to Graham, the danger of the rocks. Phillip shone a light out into the water, but it was caught up in the fog. Graham slowed the boat right down, and then came to a halt. Floating there, bobbing in the gentle ocean, they let the Night Watchman sail away, its secrets still remaining just outside his reach.

The crew, fatigued, turned the boat around and headed back to the docks to return to their homes to sleep. They left Graham caressing Hastur, watching the ocean, and waiting for the Night Watchman to return with its nightly fill of fish. They would return here later in the morning when the fog was cleared and the Night Watchman was safe at the docks. They would have time to search the area without the fear of being watched by those mystery men with the air of violence wafting about them.

***

Graham marked out that portion of ocean on his map, forming a path to a patch of blue where they ran into the fog and rocks the night before. On the map there was nothing but clear water. The Yellow Maiden found her way back there, retracing her steps to the jagged rocks sticking out of the ocean. In the clear morning air the crew could see the rocks were vast and many. They circled around an unmapped island, which they surely should have noticed before, but maybe the rocks had kept people away until now.

William and Phillip saw the drive within Graham and knew it was pointless trying to convince him that the dangers weren't worth the rewards. The Yellow Maiden steered its way carefully around the rocks, unsure precisely where they were heading, but they knew there was nowhere else the Night Watchman could have gone.

The small fishing trawler curled its way towards the island, sailing through a natural archway formed out of rock and covered in moss. The archway brought them into a lagoon. There was a white sand beach curving around, with few trees surrounded by a steep wall of rock. The water was still, reflecting a mirror-image of the bright and healthy sky.

The crew released their nets and wondered how the Night Watchmen were the first to discover this place and reap its rewards. How could they catch the strange fish out of nowhere? How could they work only by the moonlight?

They cast their nets all morning and caught nothing. The water was a stunning blue, and so goddamn clear. They could see right through it to the bottom in some places, and there were no fish. Further out from the beach, the lagoon waters got real deep real fast, they couldn't see the bottom. They continued on into the afternoon and caught nothing.

Soon the darkness would set in and bring with it the fog and the Night Watchman. If they continued much longer, the midnight fishermen would catch them in their spot, and who knew what would happen then. There was no place to hide a boat inside the lagoon. There was no place near it amongst the rocks where it would be safe. There was nothing hidden here except the fish.

They came in to the docks as the evening was setting in and the Night Watchman was preparing to leave. Graham wanted to follow it again tonight, but his crew needed rest. He needed rest too, although he doubted that he would get it. He circled around countless clues but found no answers.

***

Graham gave William and Phillip the next day off. They were overworked and underpaid, and while Graham struggled to make his own payments, there was still this taunting secret fishing spot haunting him. He couldn't let that tear his crew apart, but it was the sort of thing that would change his life, reinvent his failures as successes. If only he could find those fish.

He rented a small motor boat and took it out in the night-time. Again, he followed the Night Watchman. Again, he found himself moving through the fog on the water, trying to navigate the rocks on his own. The brightest torch he had was quickly swallowed up by the fog. He tried to follow his instincts, guiding loosely along the path, but he was unsure whether he should have been following the boat, or trying to recall the memories from the day before which guided them clear and safe into the lagoon.

The fog bred doubt. He *knew* where he was going. He had been there before. But if you cut out your own eyes, you can no longer see. Where you trusted so much on your sense of sight, you would find yourself doubting everything you thought you knew once the darkness set in.

Now, it seemed that everywhere he looked there was a jagged rock jutting out and blocking off his path. He couldn't remember if they were there before. It looked as though everything had changed, moved in the night.

The Night Watchman was gone somewhere into the lagoon, disappeared like a ghost ship, and Graham spent hours navigating from rock to rock to rock, getting nowhere, circling around all the ones he thought he'd passed before. He struggled to remember the way back home.

***

He knew the fish were there. He saw the Night Watchman disappear there with empty barrels and come back full of fish. The fish were there. They had to be. He had to search more thoroughly. He had to go deeper into the dark waters of the lagoon to find the fish hiding within.

This time he went in the day time, he went again alone in the small motor boat. This time he loaded up the boat with diving gear. One way or another, he would find those goddamn fish. He scratched Hastur's head and assured her that he would find the fish.

Again, by daylight, he navigated through the rocks with ease. He navigated his way into the lagoon with ease. He didn't know why in the night-time in the fog it became impossible. He pulled right up to the beach and laid out his things on the soft sand. Hastur curled up on a blanket in the sun while Graham changed into his diving gear.

He swam out into the cold water beneath the warm sun. Beneath the surface, through his mask he could see clearly through the water. The sand on the lagoon floor was so clear. There was nothing else here. He swam further from the beach, where the floor dropped into darkness. He lit a torch which penetrated part way through the water, but it wasn't quite enough to gauge the depth.

He dropped to the point where the lagoon floor plummeted. He grabbed the edge where the sand turned to rock and became a sheer cliff in the ocean. He held the torch tight and knew if he let go he would never see it again. He took a deep breath and plunged into the giant chasm.

At first he stayed close to the cliff face, holding on to it and using its grip to pull himself down. The cliff was wide as the beach, as the lagoon itself was wide. He wondered if the fish were hiding in pockets, little caves and crevices in the rock. He thought maybe they came out in the night time only to be caught in the Night Watchman's nets. He searched across the rock face for a hidden space like that but found nothing. It would take days, weeks, months to search the whole area section by section, he was hoping he would happen upon it by random chance, if they were hiding in a space like that at all.

He wasn't even that deep yet. The sun was clear in the light above, the water still a light blue, the bottom still invisible beyond his sight.

He could have spent hours down here. He went deeper and the water got darker, and it became harder to tell how much light was left in the day. He thought about coming up to check. He thought about what if he stayed down here too long and the Night Watchman came and the fishermen caught him in their nets? He would know the fish were here for sure. He would see where they came from, but he didn't like that risk very much.

He went deeper and found nothing in the cliff. It cut away in stages, the water coming in beneath the rock, beneath the island, and there the water turned black in the shadows. Beneath the cliff he couldn't see the sky, but the light shining didn't catch upon any fish either. There was still no sign of the bottom, and there was still no sign of life. Not even the smallest fish, or aquatic plant, or crustacean living here. Nothing.

He ventured out from the rock to explore the lagoon waters, to see if there was anything else besides the clear blue descending into nothing. He knew the fish were deeper. They had to be. They were hiding from the light. Perhaps they only came to the shallows at night. If the fish were hiding somewhere in the darkness of these waters, they were hiding deep and they were hiding well. Graham swam straight down, searching for that elusive ocean floor.

With each stroke and each kick, Graham could feel the pressure building against his body. His chest felt tight and his limbs felt heavy. His eyesight was plagued with the dark blue of waters the sun couldn't quite reach. In every direction there was that trap of not knowing which direction was which. He'd be lost if not for the bubbles rising with his every breath.

His head felt light and dizzy. There was nothing here. No fish. No movement. No life at all. As much as he wanted to dive deeper and search longer, he was already pushed beyond his limits. He slowly paddled upwards, still watching for movement in the water. From the surface, he couldn't believe the size of this place. Between the beach and the surface of the water, it seemed so small now, compared to what was beneath. It felt like he went hardly anywhere at all, and yet he had disappeared for so long.

Hastur was still curled up on her blanket on the beach. There weren't even any birds or insects for her to hunt. There was a strange silence here only washed through with the gentle sound of crashing waves outside.

Graham changed into a dry set of clothes and thought what could be happening here. Logic taught him that perhaps the Night Watchmen were so obsessed with the secrecy of their fish that they never really came to the lagoon at all. Perhaps they used the surrounding rocks as a disguise, to lose the tail of anyone who might be following, for anyone who might be after their secret fishing spot. As paranoid as Graham was about these people, he thought perhaps they were even more paranoid.

He wouldn't give up this easy though.

Graham and Hastur came back to town, and on the way Graham formulated his next plan. He couldn't sleep. These people were everywhere in his mind, gradually consuming every part of his waking life. Laura was a distant second. She watched from the distance of her front window, the man she married transforming into the shadow of a madman. She didn't see him, didn't talk with him, didn't get to hold his hands which smelled always of fish. Didn't get to kiss his scratchy, bearded cheek.

He didn't sleep at all. He didn't go back home because he knew it wouldn't do any good. He sat by the docks until dark, watching the Night Watchman and its crew going about their work. He had one more idea and he knew after this there would be no more. It was his connection back to Laura. It was the one thing that would bring this madness back to some form of functioning life. And he would have his goddamn fish.

***

Graham had watched the Night Watchmen for long enough to know their habits. He knew their mannerisms and their modus operandi. He watched them now and knew the drill. He waited for them to load up their supplies, and while they were checking the equipment, he ran as quiet as he could across the plank and disappeared below deck where the empty barrels were. Hastur ran silent in his shadow. Neither of them knew what would happen if someone found them. Graham made himself a little smaller and a little quieter, as thoughts began to creep into his head of what they might do if they found him here.

The boat began to move. He was trapped. Staring between the barrels at the stairway to the deck, listening like hell for any small piece of information which might help him figure out this puzzle. He could picture the thick fog and the rocks in the dark water and the boat floating right through with ease. He could picture the captain navigating these waters with his eyes closed. He could smell the fish. Their scent was impregnated in the wood. So strong, he could almost taste them in the air. Hastur certainly could. She purred gently, leaning against Graham's lap.

He felt the shadows of the cavernous rock formation passing overhead as they entered the lagoon. Surely this was the place. The same place he dived before, now dark and thriving with fish. He wanted nothing more than to see it. To cast his own net and reel in those beauties for himself. This was everything he waited for, everything he needed.

The crew would all be working the nets right now. They would be focused solely on the water, Graham could go up top and watch from the shadows, and see first-hand for himself these goddamn fish in this goddamn lagoon. Hastur meowed softly at him like a warning not to go, but he couldn't come this far only to back out now. He could hear the fish slapping against the hull of the boat. An erratic rhythm which signalled to the few men on board that this was a school of many. He couldn't hear his own footsteps over the sound of drumming fish against wood. The crew wouldn't hear him coming either.

He climbed up top and out into the moonlight, the lagoon glistened, the dark water rippled with the silver of the night. He moved quick to squash himself flat against a wall covered by crates. There were slats wide enough to peep through, to watch the crew work.

They hauled in their first net. Swollen with the weight of the fish, the boat tilted under the strain. The hoist struggled. Slowly, but surely, the net lifted out of the water, the writhing fish rippled against the net and made it look alive. The net came in and lowered over a large tub, to catch their fill and sort them into barrels at the end of the night. Graham's own boat had a similar set-up, but on a smaller scale.

Through the sound of men calling to each other and the sound of hundreds of fish flopping helplessly in the tub, Graham strained his ears. There was something crying. Multiple somethings. His eyes fixated on the tub. While the fishermen cast the net back out, two others with arm-length gloves shoved their arms through the fish, pushing and pulling, sorting through the mess. One pulled out a fish whose cry rang loud throughout the lagoon.

Graham looked carefully at the fish and recognised the shape.

Not a fish, but a human child.

The second fisherman pulled up a second baby. From below deck, there formed a procession of men who came up and collected the babies from the fishermen and returned below deck. The two then returned to rummaging through the fish-muck for babies.

Graham watched the first of the carriers pass nearby, heading down below. The baby screamed its lungs out. Its skin caught in the moonlight, wet and shining, scaled like a moonfish. Eyes gigantic and black.

Graham wanted to scream. He wanted to throw himself overboard and swim back to the docks. He wanted to grab Hastur and get the fuck out of there. But he was stuck. He couldn't swim that far. The moonfish and fish-baby infested water was a crawling nightmare. The screams haunted him into a frozen stupor. And the two fishermen digging through the tub kept pulling up babies and the carriers kept bringing them right past him.

There was a short break in the procession as the diggers worked through the tub but found no babies. They waited with the carriers for the next haul to come in. Graham waited for the path below deck to become clear, and took the moment to dart quickly down. He heard the cries of all the babies, but the deck was empty but for those barrels. He checked on Hastur, scrunched up small and fearful in the dark. He stroked her fur to let her know he was okay.

He followed the sound of the babies to a corner where there was an open trapdoor and a ladder leading down. He knelt by the trapdoor and peeked through it. There, in the dim candlelight in the guts of the ship, rows and rows of cots stacked five high and filled with scaled babies, one of the fishermen down here tucking them in and feeding them mashed moonfish from a wooden bowl.

There must have been at least a hundred of them, all crying, all being calmly fed by the freakish fisherman kindly acting as their fish-mother.

A cold hand grabbed Graham's leg and pulled him from the trapdoor. The fisherman passed his baby off to the one behind him and seized Graham by the neck, saying something he couldn't understand.

Hastur shot out from the barrels like lightning and launched at the fisherman with claws out, digging and slicing into his slimy flesh. He let go of Graham and grabbed at Hastur, but she was too fast. She launched off his back and stood by her master's side, hissing and growling at these nocturnal freaks.

More of them passed their babies off to each other, delivering them down below, gradually forming a mob surrounding the man and his cat. Graham hadn't realised until now how large and daunting they were up close. He didn't realise how many of them were aboard the Night Watchman.

One of them stepped forward, and Hastur lashed out, slashing at his hand. He grabbed at her and she bit his hand several times. He flinched a little, but didn't move back. He snatched her by the head and lifted her up. She writhed and kicked like mad, but he didn't let go. He grabbed her body with his other hand and flicked his wrist and her body went limp.

Graham threw himself at the fisherman and punched at him and yelled, but he was too weak. He was cornered and he was incapable of fighting his way out. They lifted him by the limbs and carried him above deck, where the others were still casting out their nets and sorting the fish from the babies.

They sat Graham down and tied him up and left him there helplessly struggling while they continued to fish and sort and carry the babies down below. He noticed not all of the babies were going into the arms of the carriers. Some were simply tossed into nearby barrels. Lifelessly, they bounced off the wood and filled the barrels up.

91

Hastur too disappeared into one of the barrels. Graham stared at the barrels. He now knew where the fish came from, although he no longer cared. These people were barbarians. Their babies were freaks. He could see them forming a fleet once their young grew up. They could take over Dunpeal, spread from fishing village to fishing village. They could take his boat and take his home. He didn't think he would see Laura again. His stomach churned at the thought that her last memories of him were these obsessions over a goddamn fish.

The last net for the night was only a quarter full. The thick drumming of fish against the boat had died down and the frenzy on the surface of the water had died down. The babies were sorted dead from living. The cries sealed below deck leaving silence in the lagoon.

The fishermen began to toss the dead babies overboard, floating on the surface, they tossed about a dozen in then waited by the edge of the boat.

The water rumbled, the boat began to move.

A gaping maw spurted from below the surface and swallowed the floating babies. Its head was slick black, with a crown of white eyes surrounding its mouth. Its mass took up the majority of the lagoon.

The fishermen cheered and yelled unintelligible words.

The beast withdrew and returned the water to calm. The fishermen tossed a few more babies overboard. Graham noticed Hastur's body in this batch, flying out into the water.

She was gone, and now he felt truly alone.

Again the beast snatched up the offering and returned below.

The fishermen tossed out the last of the babies and cheered as the lagoon monster swallowed them up.

They turned to Gregory as the monster behind them returned beneath the water. Gregory kicked and writhed and screamed. The ropes burned against his skin. They rubbed raw and tiny drops of blood appeared on his flesh.

The fishermen untied his knots. He kicked and pushed and screamed and wrenched himself free from them. He leaped up and threw himself forward. He bounced off one fisherman with silver teeth and ran in the other direction. He crashed into another fisherman. This one was missing half his ear.

He threw his weight into them, but they didn't move. They didn't try to grab him again either. His breathing was short and sharp and erratic. The stars above began to spin. His skin burned from the rope marks. It felt like he was on fire, like there was something on the rope which was reacting with his skin. He propped himself up against the railing. He threw up overboard, chum to feed the few remaining moonfish.

92

He hurled himself across the deck and slammed into the hardwood walls. Before he knew where he was going, he looked up and saw the water rushing at his head.

He tumbled overboard and in the water he could hear the muffled laughter of the crew above.

They cheered in anticipation of the rising beast below.

Graham could feel its movements in the water. He tried to find the direction of the beach. He flapped his arms in a swimming motion but it felt like he was going nowhere. He looked down and gazed into its dazzling mouth of shredded teeth. Its ring of eyes slick, gazing right back. The deep groan of its hunger.

He saw the consequences of his future, either dying of starvation on the beach of the lagoon, or consumed within the belly of the beast, joining Hastur in the brine-washed oblivion.

THE WHEEL HOUSE

Bram Riddlebarger

"Watch out for the Rabbits, son," said the father.

Their canoe, a green fiberglass model, bumped across the water. The river was low, but still contained a number of holes and stretches of deep water, most of which would not be more than chest-high to the average adult. There was a story, from the turn of the last century, about a newlywed couple that had drowned crossing a ford of this river, with a small team of horses, when the water was said to be low. The father had grown up hearing the story in the town. He had heard the rumors of a hidden chasm, or sinkhole, when he was a boy himself. Then, a year or so back, while eating breakfast at his kitchen table, the father saw that a local man had found a wagon wheel, spokes and all, nearly complete, in the river. The man's picture had been on the front of the town's daily paper, smiling, with the old wheel. No one was quite sure where the hole might be. The newlyweds had dreamt of life and of carnal desire, like a release from coarse linen, but they had found eternity instead. Now, the father and his five-year-old son floated the river. The canoe was rented, but solid. They wore orange life jackets that fit snugly and too high, as was usual with the sort at commercial liveries, but they would do. The father had made sure that his son was secure in his vest. Now, he sat in the rear of the canoe and pushed with steady J-strokes of confidence, enjoying the fine summer weather. Tulip poplar petals fell like haiku poems around them in places and the father felt at ease. His son held a small, child-sized oar in the bow and attempted to help to propel them at times. More often, he sat and listened to the river, somewhere else in his five-year-old mind entirely—his imagination bringing terror to the Rabbits that his father had convinced him were lurking out there, somewhere on the river. His father kept close watch. The water was low. The canoe scratched the rocks if they did not keep to the deeper current of the river, which flowed like a corkscrew from a meandering bottle.

***

His reaction when she walked into the room was one of resignation rather than love. The worry of parenting and being locked in a war of

94

endless duty did melt somewhat away. Relief shone on his face. But the other emotion, the one that she saw, was not love.

She looked back with rippling disdain.

"You guys going out on the river tomorrow?"

"Yeah, I'll take him."

"Good."

She left the room.

He adjusted his glasses. Everything was ready. There would not be many chances left.

***

The boat ground to a halt on a large rock near the bank. The father could not navigate so well when the water began slipping over the rapids of the low rocks with his son in front, partially blocking his view. Nor was his son an adept lookout. Rights became left and lefts became right. The rocks were slippery near the bank, moss-covered and slimy in the shade of the trees on the bank. He had worn his contact lenses, which he only wore when swimming or boating, and they drove him crazy with a feeling of restriction like a pressure of time. Although, in a sense, he could see better without the black plastic frames that he normally wore, which obscured part of his vision, the feeling that he had with the contacts was one of restriction—a tightening of the world pulling in on itself, a neurosis.

"We're stuck, dad."

The father pushed his oar into the bed of the river to free the canoe. He pushed on a rock.

"Switch me places, buddy."

A group of sleek, blue, yellow, and red kayaks slipped down the rapids on the other side of the river, able to transverse the shallow water with their lighter build and lesser weight.

He pushed against the rock that held the canoe. The boat turned and began to take in water. The rock, a boulder really, was fixed in the stream. It jutted from the water like the head of an expired parking meter of significant girth. Suddenly, the boat took in more water, as the rapids beat in, and the boat slipped perpendicular to the line of the earth. The boy tumbled into the water with a screech. The father managed to fall and slip and come back up with some grace, losing his hat to the rapids, but, as he stepped to grab the canoe, now free, his canvas sneakers slipped on the mossy rocks. His ankle snapped. He fell into the river, as the canoe floated downstream. He still held his oar, but everything else was floating away. Pain welled up like lightning in the sky of his ankle.

95

His son stood with his life jacket dripping water onto the shallow rocks. And then he too fell, unable to stand up on the slippery rocks with the force of the rapids upon him. They were four miles from their take-out point.

***

The seismic activity of the breakfast table was curtailed by the boy's entrance into the room.

"I love you, mom."

"I love you, too, sweetie."

The father held his hands to his face. The contact lenses that he had put in that morning were like a snake constricting his eyes and his brain. He did not know if she would be here when he and the boy returned that afternoon from the river. The years had become contact lenses that each of them was ready to take out.

***

The father used his oar to push himself over to his son, now crying and unable to stand in the water, and then on to the bank. The haiku poems of the trees had gone away, and the weather was hot now in the early afternoon.

"Dad, are you ok?"

"I think I broke my ankle."

His ankle, once he could see it clear of the water on the bank, was already turning yellow and blue. His low-cut canvas sneakers were full of sand.

"We need to get the canoe. Can you see it?"

The father had placed his keys and cell phone and his wallet in a zipped, plastic bag inside the canoe, secured in a bag with extra clothes and a few snacks and a water bottle, all tied to the wooden thwart of the canoe. Now, it was all floating away.

"I need to get my phone and call your mom. Can you see the canoe?"

"Dad, are you ok?"

"The water's low enough, we should be able to find the canoe and call your mom. We'll have to try to get it. We'll go a little way and if we can't find it, we'll find a house or something and call. Can you do that?"

"Ok, dad."

They moved along the bank, which was thick with summer growth, for twenty yards or so, until they were forced back into the low water of the river. The water was calmer, now, after the rapids, and smoothed out for a stretch. The water was waist-high on the father. The water felt good on his ankle. His son floated in his jacket. The father towed the boy along. At least, he still had the oar. They rounded a bend in the river, full of downed trees. Soft-shelled river turtles plopped off the logs, and then into the safety of the stream. There, several hundred yards downstream, just past another low stretch of water, the father thought that he could see the canoe hung up on some rocks. He was not quite sure. His contact lenses played tricks on his vision, and the canoe was dark green against a backdrop of green and black.

"I think I see it. Just a little farther, buddy."

He hoped that his phone was still there. He had tied the bag tight, but he did not foresee them overturning in the low water of the river.

Dragonflies whizzed around them.

They moved through the low water, less full of cumbersome rocks here and more full of sand. The father limped along with the oar and his son. There, ahead, was indeed the canoe, caught up, not on a rock, but on the exposed roots of a tree, cut out by the meandering of the river into the bank.

"I see it, dad!"

They crossed the ford and reached the boat.

***

He sat in the chair and shook his head. No, no, no. This was not how it was supposed to go. The table, for one, was too clean. And he had not drunk nearly enough beer. No, this was not right.

The chair scraped back on the dirty, worn vinyl flooring and hung up on a loose tile.

"Maybe we should see someone," she said.

He shook his head. No. This was not how it was supposed to go.

He stood up and got a bottle of beer out of the refrigerator. The beer was cold. He took a deep swig from the brown glass bottle. The cold beer stung his throat and felt good.

"You're such an asshole," she said.

He drank. Little spurts of bottled gas rose in his mouth, and he puffed them out.

"Pfft."

Lips and glass.

It was all over anyway.

***

97

"She's not answering."

The boy was sitting in the canoe, eating fish-shaped crackers from a plastic sandwich bag. The father stood in the river. The cold water was keeping the swelling down in his ankle. The sun was overhead and very hot. They had planned to be off the river, not long from now, after noon.

After texting and calling three times, the father zipped the phone back into the plastic bag with his keys and secured it at the bottom of their daypack tied to the thwart. He had taken off his life jacket, which now lay in the tepid water that had collected in the bottom of the canoe. They had not seen anyone else on the river since the kayaks had passed by them just before they had capsized on the rock.

The water was very low here. The father had been standing in a small pool close to the bank, which kept his ankle submerged. The canoe was hung up on the tree roots, but also now on the rocks in the river, with the weight of the boy back inside the canoe.

"I'm going to the have to get us back into the current. We're just going to have to get to the take-out point."

The boy ate his crackers. He still had not seen the Rabbits that had already bitten them.

The father placed the oar in the canoe and began to push it over the low rocks toward the deeper water on the other side of the river. He had maybe twenty yards to get the canoe to where he could sit down in it, with his son, without foundering. There were rapids here, as well, and, as he pushed, the water picked up speed. Several large boulders protruded from the rapids like fists. As he passed by one of these larger rocks, he slipped and overturned several river stones. He came down on his ankle. He did not realize what happened next, but he heard the sucking sound and his hands no longer held the fiberglass of the canoe. He did not hear his son screaming. He did not see the canoe stop again on the rocks in the low water of the river.

Down inside the death hole, things bumped against him. The water was furious. His contact lenses pressed against his eyes. The skeleton of a raccoon or a small dog came and went and then his lungs began to burn. Above him, a small point of light emerged from the chaos and then the bride and the groom arrived.

***

Does the spray over the river stones ever repeat itself?

Is the sound of the river really ever the same?

The rocks reach like hands from the spray, as unable to grasp the air, as we are able to understand.

YOU'LL LIKE IT HERE

Sam Reeve

The mountains loomed beyond Tatariv's small train station, encircled with mist like a lace shawl around an old woman's sagging shoulders. On the other side of the track, along the tree line, a couple stray dogs picked at trash and nipped at each other's legs. Masha hefted her bag and looked at Dylan, who smiled back nervously.

"Welcome to the Carpathians!" she said. "You'll like it here, it's peaceful."

Two grey-haired babas with scarves tied over their heads approached them, offering to sell them fruit and fresh milk. The milk was in old plastic water bottles, the faded labels still attached.

"You want to try some?" Masha asked. Dylan hesitated. Masha said *tak*, "yes." The woman unscrewed the cap and poured a few drops into it and handed it to Masha, who put it to her lips and sipped. "Not bad." She pulled a few crumpled *hryvnyas* from her pocket and paid for the bottle, stuffing it in her tote bag.

Masha led them from the train station crowded with old Ladas and more women selling homemade goods.

"Is it like you remembered it, this region?" he asked.

They walked down the road, past two men leaning against a taxi. The men ate sunflower seeds and smoked unfiltered cigarettes, and said something to them as they walked past. Masha shook her head to them and then smiled at Dylan.

"Nothing has changed."

***

In front of the hotel that rented the canoes was a car with two rusted tanks affixed to the back bumper, and two hoses running into the back of it.

"And what is this?" Dylan asked. "Is this one of those car trunk meth labs?"

Masha laughed. "No, of course not. This is a wood-fire car. It saves on fuel. There is plenty of wood around here, yes?"

Dylan continued to inspect the vehicle while Masha went to negotiate a price for the canoe.

"And where are you going, little lady?" the hotel manager asked, eyeing her husband who still eyed the strange car.

"Up the river, there's a lake to the north, right? The one famous for its large fish?"

The man gave her a strange look, shook his head. "This is unwise," he said.

"And why's that?"

"Because this is a remote region, you know? Full of bears, wolves. Must be careful."

"Ahh, you afraid we'll catch all your big fish or something? Don't worry, we're just camping."

The man shrugged when Masha handed over the cash, and nervously played with the bills as she filled out a rental card with her passport information.

***

All day they paddled against the lazy current. Sticks and leaves gently floated past them, down the small tributary to join the much larger Prut river. Birds crisscrossed the sky above them, to and from the dark trees that lined the shore. Roots hung over the edge of the bank, reaching for the water with their twisted fingers.

Several hours into their journey, the river narrowed, and up ahead they could see trees where they expected the river to continue.

"What the..." Dylan trailed off, confused as they paddled up to a wall of green. The river seemed to end. Masha squinted at the map saved on her phone.

"This doesn't make sense, the lake is supposed to be up ahead, isn't it?" Dylan asked.

"Yes, of course it is, but as you've already experienced on this trip...not all Ukrainian maps are accurate. In fact, most aren't."

"Well?" Dylan crossed his arms and stared up at the trees. He had never seen a river end like this, as if it was just cut off suddenly. He shook his head, frustrated.

"What did you call those men, the ones you said carried canoes?" she asked.

"The what?"

"The ones you said you read about in school."

"The *coureurs de bois*?"

"Yes, we will do as they did then."

***

Masha carried both her bag and Dylan's, his strapped to her front. Dylan hoisted the heavy canoe over his head, the yoke resting on his shoulders. Water dripped down onto him from the hull, mixing with the sweat that poured from his brow as he navigated the rotting stumps and clingy brush of the forest floor. It was strangely silent, and they heard only the sound of their huffing and cursing.

After many breaks and roughly an hour of portaging the canoe, the navy glass surface of a lake peeked through the branches up ahead. They made it to the shore and looked out. Dark, still water reflected the trees, and they quickly cleaved through the surface with their canoe, making for the far side of the lake where they could see a pebbly beach.

The sun had just begun to dip behind the nearby mountain, threatening to cast them in the dark. They had almost reached the far shore when something bumped the boat.

"What was that?" Dylan asked, white knuckling the side of the canoe as it rocked back and forth.

"A fish," said Masha, looking back at him. "There are legends about the size of the fish from here, and its remoteness keeps many away."

"I'm sure the whole dead-end river thing helps," he said.

They made it to shore, pulled their canoe up the small beach, and sat down to rest at last.

"My arms are aching," said Masha, stretching as they peered out across the lake. The cherry blossom sunset reflected on its surface, and just then a fish's tail breached the pink water. "See," she said. "Big fish."

Masha and Dylan set up camp for the night, which consisted of a two-person tent, a fire that Dylan managed to get lit only after much cursing and embarrassment, and a small pan in which they cooked some potatoes and rice. Their night was simple but they were happy, and slept soundly if not for the occasional splashing sounds as fish jumped from the lake to catch bugs in the night.

***

At the first hint of dawn, Masha awoke, suddenly, and decided she could no longer sleep. Sporting warm leggings and a hoodie, she ventured barefoot down to the beach to wash her face. Mist rose from the lake as the sun inched above the imposing mountains and warmed its surface.

Masha kneeled down and reached into the freezing water, cupping it with her hands. She splashed it on her face, gasped, shocked at how cold it felt. She looked up as she did this, and saw a man standing up in the middle of the lake, maybe two-hundred feet away, the water at waist height despite being at least ten feet deep where he stood. She blinked in disbelief.

The man had long grey and white hair, and appeared to have black, shiny skin in some places, like a mold creeped over him. He was grinning, and his teeth looked rotten, even from that distance. Wide, dark eyes bulged from his head and his mouth protruded oddly from his face, like it was swollen.

Masha cried out and quickly wiped the water from her face with the sleeve of her hoodie. The man was gone. A large fish's tail splashed up from the water where he had stood, and she continued to look out, mouth agape. *I must be sleeping*, she thought. She called out anyway, wondering if they were really alone.

"Hey, what's up?" Dylan said, walking up behind her from their camp. Masha looked back at him, shaking, both from the cold and from her strange vision.

"Nothing, it's fine," she said, standing and wrapping her arms around her body. She headed back for the camp to start on their breakfast.

***

Masha and Dylan spent the day exploring the surrounding woods, picking wild mushrooms and berries like she had as a child with her grandmother. Being summer, it wasn't high season for the mushrooms, but they found enough for a small meal. Later she fried them in their pan, along with a few more potatoes, and Masha kept watch of the lake out of the corner of her eye. She couldn't forget the strange man she'd seen, real or not. Dylan noticed her odd behaviour, and raised an eyebrow.

"You look worried," he said. She smiled and waved her hand, dismissing the notion that anything was wrong. Content and weary from their day of hiking, they fell asleep after their meal.

***

Sometime in the night, Dylan awoke, needing to pee. He decided to walk down the beach to the black lake. As he relieved himself he marveled at the stars, how bright and plentiful they seemed out here, away from the city lights. Somewhere out on the water a fish splashed, sending ripples towards the shore. He looked down, and noticed a playing card in the muddy sand at the water's edge.

Mud-stained and frayed at the edges, the bold reds and yellows of the playing card were a strange sight on the beach. Dylan bent down to inspect it, a queen of spades.

***

Masha awoke the next morning cold and stiff. She rolled over to Dylan, who wasn't there. She rubbed the sleep from her eyes, tied her hair into a knot atop her head, and exited the tent. Dawn was breaking and mist once again hovered over the lake like a phantom sipping at its surface.

"Dylan?" she called out. No response. She walked down the shore, looked at the canoe, which was still there with all their gear. She didn't see his shoes anywhere, but his day pack remained. She figured he must be in the forest for a morning bowel movement, or perhaps searching for more berries for their breakfast. Masha smiled at the thought of him waking up early to forage for them.

An hour later, Masha's smile had faded and her face twisted, anxious. Her eyes kept darting to the lake. *No*, she thought. *He's lost in the forest.*

The rest of the day, until the darkness crept in from the sun's retreat, she searched for Dylan. She found nothing, no footprints, no sign of him. She called his name, heard nothing in return save for the rushing sound of the pines in the breeze.

Masha walked back to their camp, alone, head down in defeat. Her lip quivered as she fought back tears, wondering what could've happened to Dylan. He wasn't an outdoorsman but also not stupid enough to get lost by himself. As she approached the rocky beach, she noticed imprints in the sandy part, close to the water.

Cautiously, she approached. They were human footprints, barefoot, too. She could make out three prints in the muddy sand before whoever made them had stepped onto the rocks. She whirled around, and called out once again for Dylan. Silence.

Masha's hands shook, for she was not alone. Someone was out there, and she was sure he was watching her. She slowly reached into her pocket for her mushrooming knife, unfolded it, and walked to their camp. She decided to leave the tent, that way if Dylan returned he would have shelter. She left his bag, as well, with some of his clothes and a few potatoes. He would have enough to survive until help came.

Panic set in. Masha grabbed her things and ran for the canoe. Unsure she could get far in the dark with the heavy boat on her back, she decided to take her chances on the water. If she had to, she would sit in the middle of the lake all night. There's no way the man could sneak up on her from the shore without her noticing.

Masha paddled out, slowly, and turned around every few seconds to watch the surrounding trees, which she could barely see through the dark now. She turned on her headlamp and brandished her canoe paddle like a weapon, the heavy wood feeling better in her hands than her small knife. She continued to eye the shore, mentally daring the intruder to show himself.

Water lapped at the side of the canoe, and it rocked gently in the chilly evening breeze. Masha looked down, and saw a white face floating, mouth open. It was Dylan. She gasped when he suddenly blinked, his pale hand reaching up for her.

"Hold on," Masha cried out, reaching for him. A hand emerged from the water, reaching to meet hers, but it wasn't Dylan's. Black scales dotted the grey flesh, the fingers ending in filthy claws. The stench of rotten fish instantly hit her nostrils and she cried out anew, swinging her paddle towards the hand. The long-haired man erupted from the depths, Dylan nowhere in sight, and grabbed hold of Masha.

She fought at him with the paddle, hit him on the side of the head, but he held on tight and threatened to capsize the canoe. His bulging lips made sucking sounds, blackened teeth gnashing in her face.

With more strength than Masha expected from a frail-looking old man, he ripped her from the canoe, and plunged her beneath the icy mountain water. She fought for air, grasping for the canoe to pull herself back in. A clawed hand held her by the wrist and dragged her down. She turned, eyes open underwater, and saw Dylan down below her.

"Help me," she mouthed, looking at him with confused eyes.

"Come with us," he seemed to say, smiling and waving her down towards the bottom of the lake. "You'll like it here."

YACHT ROCK

Matt Serafini

Music is another way to dream.

That's what Dennis Bouchard thought as his yacht, *Cannon*, rocked slow on mild Atlantic waters. On the radio, Dobie Gray encouraged the boat's lazy pace, crooning *Drift Away* through the deck-by-deck stereo system.

It cost a pretty penny to wire the *Cannon* this way, but Dennis wanted the best. Scratch that. *Deserved* the best. A man needed access to these soothing sounds whether he was sloshing drinks at the teakwood bar below deck, or swept up in the ocean breeze while stretched out in the aft lounge.

Dennis closed his eyes and pushed his face beneath the shower stream so the water could rinse him clean. It was mid-afternoon and the *Cannon* bobbed toward France. He hoped so, at least, because they were supposed to be there yesterday. And would've been, had it not been for the sputtering and stalling engine. By the time black smoke filled the motor compartment, it was too late to deny there was a problem.

Dobie Gray wanted to *Drift Away* and Dennis was terrified they were actually doing it.

His heart pounded as he forced a smile beneath the cleansing water. *It's 1985*, he thought. *This is the future. Nobody gets lost in it.*

The music lulled him. Its rhythm calmed his racing heart. He always counted on it to shift his mindset, and it was reliable that way—like an old playground friend. Music could get you to step outside your reality, to break from a waking nightmare. Today, Dennis' only nightmare was that this life was a dream, and his old one was in the shadows waiting to spring. That fear woke him from time-to-time with cold sweat. And each time he'd think *"thank Christ"* before reaching for the whiskey bottle and pouring one off to send those 9-to-5 memories scurrying.

Because this life was *exactly* where Dennis wanted to be. His problems were back there beyond the Miami marina, somewhere in early 1983. The drugs made it hard to remember all the ways in which it had gone wrong back then. The years before Frank had come knocking with an offer.

With an investment.

A "sure thing."

A horror picture called *Night Slash,* about a guy in a ski mask who hacked up a bus full of cheerleaders after they broke down in the Ozarks.

Dennis had been 44 then, stricken with a soul-crushing case of *is this all there is?* Sleeveless button-downs. Plaid ties. Black socks. Co-workers who loved punching a clock. Arguments about who got to have time off at Christmas.

Who needed it?

It was the music that pulled him through that drudgery. The melodies stoked fantasies of escapism and promised another life.

Is this all there is?

That question plagued him in bumper-to-bumper traffic always, and his hands would coil around the steering wheel as his jaw clenched and teeth gnashed and he'd think, *"Not if I can help it."*

For Dennis had a tiny nest egg stashed away. In *his* bank account, not that husband and wife joint thing everyone got scammed on. Frank was his pal from way back, and might've heard about the "rainy day" fund a time or two before, usually after a Thursday night spent crushing Miller Lites and extra saucy buffalo wings, when secrets were apt to flow a bit looser. He'd come knocking in search of it.

"A couple of hundred grand can get a lot done on a picture like that."

It was a gamble, but Dennis was hungry for change. Anything was better than the grind.

The music had wanted him to go for it.

He had been rotting in traffic on I-95 listening to Seals and Crofts revere a *Diamond Girl.* It was that melody specifically that had opened a window into the future and showed him this moment. All that could be possible if he'd only put his money where his thoughts were.

Night Slash was a gamble, sure. How many horror pictures had hit the market around that time only to die a woeful box office death? But Seals and Crofts hadn't steered him wrong. The $41 million box office haul was astonishing. Bidding wars on foreign sales in thirty territories. The first thing Dennis did was go out and buy himself a divorce, hoping one day he might forget that life as quickly as he'd forgotten her name. Next came beachfront property, and then another six million for his pièce de résistance. This bobbing baby.

"Drift Away" passed, seguing into the aggressively soothing trumpet of Chuck Mangione, which chased away what little trepidation remained embedded beneath his ribs. *Feels So Good.* This is the life. This was sweet freedom.

Dennis stepped from the shower and wrapped a towel around his waist. There was one errant bump remaining on his cabin's bedside table. A shot of candy disappeared up his nose with a quick sniffle.

"I can't find anyone," Sybil said. His very own Diamond Girl leaned against the doorjamb in a skimpy golden two-piece that matched her curly blonde locks. Her other hand dusted her hip like this was another of her sultry photo shoots.

"Feeling better?"

"Took a Xanax to knock me out, so yes. Headache's passed."

"Good," Dennis said and eyed the bed. "Round two soon?"

She brushed the question aside with a roll of the eyes. "Where is everyone?"

"This boat's 100 feet from bow to stern, baby," he said with violent assurance. Teetering on defensive for reasons he didn't understand. Sybil's brow furrowed, and suddenly he knew he was close to blowing it. Shit. He couldn't blow it. Not with the Austrian goddess. A year ago, he'd been jacking off to her Playboy spread—one of three issues he was able to stash in his garage without the wife knowing. But today she was ten feet away, and looking like his memory had projected her centerfold spread in front of him.

Music wasn't just another way to dream, it could actually create new realities if you believed in its power.

"I mean...I know they're screwing," Sybil said. "I think Frank wanted me to join them. Left a note on my bag saying I should meet them when I wake up."

Dennis balled his fists as the anger worked through his system in tandem with the Colombian blow. He felt like finding Frank. Barbie, the 1982 Playmate of the Year, wasn't enough for him? In a way, he was surprised Sybil hadn't gone for it on the promise of starring in more schlock. A body like that would look good in loincloth, and they had not one but two barbarian scripts on his desk. Girls have done a lot worse for a lot less.

Maybe Sybil was a more honest girl than he had suspected, and he suddenly felt guilty about making assumptions. Sure, Hef had already pawed her a half dozen times, but that was the cost of doing business in this industry. She also happened to be the goddess from his fieriest fantasies—gorgeous, with buku brains to back her scrumptious rack. She even voted Republican.

Still, Frank was supposed to be restarting the yacht's engine, not revving his own. What were they going to tell the girls if they couldn't get it up and running? *Sorry ladies, no Cannes this year, but we'll make it up to you by putting you in the pictures?* If they couldn't get their latest sold, there would be no more pictures.

The communication equipment also needed repair. If they couldn't do that, it would be even worse because who knew where they'd end up? Dennis had taken a few navigation classes in pursuit of his Captain's License, but he didn't trust himself to remember a word. Something about using the stars in the sky to find your way home. *"Just look for Polaris"* or some shit. Was that the star that never moved? Was that even accurate? He couldn't remember because he'd been too coked out to care.

Why bother? This was the 80s. You shouldn't have to use a fucking sexton when you float out to sea.

"I guess it doesn't matter where they are," Sybil said. "I'm up and feeling better. Why don't you and I go have some Mai Tais?" She watched him dress and, when he was finished, placed the white captain's hat atop his head like she was decorating a Christmas tree. Then backed out of the doorway with a playful grin that dared him to follow.

Dennis followed all right. His mind stumbled over subconscious panic, unable to focus on the wiggling ass leading the way. If Frank wasn't worried about being stranded, he shouldn't be, either. It was usually his yacht they were on, and they'd made similar voyages a dozen times without incident.

Just my fucking luck, he thought.

Sybil tugged loose her bikini strings. With a delicious grin, the straps slid off her shoulders. His eyes, among other things, bulged at the sight.

On the yacht-wide PA, Pablo Cruise assured him that *Love Will Find a Way*, as if on cue. The cool Atlantic air pacified his fears about being lost at sea, at least temporarily, as the music promised everything was going to be fine.

Sybil sauntered toward the *Cannon*'s bow, dropping into the rounded seat cushion that overlooked the sprawling blue void. She turned back with a smile and lifted a bottle of Asti Spumante that she must've planted there. "I was going to save this until you sold your film, but we'll just get another." She uncorked it and poured a little across her chest as Dennis got there, cupping her breasts in his hands and lowering his mouth to taste alcohol-soaked flesh.

They could float all the way to Japan for all he cared. Life was meant to be enjoyed, and he wasn't going back to his old one. Nope. He'd won. And after the next multimillion-dollar payout, Robin Leech might finally come calling.

He went at Sybil like an animal, fueled by the cocktail of coke and Asti that reduced his mind to mush. Screwing the woman of his dreams was a blur. Her body was soft against his, and her legs wrapped around him in a loving way that only encouraged him.

By the time he finished, spilling on her thigh after slipping out in a clumsy attempt to prolong the gesture, the blue sky was no more. It was as if they'd sailed to the edge of the world and found only darkness beyond the yacht lights. He grunted and groaned his finishing cries and she moaned *"no, no, no"* before her own whines settled into frustrated acceptance and their muscles went limp together.

"Let's just enjoy the evening sky," she said, not wanting to hear his excuses.

Dennis looked up and saw a thousand glowing stars trained on them like leering eyeballs while the ocean beneath heaved. He stumbled upright into brisk night air as Olivia Newton-John's *Magic* greeted the darkness with pop atmosphere.

This time the music brought no relief. There must've been interference from another ship's intercom, because the speakers pushed through static, drowning Olivia in a wave of crackles. A faint hum surfaced, gaining on the static and pushing Ms. Xanadu off the air entirely.

Here was new music, steady and melodic. Ancient—almost as soothing as his mix but unlike anything he'd ever heard.

"What the hell is that?" Sybil said, sliding her long tanned legs through the thin bikini bottom.

Dennis was far too disoriented to acknowledge the question. The veil of lust had been lifted and his chemical high receded. His thoughts reshaped into something resembling priority. Time to start thinking about getting this hunk of junk moving again.

"Frank," he called and wondered why there was still no response.

Sybil moved closer to the railing, her arms covering her breasts as she squinted into the night. "I think I see something."

He turned to tell her to stuff it, but his irrational anger was stymied by a silhouetted landmass in the distance. Was it France at last? Had they made it? Beneath them, the rocking water intensified. The stalled vessel lifted and ebbed toward the island on a steady crawl.

"Where are we, Dennis?"

"France," he said with the kind of certainty that wouldn't fool a conch shell.

Sybil snuggled against him, crystal blue eyes swiveled up with an affection that made his knees buckle. Her fingernails pierced his arm as she shook.

109

Drifting in off the sea, a pleasing voice called out, somehow blaring through the yacht's speakers while filling the night sky. An inescapable song.

It invaded Dennis the way a bedroom voice seeped inside your unconsciousness and manifested within your dreams. He wanted to ask Sybil if she heard it, but it was far too beautiful to interrupt.

He trained his ear and held his breath as the island loomed closer.

The song rose and fell, scored by ethereal strings he could not identify, and sung in a language he did not understand. This tongue was more than exotic, it belonged to an age long past.

Sybil pushed away, clamping her palms over her ears and bending over like the auditory invasion was killing her. She tried to speak, and maybe she was, but Dennis either couldn't hear or wasn't listening. He was a captive audience, and this new music was the only thing that mattered.

That's when Sybil launched at him, throwing a frustrated shove that sent him staggering.

The fugue spell broke and Dennis was suddenly furious. He raised his hand to her, and felt the urge to slap the stupid vulnerability off her face. But the music came for him again, a warm burst in the center of his chest that made the anger dissipate. The voice locked him in place, growing louder as the current continued to ease the *Cannon* straight for it.

Sybil came and went, stomping off and returning more than once, each time bringing a different declaration or interrogation: *Frank and Barbie are still missing! How can that be? What if they went overboard? Dennis don't you care?*

He should care, but nothing seemed as important as the music.

Music had never steered him wrong.

The island had become a sizable landmass before his eyes. Dennis felt a swell of excitement at the thought of reaching it as the boat buckled. The electric hum signaled the dropping anchor and interrupted the honeyed sound. The *Cannon* was locked, trying still to inch toward the music like a leashed dog in heat.

What had Sybil done?

Just like the whore wife whose name he was beginning to forget, she too was sabotaging him.

"What is that?" Sybil cried from the sun deck above.

Dennis turned with rage in his eyes, and found her pointing to the nearest outcropping of rocks.

Pointing at a woman.

A buxom outline stood beneath the moonlight on an edge of stone like a sculpted statue. Two hundred feet away, but her shimmering cat-like eyes were clear as day. Her shoulders bucked and her chest rose as her song purred in the air, somehow amplified by his speakers.

He wanted to call to her, and was about to do it when Sybil's palm curled around his mouth. She was stronger than she looked, hooking her other hand under his shoulder and dragging him across deck. Her skin, previously so pleasing, repulsed him like touching a rotted banana peel.

Dennis fought, but the music had done more than lull him. His eyelids were heavy, his muscles lax. He wanted to push her away and rush right back to his personal concert, but Sybil had other plans.

She pulled him inside and closed the door where the music persevered. The reflective eyes on the rock watched with a gleam that might've indicated a smile.

"What have you done, Dennis?" She wiped her eyes with the back of her hand as she asked, and backed away, brandishing an icepick like a weapon. Her leather jacket hung off her shoulders, but the gold bikini bottom was the only other article of clothing she wore. Even in distress, she was ready for a photo shoot.

Everything about her irritated him now.

"I found them, Dennis." She motioned to the aft sliding door. He stared at her before understanding she wanted him to look.

Dennis got to wobbly feet and shuffled to the glass. The engine compartment was open, the inside latch covered in blood. From here he saw Barbie's severed head. Her dead gaze staring from the top of a pyramid of mutilated body parts.

That's when he remembered. He'd heard this song before. It came as a whisper on the wind, late this morning, little more than a tickle in his brain. Its suggestion had been no less powerful, though. Taking the fire axe in his fists was palatable as he strode aft and found Barbie riding Frank like he was a bucking bronco.

He'd wanted nothing more than to kill her, and she broke and cracked apart like firewood, only the spurting mess was ungodly. The hungry blade decimated her breastbone and the blow flung her aside, tearing the weapon from his hands because it was embedded inside her. That's when he knew Frank had to die next. Unarmed, Dennis did what came natural in the moment: he jammed his thumbs straight through his friend's eyes.

The worst part had been the thrashing struggle as fingernails scraped warm bone at the back of Frank's skull. It took a long time for life to vacate the body—the entire length of Christopher Cross' *Ride Like The Wind*, to be exact—and Dennis couldn't help but fixate on Frank's shriveling penis as it reverted back into a flaccid pod. Life's indignity never more clear than in that moment.

Is this all there is?

He'd rushed back to his cabin then, eager to shower. Xanax had Sybil out cold on the sun deck above, and that time needed to be used wisely. Hacking two bodies into pieces and then stashing them tended to be messy.

Tears streamed off Sybil's chiseled cheeks as the blade in her fist wobbled. Blood dripped from her earlobes and rappelled down her golden earrings.

Dennis realized there was only one way to get back to the music. It was a craving, the way addicts got all twisted and manipulated by chemical addiction, and it had to be enjoyed without distraction.

He took a step, and Sybil was wound so tight she slashed at him. The crazed look in her eye begged him not to try again. He did, and the blade caught his wrist as he lashed out, gasping at the sudden spring of pain while she dashed for the door. Her bare flesh sprinted past the window darting for the bow. Beyond her, out on the rocks, glimmering eyes narrowed with waning patience.

Dennis knew what he was supposed to do. He returned to the deck, stalking this bitch to the music that swirled through the ocean breeze. It scored his pursuit as if this were a movie where characters could hear the music that accompanied their actions.

He found Sybil with her back to the sea. The blade raised high. Sputters tripping past her lips. At fifty feet, she managed to scream, "Keep your distance!" That didn't deter him. She tried supplementing her threat with "I mean it!" But her voice was lost in the wraithlike melody that filled their ears.

That music pulsed and Dennis' fillings shook. He approached his prey with a slow skulk and tried to smile in a way that belied his predatory intent. "Take a drink with me," he said as he neared the cushions that had been the spot of their lovemaking. He lifted the bottle of Asti and took a quick swig. It was tepid.

"You have to get the engine running," Sybil said. Her eyes were no longer crystal blue, but bloodshot cherry red. "Please, Dennis, the noise is killing us. It's squeezing my thoughts...my head feels like it's about to crack."

"You're right," Dennis said. "It's awful." But it wasn't awful. He glanced toward the rocks, at the singer. Her high notes were hooks into his soul, stirring him from a distance. In that instant he was back on I-95, miserable, save for his car stereo. The music propelling thoughts about the future. Seals and Crofts making him realize it was out there, ripe for the taking.

That's how he felt today.

He smashed the glass bottle of Asti on the yacht's railing and gripped the neck like it was a hungry knife. Sybil's gorgeous eyes popped wide as he stepped to her, catching a defensive icepick stab through the top of his hand. There was probably pain, but the music wouldn't allow him to feel it. Instead, he jammed the bottle's jagged edges up through her jaw, forcing it into her mouth while warm blood coated his arm.

With a heave of strength he wouldn't have thought possible, he pushed up so the entire bottleneck disappeared inside her head. Her mouth gaped and the dark glass at the back of her throat twisted up like a drill, boring into her brain. Blood squirted from her eyes to escape the pressure, while brain matter oozed from her ears and nose like a runny bowl of Quaker Oats.

Sybil landed against the bow's tip and her arms dropped over the rails, half-propped like a disheveled scarecrow. The once flawless figure was a lifeless husk that stared through Dennis with cold apathy.

There was immediate regret, but that notion was buried deep. He didn't have time to contemplate it further because he was already looking toward the rock, desperate for his favorite singer's approval. She glided from one edge of the natural stage to the other, her song pitched high. Musical gauze wrapped his thoughts so this act of annihilation became nothing but a hazy memory, and easily disposable.

A slat of moonlight caught the rock, bathing her in a heavenly glow. She was a nude figure moving without the sin of shame. She lifted her arms to the sky and spread them in a slow and commanding motion.

There was only one thing left to do.

Dennis went back to the anchor control and retracted it, allowing the boat to drift again. The anticipation in his body was like nothing else. The *Cannon* neared the outcropping, and he understood why the music was so loud. There was more than one singer. His soprano was close by, maybe fifteen feet off the starboard side, and Dennis was spellbound as he floated past. Their eyes locked, and her face changed in the shifting moonlight. Sickly pale skin. Eyes like nothing from this plane of existence—lit with a color he had never seen, light and dark all at once. When she opened her throat wide to hit a high note, her tongue was forked.

He didn't judge. This was the most beautiful sight.

Land was less than a hundred feet off, pocked by the silhouettes of a half dozen songstresses. Some were perched on their own rock stages, and another stood expectantly in waist-deep water—arms outstretched in welcome.

This was more than a dream come true. This was actually paradise.

Dropping anchor made sense now as he could easily swim the rest of the way. But it was already too late. Deep down, he knew that. And wanted this.

Beneath him, the *Cannon*'s hull scraped along rocky shallows, the fiberglass hull protested the sweeping current lassoing the yacht, tugging it close. The ship's bottom could only warble so much before giving, and he wasn't surprised when the splintering cracks were loud enough to feel. That physical distress signaled a loud echoing puncture and then the *Cannon* was really in trouble.

The music in the sky stopped, every voice silenced at once.

Shining eyes lit the night, each pair locked onto him. The woman in the shallows waded in up to her shoulders and Dennis thought he saw her wink before vanishing beneath the Atlantic.

Splashing water sounded behind him. Dennis turned and found a blotch of moonlight looking down on the rock cluster like a spotlight. Only his soprano was missing, and a quiet ring of water radiated outward, as if its performer had never been there.

Or had suddenly slipped away.

Diving bodies splashed all around him, and Dennis whipped back to survey the shoreline. His welcome party had vanished, and he imagined a half dozen women knifing through the water on a path toward his sinking boat. The hairs on his arms rose and a spike of terror crashed into his heart.

On the speakers, America's *Horse With No Name* started up and the irony was so brutal that Dennis couldn't even laugh. He looked at Sybil's corpse, certain there was a slight smile at the corners of her mouth.

"I'm sorry," he tried to say, but the best he could do was mouth the words. The dead weren't interested in apologies.

He ran aft toward the life preservers, gasping when he found an empty rack where they had been. Memories of his blood rage thundered back. Breathing heavily over the stashed corpses of Frank and Barbie, thinking that nobody could leave the *Cannon* alive. Before he ruptured one of the engine lines with that fire axe, he had hurled all the life rafts overboard, ensuring this boat would become their collective tomb.

Oh Christ!

America seemed to mock him in mayday. His yacht mix had been a harbinger of better days, but this song suddenly felt like a betrayal. It crashed through the speakers, turning a soft rock classic into aural violence.

He wanted his songstress back. Her music had been like nothing else, and would take his pain away. But they all refused their gifts now, because he was already stuck at the center of their spider web.

Water lapped at the *Cannon*'s deck, ensuring his boat's days were numbered.

The women surfaced and surrounded the bow. He headed up front to see them, to plead his case, his feet splashing through water that was suddenly ankle-high. They bobbed up and down in silence, hovering like expectant animals waiting to be fed. Their faces were barely human in the deck light's glow: grey scaled flesh, eyelids that lifted and revealed button orbs and serpentine half-moon irises. Their mouths hung low, with drool dangling from fangs that seemed far too large, too erratic to fit naturally inside them.

Dennis was nearly submerged. "Please," he cried, knowing it was too late to escape. "I did everything you asked." The water rushed up to his hips and lifted Sybil off the railing. It looked like she had returned to life for revenge, her neck lifted and her arms pulled forward, but it was only the weight of the Atlantic rearranging her.

Her once flawless face was a pulpy mash of jagged gashes and dark blood. Her beauty destroyed. Stubbed out because their music had fooled him into thinking he deserved better. Music was dreams. And dreams were impossible things.

Two of the women shot forward, claws slashing into Sybil's flesh, drawing pools of red wherever they dug. When they had her, their eyes bugged wide with a hiss of satisfaction, dragging her over the rail. They shredded Austrian flesh like kids tearing at giftwrap. Bladed teeth tore her apart. Then they slipped beneath the sea with their prey.

Dennis went from standing to floating as the *Cannon*'s deck disappeared with them. Mercifully, America shorted out like a smoldering cigar mashed against the sidewalk. He was thankful for small favors.

Two more creatures swam past, and Dennis didn't have to look to know what they were after. Pieces of Frank and Barbie would be floating back there somewhere, a spilled chum bucket. His role in this was little more than glorified waiter, delivering a meal in exchange for a song.

His songstress lifted through the surface and hovered few inches from his face. Her monstrous visage prompted Dennis to scream as the water around them turned to blood. The sounds of tearing flesh and smacking lips were the worst in the world.

Dennis slipped willingly into her arms, embracing flesh that was colder than ice, his hands roving hardened body scales. Her snake's tongue was like sandpaper dragging across his cheek as she lapped bloodstains off his face, grinning at the taste of Sybil's blood.

"Sing to me," Dennis said in fleeting breath.

Around them, the others were too ravenous to consider his request, but not her. She pulled back and cocked her head, granting him a moment of consideration. Then she took him close, her wet, sticky lips hovering over his ear.

Her talons sliced into his chest and glided upward, ripping bone as if it was tissue paper. But she sang. All for him. And Dennis was at peace as he spilled into the Atlantic, that serenade stirring him to dream one last time.

LAMPREY LUAU

Amber Fallon

Rebecca Marsh was absolutely giddy as she stared out the window of the airplane. The view of the Pacific Ocean was breathtaking. She was in love. She and her fiancé, Shelly Sanchez, were heading to Hawaii to get married. She sighed happily, watching the sun glint off her engagement ring. The effect was dazzling.

"This time tomorrow, we're gonna be married!" Rebecca nearly squealed, drawing the attention of several of her fellow passengers. She took Shelly's hand, squeezing it tightly.

"I know, silly!" Shelly smirked, "I'm the one that got us the island, remember?"

"The island! I almost forgot!" Rebecca exclaimed more loudly than she should have, this time earning herself glares and a few *shhhs!* from those around her.

Shelly couldn't help but grin. She had fallen in love with the quirky freckled redhead because of her childish sense of wonder and enthusiasm. Every day with Becky was a new adventure and even normal, boring things like going grocery shopping and doing yardwork became epic quests. She had found a partner that made her laugh and smile almost daily. What could be better than that?

"How could you forget about the island?" Shelly asked, playfully swatting her fiancé, "How many people get to have a whole island to themselves to get married on? You must be pretty special!"

Rebecca giggled, "Or lucky! It's your grandfather's island, after all."

"True," Shelly said. "I haven't been there since I was a little girl. I remember him taking me and my brothers fishing and swimming, running around on the beach and sticking my toes in the warm sand... I don't want you to be disappointed, though... It's a pretty small island."

Rebecca took Shelly's hand and kissed it gently, "It will be perfect. We'll say our I do's and party under the stars to celebrate! Roast pork and camping! I even brought a ukulele!"

Shelly's eyes went momentarily wide. One less positive thing about Rebecca was that you could never be quite sure whether or not she was being serious when she said some completely ridiculous thing. Knowing her, a ukulele was completely plausible.

"Kidding!" Rebecca broke into a fit of giggles as the pilot announced that they were beginning their final decent into Hawaii's Big Island.

***

Far below the plane, in a small underwater research station, a secret terror dwelled. The product of military science and genetic splicing, a huge insulated interior tank writhed with altered lampreys.

The fish weren't especially dangerous in their natural state, at least not to humans, but when you added in growth hormones, DNA from half a dozen other species all selected for their most deadly traits, and brains manipulated to promote aggression, they could do some real damage if they ever escaped into the open ocean. Which is precisely why that should never be allowed to happen. At least, that was the direction of the program's head overseer, General Benson Briggs.

Briggs called up the head research scientist, a man named Michaels Clausen. Clausen had given years of his life to the project, spent countless hours in the laboratory, building monsters that would be capable of taking out class 1 submarines, should the need arise. They were big, they were aggressive, they were the perfect killing machines; born and bred to do one thing: Destroy.

"We have to pull the plug on Project Tri Tooth." Briggs was calm, detached almost, as he delivered the news.

"WHAT?!" Clausen spat, fists clenching in anger, "What do you mean *pull the plug?!*"

"I mean," replied Briggs, "that the project has been terminated, effective immediately. You are to destroy all living specimens, ship any collected materials back to HQ, and vacate the premises by 0800 tomorrow morning."

"But... but... but sir! This is absurd! We're just on the brink of an advancement that will..."

Briggs cut Clausen off mid-sentence, "Clausen, I am done with your delays, your little side projects, and most of all, I am done with you. Now clear out! That's an order."

The line went dead. Dr. Clausen ripped the Bluetooth earpiece off and threw it angrily to the ground. They couldn't do this to him! Not after taking years – YEARS! – of his life away! He had worked so hard, done everything asked of him, even against impossible odds, and this was the gratitude they showed him for it? Tasking him with killing his finned children? The product of exhaustive amounts of work and tireless hours of effort? No. This was NOT how it was going to end. He'd see to that.

***

A troupe of pretty young island girls greeted the deplaning passengers at the airport, welcoming everyone with brightly colored leis and warm alohas. Rebecca smiled as she disembarked the plane, stepping in to a warm Hawaiian sunset that looked like something out of a movie or a painting. She gratefully accepted a lovely purple orchid lei that matched Shelly's and together the women made their way into the airport proper.

"Everything is all set!" Shelly, the planner of the pair, smiled as she finished loading their luggage into the rental car. There'd been a little bit of friction with a stewardess who'd been unhappy about being asked to stow two wedding dresses in the captain's closet, but other than that things had gone off without a hitch. Now all they needed to do was make their way to the dock at the end of the island before sunset, where a boat was waiting to take them to the island to meet the small group of family and close friends they'd invited.

According to texts sent while they were in transit, all of Rebecca and Shelly's invited guests were already on the island and waiting eagerly for the girls to arrive so that the festivities could begin.

In lieu of bachelorette parties, the pair had decided to camp out on the beach the night before their nuptials, get married in the morning, and spend the day partying and having fun in the sand and sun before sharing a traditional luau feast of poi, poke, and roast pig with their guests.

Shelly, true to form, had ordered tents for everyone as wedding favors. It would be a weekend to remember, if all went according to plan.

"Do you think we can stop somewhere and pick up some marshmallows?" Rebecca asked. "I want s'mores for dinner!"

"Aren't you worried about fitting in your dress?" Shelly joked. Rebecca pouted in response, tucking herself into the passenger seat of the couple's rented Fiat before they hit the road.

***

"Are you sure this is the right place?" Rebecca asked, raising one eyebrow at her fiancé.

"That's what the GPS says…" Shelly trailed off, clearly feeling the same way Rebecca did. The couple sat in the parked car staring out at a rickety dock with a pair of ancient canoes tied up to it. A ramshackle shed hunched a few feet away.

"I'm not sure I want to get out of the car here... let alone get into one of those boats..." Rebecca stuck out her tongue indicating her disgust.

"Fine, then you can stay here and watch our dresses. I'll go see if there's anyone around." Shelly got out of the car as her fiancé watched warily.

Rebecca almost grabbed a 3 ounce bottle of body spray to use as mace when a tattoo-covered giant of a man emerged from the shack and grabbed Shelly. She relaxed, however, when the man swung her fiancé around in a circle and Rebecca could see Shelly's smiling face over one broad shoulder.

The man set Shelly down before turning to grin at the car and its still somewhat terrified passenger. Shelly gestured for Rebecca to join them, and she did, hesitantly.

"Rebecca, this is my great uncle Makoa. Uncle, this is my wife to be, Rebecca."

Rebecca extended a hand in greeting, though she had a sinking feeling that she was going to be pulled into a bear hug. She was right. The large older man smelled of the briny sea and his skin was warm to the touch.

"Uncle Mak, I didn't know you still owned the place! No one said anything when I made the reservation."

"Of course I do!" Makoa chuckled, "Who else would do this work? Pah. Not the same after your granddaddy died though."

"Hey, come on. It's a happy occasion. We're getting married. Oh! You HAVE to stay for the wedding. Say you'll stay? Pleaase?" Shelly begged.

"Of course! I wouldn't miss it! I am honored to be part of your celebration. Now, let's get out to the island before it gets too dark."

Once they had everything loaded into the larger of the two boats, the trio made their way to an island that seemed a lot closer than Rebecca had been led to believe. There was a huge bonfire burning on the beach and half a dozen matching purple tents surrounded it. As they drew closer, Rebecca could see her sister, Rose, and Rose's husband, Kyle, and her best friend, Tina. Shelly's brother, Chris, was roasting fish of some kind on a stick. A few other guests were too cloaked in shadow to make out clearly.

***

120

Clausen stood on a metal catwalk spanning the two huge tanks inside the underwater lab. "I'll show him," he grinned maniacally, face lit greenish blue by the dancing waters in the tanks below him, "I'll show them all! Think they can shut me down! HAH! We'll see about that…"

Still cackling to himself, Clausen punched a big red button mounted on a stand between the tanks, opening the outer release hatches and freeing hundreds of his genetically altered lampreys. Then, he took a syringe from his pocket and plunged it into his arm. He was still laughing when his skin began to crack, just before he lost his balance and pitched over the side of the catwalk.

***

"This is GREAT!" Rebecca laughed, holding a stick with a roasted fish in one hand and another with a half dozen burnt marshmallows in the other. "Shelly, can we stay here forever? I LOVE HAWAII!"

Shelly smiled, watching her fiancé dance around the flames and take alternate bites of fish and gooey sugar from the sticks Chris had given her. She sat beside her uncle on a log near the fire. The two had never been very close, but she was glad to see him all the same. They'd fallen out of touch after his brother's funeral, when Shelly couldn't deal with the loss of the man who'd raised her and instead turned away from the islands and all she'd known to make a new life for herself in California, where she'd met Rebecca and fallen in love. After that, picking up the phone to call her relatives hadn't seemed so important. So she just hadn't.

But here they were, back together on the island where she'd spent her springs and summers, Christmases, most weekends… A place of safety and sanctity where in less than 12 hours, she'd pledge her life to the woman she loved. It seemed fitting.

"Hey, we're going to go for a dip in the ocean. Wanna come?" Rose asked Shelly, interrupting her reverie. She glanced at her uncle as he stared into the flames.

"No, I'm spent. I think I'll just rest up by the fire. You guys go have fun."

"Suit yourself!" Rose laughed, already halfway to the water, neon pink bikini standing out in the dim light of the fire. There was a splash, followed by another, then laughter as Rose and Kyle played together in the warm, tropical waters. Rebecca sat down next to Shelly and Makoa and offered them some of the remaining morsels on her precious sticks. Both demurred.

After a few moments of peaceful quiet, Rebecca started belting out lines from her and Shelly's song, before pulling her to her feet, fish and marshmallows all but forgotten. Shelly moved, reluctantly at first, but eventually she and Rebecca were joined by a chorus of their friends as they danced by the fire, singing to one another. Only Uncle Mak didn't seem to know the words, but he clapped along anyway. It was a perfect prewedding moment. Until a scream shattered the romantic atmosphere.

Shelly turned towards the sound, sharp and alert. Makoa stood, clutching Rebecca's discarded, marshmallow-covered stick in one hand; the closest weapon he could find.

"Rose?!" Rebecca cried, "Rose, are you OK? Kyle?" She darted out into the waves and was knee deep before Shelly even realized it.

"Rebecca. Becks, get out of there. Now." Panic edged into Shelly's voice as Rebecca froze. Rose's pink bikini top washed up on the shore, bloodstains evident even in the firelight.

Rebecca shrieked when she saw it and darted back onto the sand.

"Everyone, stay calm," Shelly said. "Stay out of the water and stay calm."

"Calm?!" Tina cried, "Where are Rose and Kyle?"

"I don't know yet. But I don't want anyone else getting hurt until we figure it out."

"ROSE!" Shelly called, "KYLE!" but there was no answer.

"Does anyone have a cell phone?" Shelly asked. "We need to call the Coast Guard."

"No good." Makoa shook his head, "No reception out here." Sure enough, everyone who'd pulled out their phones hung their heads in dismay.

Makoa pulled his keys from his pocket and turned on a small flashlight he had clipped to them. Aiming it at the waves, he knelt down to pick up the bloody scrap of fabric when something darted out from beneath it and bit his finger.

Makoa swore loudly and leapt backwards, blood running down his arm.

"What the hell was that?!" Rebecca gasped, staring out at the dark water.

"I don't know," he said, "But I think we'll be safe if we stay on the land." Rebecca stared at him wide-eyed and started to cry.

Shelly put her arm around her fiancé as tears streamed down her own face. What the hell was going on? The water off the island was supposed to be too shallow for big predators like sharks or barracuda, so what had happened to Rose and Kyle? And what had bitten Makoa? This was not

122

how she envisioned their time on the island, she thought, as she stared out at the water.

Not far off shore, something broke the surface. Shelly pointed, straining her eyes to make out what it was in the near darkness. At first, she thought it was Kyle, but then why wasn't he answering them?

Makoa picked up his makeshift spear again and shined his small flashlight in the direction of the thing that was approaching the island. As soon as the light hit it, Rebecca and Shelly screamed in unison.

It was a man. At least it was man-shaped, but that was where the similarities ended. Huge lidless eyes reflected the light back at them. A round mouth gaped open, revealing three enormous, sharp teeth. Water, drool, or both ran from it down a chest covered in scales between two muscular arms. Some kind of mohawk or pointed hat stuck up from the thing's otherwise bald head. Bits of blood-stained white fabric clung to its shoulders.

"I am king!" it hissed in an oddly flat voice, pointing a finger at the party goers.

A wave of writhing, squirming fish flung themselves up onto the beach. They were long, more like eels, with gaping three-toothed mouths like the creature that commanded them. Their scales shined in the firelight as they flopped ever closer.

"Shelly!" Rebecca cried, clutching the woman she loved so tightly she left bruises.

Makoa lunged forward, spearing one of the things with his sharpened stick. It shrieked a high-pitched cry as its brothers, shockingly, flopped toward its assailant. Makoa flung the thing into the fire just before one of them managed to latch onto his ankle. He cried out in pain and tried to rip the thing free, but the others were already on him, their mouths like suckers seeking blood. Rebecca looked away, but Shelly could only watch as more and more of those awful eel things crowded onto her great uncle's body, biting and snapping and swarming like a school of ravenous piranhas.

Meanwhile, the thing that had been Clausen emerged from the waves and bowled something towards the women. It rolled and bounced before landing at their feet: Rose's head.

Chris lunged forward and grabbed the end of a log from the fire, wielding it like a torch in front of him as he advanced on Makoa, using it to ward the eel things off, but he was too late. Makoa fell to his side, dead, bloody holes oozing on the sand.

The fish creature laughed and pointed again, sending his hideous lamprey minions after Chris, who swung his burning weapon for all he was worth. He managed to take out a few of them before he became overwhelmed, falling to his knees in the sand, his blood leaking from holes the size of highball glasses.

Rebecca was screaming "NO! NONONONONO!" in an ever-climbing pitch as Shelly surveyed the situation. There were at least a few dozen of those eel/fish things and one badass mutant creep who seemed to be their leader.

The man fish was fully out of the water now, stalking toward the remaining guests with murder in his cold, silver, dinner plate eyes. The smaller things flip flopped on the beach, advancing further and further with each movement. They didn't seem to be suffering from lack of water, but given their leader, that was hardly the oddest thing about the evening.

Rebecca squealed once more and ran off in the opposite direction, not that there was much more to the island. Aside from a few palm trees and some scrub brush, it was basically a small flat beach with very little cover.

Shelly stood, watching as the things advanced like some kind of freakish army, led by a mutant general of unknown origin. There was no way in hell she was going to let that thing win. She couldn't allow it to kill any more of their friends, or god forbid Rebecca.

Her training and muscle memory after years on the force kicked in. She watched as the eel things advanced on Tina, then seized her moment and shoved their leader into the flames.

He let loose a shocked, garbled cry as his skin blackened and burned. The fish things seemed to have lost their herd mentality and were easy enough to either step on or avoid.

Shelly looked over to where Rebecca was hiding (poorly) behind a palm tree. Rebecca looked up, a palm frond clasped to her head.

"Can we just get married in Vegas?" she asked meekly.

THEY WAIT

Christine Morgan

Diving is the best.

No matter how awkward we might feel on land, how heavy and clumsy, the moment we're in the water, we become sleek grace and weightlessness. Each supple turn, each rippling roll, pearly bubbles streaming up in long glimmering trails ... such beauty, such freedom, such wonder and joy.

Leo bumps me. A friendly gesture, but there's flirtation behind the playful affection, and I know it.

It isn't that I mind Leo; Leo's okay ... he's cute, a great swimmer ... catches lots of fish when he puts in some effort ...

He likes me, but Selah likes him, and Selah is my cousin.

Anyway, I like Pip better, though Pip is with Jaya now. They'll probably be king and queen of the beach this year.

I shouldn't be jealous or disappointed. I'm sure I'll find someone. It isn't as if I'm going to end up with one of those scrawny losers who lurk around the edges of things, hoping for a lapse of judgment from the lonely or desperate.

Leo nudges me again. I look over, and he's goofing around, doing twists, showing off. Selah's below us. I see her watching him too. Watching him show off for me, anxiety dulling the dark shine of her eyes.

So, because I'm a good cousin, I splutter a rude string of bubbles to indicate the degree to which I am unimpressed, then arch my body and dive deeper. I skim over the rocky ledges – teeming with life, stars and spiny urchins, wavering fronds, crabs creeping sideways on skinny legs – toward the dropoff.

We know, of course, not to swim too far. We know the dangers, what's down there, what's out there. What waits, always hungry. Gaping maws. Gaping jaws. Rows of sharp teeth ready to rip and to rend.

We know, but we're young, we're confident, we're having fun. We're sure nothing bad will happen, not to us. To others, maybe. The careless or unlucky. Or, like Big Ro, the stupidly brave. Thinking he could take on a shark and win; was it any wonder he ended up shreds of gristle?

Shreds of gristle, adrift in dispersing blood.

A memory I could have done without.

A memory easy enough to shake from my head as I propel myself onward. The water parts around me and I am one with it. I'm not wallowing on the shore, trying to get comfortable, heaving my bulk around.

I am sleek, effortless, limber grace.

This is better.

Diving.

Diving is the best.

Selah paces me and Leo brings up the rear. We are well away from the beach now. Well into the bay, slipping through liquid indigo silence.

Silence, but for distant whalesong thrumming and warbling from the deep. The serenades of mating, of mothers calling to their calves, of bulls sounding challenges. It is their music, their melody. Oceanic arias in a cetacean opera.

Peacefulness. Serenity.

If only we could stay here forever.

But, sooner or later, we will have to surface. We are not fish to swim eternally while drawing with gills. We must breathe, and are limited to what air we can hold.

Our bubbles stream and trail and glimmer, rising from us, vanishing. I bump Selah and she bumps me back. We twirl around each other, play-fighting with slaps and swats. Leo joins in. We are a tussling tangle of flippers and slick wet fur, noses bristling with tickling whiskers.

I break from them first, disengage as they wrestle and roil. A small school of herring flit by. I dart and snap and catch one. It wriggles in my mouth. I bite. Fine scales and soft meat and a quick burst of juices. Gulp, gone. I want more, but the school whirls away and a constricting pressure in my ribs tells me it's about time to ascend.

The sea-ice hangs thick overhead. Pale arctic silver, shades of pure glacial blue. Its underside forms inverted canyons, ridges and ravines. Sunlight beams down in shifting, wavering shafts from jagged cracks and smooth-edged holes.

Up and up, I swim toward the shining gleam. Toward the promise of air, of life-giving breath. I exhale more wobbling bubbles, a billowing cloud of them, seething around me in coursing undulations.

My muzzle splashes up into the bracing cold. I puff out a last pluming gust, my own little imitation of a mighty whale.

White, it is so white and so bright after the beautiful gloaming in the depths! The sides of the hole are sloped, ridged with marks made by others before me who've scraped and scoured and dug to keep it from closing over. I add my own contribution, the stubby claws at the ends of my flippers gouging at the ice even as my lungs swell with –

I see the sudden lunging shadow and twitch with shock, recoiling.

The twitch saves me.

Something deadly shears past my face, close enough to flick my whiskers. It crashes into the icy edge. There is a miniature blizzard of flying hail but I am already dropping, dropping straight down rump-first with my hind-flippers tucked and my front-flippers folded against my chest.

The shadow looms, menacing, furious, uttering some horrible noise. I curl in a somersault, I dive as fast as I can.

Leo and Selah …

… are not wrestling anymore, but rising themselves, rising side-by-side in tandem. They look good together. It is their moment. Like a dance. A thing of beauty.

Which I ruin by plowing right into them, but I don't care. I don't care that Selah actually snaps at me in irritation, or that Leo gawks at me as if I've been chewing on the kind of anemones that make bulge-heads swim in circles.

Selah pushes past me. I grapple at her, prod her with my nose. She spins, and this time it is no play-fighting slap. It's slowed by the water; if we'd been ashore, she would have bowled me over.

Throat-grunting his amusement, Leo slings his muscular body upward. The silvery sheen of his belly-fur flashes. I squeal, but he must think I'm fooling. A strong flex of his hindquarters propels him into the wavering light.

Again, Selah pushes past me. Again, I grapple at her, and again she snaps and slaps at me. Her muzzle wrinkles, black lips peeling back to bare teeth in a snarl, nostrils sealed to shut slits.

I plead with pup-cries, like I haven't done since we lolled on the ice-floes waiting for our mothers to bring sweet milk and half-chewed fish. Selah hesitates. Her head tilts. I see a grey face in her glossy eye, and realize it is my own.

Then she shakes me off, batting impatiently at my grasping flippers, and surges up after Leo.

He has nearly reached the breathing-hole.

My squeal is so loud and shrill the whales probably hear it in the deep. Selah flinches, glancing down at me.

But Leo pops his head up through the hole in the ice.

The shadow lunges. There is a sound, a terrible sound – a grisly, meaty kind of crunch – and a dark tide of blood floods the water. Leo thrashes, flippers flailing, all his sleek grace and strength gone in a writhing and desperate struggle to escape.

More blood gushes, a great spreading cloud of its hot thick red stink. Leo screams. No, Leo shrieks. His bladder and bowels add more hot floods of fluid. The space beneath the air-hole is a vile, churning turbulence.

There is a second terrible crunch. Leo's shrieking becomes a gurgle. He convulses. His flippers beat madly at nothing, then go slack. The bulk of his body is yanked from above. It lodges in the hole, caught on the blood-rimmed edging of ice. The ice cracks and crackles.

Whatever's up there gives another tremendous yank. Blubbery skin squeaks as the widest part of Leo is squeezed through. The rest follows. I have a final glimpse of his hind-flippers, a claw snagging briefly, and then he is gone.

Gone, but the shadow ...

Gone, but the sounds!

The grisly, meaty, crunching, rending sounds.

And the blood. More blood. So much blood. Running like spring meltoff, spring meltoff in steaming, stinking scarlet.

I turn to Selah. Now I see my face in both of her eyes, her eyes so wide they're like round sea-polished stones. Her muzzle contorts. A thin, tiny whine issues from her throat. It is accompanied by a thin, tiny line of bubbles.

She needs to breathe.

She needs to go up.

Up there? Up there, where blood stains the ice? Where torn skin and gobbets of blubber plop into the sea as the thing that's killed Leo – there can be no doubt! – is ... what? Ripping him to pieces? Eating him?

But Selah needs to breathe.

We swivel, gazes searching the contoured, frozen underside for another opening, finding none. We've swum a long way, too far for her to swim back without a fresh lungful of air. She'd never make it.

I jerk my head at the hole above, encouraging her. If she goes now, while the deadly thing is busy with Leo, she can gulp a quick breath. Then we can flee far enough to find safety.

She shrinks from me, wrapping her flippers around herself. She's trembling, quivering with fear and distress. I don't blame her. The prospect of surfacing through the warm red salt-wash of Leo's blood, the way it would feel coating whiskers and fur, the way it would taste ... it's too much. Too much even without risking a similar, violent end.

128

What is it? What can it be?

I know of sharks, of course. I know of the orca, those lethal black-and-white kindred of the gentler whalesong behemoths.

None of them could be on top of the ice.

Something else is.

A death-bear?

I know of them, have even seen them from a distance. They are big and shaggy, white as the snow. They are land-creatures, but they can swim – unlike us; we are sea-creatures who can go ashore. And they will gladly kill and eat us, if they can.

Death-bears are sly, too. They'll charge us when we're on rocks or pebbly beaches, when we're at our slowest and most ungainly. They'll slide into the sea and paddle with only their snouts and wet backs poking up, slinking alongside our ice-floes as we're trying to bask, looking like ice-floes themselves.

If they've figured out our system of air-holes …

We have to surface, we have to breathe.

All they'll have to do is wait.

Selah warbles a small, pitiful sound.

Urgently, almost frantic, I jerk my head. I swat and nudge at her, trying to force her upward, but she resists. She's too scared. She knows something's up there. Waiting, just waiting for the next silly seal to stick its nose up.

I find a place where the ice forms an inverted basin, a kind of hollow. I exhale some of my own breath into it and it catches there, held, suspended, a jiggling air-puddle. I push Selah at this instead, working my head and torso under her to boost her the way our mothers did when we were pups having trouble resurfacing on our own.

She finds the pocket of air. It may not be the freshest, but I feel her gasping. Her flipper pat-strokes at me, desperate gratitude.

Desperate, possibly doomed gratitude, because now neither of us have enough breath to last long.

We explore the underside, claws ticking and scraping, hoping to find a spot we might be able to gouge through. But the ice is too thick.

There's no other choice. If we're going to make it, if we're going to live …

I squint up into the hole's murky brightness. I don't see any looming shadows. I don't hear any more menacing growls or awful feeding-noises.

Maybe it's satisfied and has already gone?

Maybe it took its … kill … with it. Dragging Leo's mangled corpse away, leaving only a long gory smear. To its lair. To its mate, or its hungry young.

Maybe it's all right now. Maybe it's safe.

Maybe just the briefest of bob-up-bob-down peeks, to check. To make sure nothing's up there … poised and patient … waiting.

Selah won't do it. I don't want to, but what else can we do?

A lot of the blood has diffused, so, there's that.

Of course, sharks and orcas may have scented the bloodspill and be coming already, strong tails whipping sinuous side-to-side or flexing powerfully up and down.

Their jaws. Their teeth. Coming at us out of the blackest depths.

Sharks and orcas won't wait.

Danger below. Danger above.

Dead either way.

I gather myself. My heart pounds, my muscles tense. Selah watches me, so much fear in her eyes … Leo is dead, and I've already given her my breath, and if I die too, she'll be all alone.

Nothing moves. Nothing makes a sound.

Cautiously, as a test, I blow a few bubbles and hang beneath them as they wibble and wobble to the surface.

No shadow. No noise.

Up!

The water thins, the light brightens, the red-stained ice sparkles and shines. The cold air hits me like a rogue wave. My nostrils flare and my mouth gawps; I suck in as much as my lungs will hold.

The sight almost knocks the breath right back out.

Leo. His belly split open from gullet to tail, layers of blubbery skin folded back to reveal sodden crimson meat and purplish innards. His head hangs back, upside-down, his frost-glazed black eyes staring dead and blank into mine.

The things around him –

They are not death-bears.

They are big, yes, and shaggy, but their pelts are of many mingled kinds and colors. Luxurious ruffs encircle their round, mud-brown, flat faces. They have curved claws like sharp stones, slicing dripping dark hunks of liver-meat to gnash at with short white-ivory nubs.

One of them sees me. A female, I think; it seems to have a pup or youngling clinging to its furs. It thrusts a claw toward me and garbles a loud call. The others whirl. Meat in their teeth, blood on their chins, they rear up on hindlimbs and waggle weird forelimbs.

Then there is a stick, a stick with a claw or a tooth of its own, jabbing at me. I flinch like before. And, like before, the fierce shearing strike passes close enough to tweak my whiskers.

Unlike before, there is another claw-tooth-stick and there is pain!

A vicious, brutal, biting pain!

I squeal.

No, I scream. I shriek like Leo did.

I try to drop but am snagged, snagged on the claw-tooth, and it digs and it grinds and I feel it shudder against bone and my blood pours down into the water as I thrash my body every wild which-way.

A pull.

A pull, and the claw-tooth catches firm, it is barbed, it is hooked, it has me. My flesh tears, my flippers smack rapid panic on the sloped, wet, bloodied ice. I am sliding, sliding upward, out of the sea, out of the hole, I am being dragged up to where Leo is a cold, gutted carcass.

I will be next, they'll open me from gullet to tail, they'll peel off my fur in silver-grey strips to add to their own monstrous minglings of pelt, they'll eat my liver while rimes of frost ring my dead eyes –

With another shriek, and another agonizing wrenching of my body, and another even-more-agonizing deep-inside slashing of pain, I am suddenly loose.

Loose and floundering on the ice, splashing in blood-slush. Clumsy and heavy, galumphing, awkward, as all around me the killers bellow and roar. Another claw-stick pierces my flipper. I heave myself forward and the grey webbing-skin shreds.

The hole!

I lunge for it. Headfirst, flippers scrabbling, hunching and flopping. They grab at me. But –

In I go, down I go. The sea closes over me. My sleek grace returns, or as much as my bleeding wounds will allow. I try to dive.

The cold numbs.

The salt stings.

I do not so much dive as sink, but I sink fast and deep. I cradle my hurt flipper to my chest and try to curl into a ball, as if it might meld my injured flesh together again with itself.

Above me, there is commotion. One of the strange-furred killers has fallen in. A big male, a bull. What was my escape and return to grace is the opposite for him. He is not made for swimming. His own pelt hinders and entangles. His broad-set nostrils do not close.

And Selah streaks out of the dark waters. Her jaws, made for nothing much larger than cod, clamp around one of the bull's hindlimbs. She drags him far below any reach of the air-hole, whipping her torso savagely, like a shark rending prey. Enormous bubbles erupt from the bull's gaping mouth.

She is in a frenzy, my cousin, a maddened rage. Blood seethes in a cloud, half-obscuring her from my view. She is a dark shape in the red gloom, a death-shape, and she releases the land-creature's hindlimb only so she can go for his underbelly and face.

Just as abruptly, Selah halts her attack. She loops away from her still-struggling victim – his bubbles have nearly stopped, and his remaining eye bulges with terror – and comes to me. She nuzzles me, rubs her sleek side along mine, makes concerned and inquisitive clicks.

The best I can manage is a mewling kind of cry. Selah, with a gentle care, burrows her head under my wounded flipper to help steady and support me.

I don't want to move, I don't want to swim, it hurts, everything hurts. The next-nearest breathing-hole is still so far away … and even if we could reach it, what's the use? Wherever we go, we'll never be able to surface safely again! Not with them up there, waiting!

But Selah is insistent. Even urgent. She will not leave me. She'll push and tug and haul me through the water if she has to. Because she knows what I should have known, what I did know but forgot.

All that blood.

All that spreading bloodspill scent, hot and enticing.

The first ominous outlines of fin and fluke have already begun to appear.

And they do not wait.

OUT THERE HAVING FUN

Andrew Wayne Adams

The yellow Jeep Wrangler careened onto the beach with its canvas top down, tires churning up sibilant blades of sand as the vehicle swerved all wild and young, just slightly out of control on its eager way to where the water and the sun were perfect. It skidded to a stop and six teenagers jumped out. Laughing, smiling, they threw down beach blankets, stabbed a few big and brightly colored parasols into the sand, swung a cooler into place and popped it open to reveal sodas on ice, and pressed play on the radio that one of them had set up on the hood of the Jeep—and from the great round speakers of that bulky silver box came the opening drum shuffle of "California Sun" by the Rivieras, followed closely by the guitar twang of its famously groovy surf riff.

The teens danced. They twisted, they shimmied: three guys and three girls, all six of them with superb physiques, a lot of skin showing. Their teeth perfect in their grins. The ocean sparkled blue and vast a bare ten yards from them, its immensity reduced to a backdrop for their swiveling hips and sculpted hair, their laughter somehow louder than its crashing. Their music overpowering the ocean, the rock song suffusing all...

Especially this part: "Where they're out there having fun... in the warm California sun..."

And the teens looked more like they were in their twenties, but whatever. They *acted* like teens. Or at least like what people *thought* teens acted like. Twisting, shimmying. The guys and the girls really digging each other. Really digging the song, the sun, the sand, the space-time they took for granted as the arena of all being.

Until suddenly "California Sun" shattered into sonic dust as a distorted bass drop intruded upon its shuffle and twang—and the cool 1960s rock song morphed into a jaggedly schizophrenic version of itself: rumbling, gravelly, spastic. Like the radio was broken. Except it wasn't.

The dancing stopped.

"Goddammit, Ben," groaned Lynda; "you downloaded the dubstep remix?"

Ben gave an innocent grin. "Oops?"

She kicked sand at him. Then the others kicked sand at him.

Paul said, "There goes the authenticity of our experiment," and he folded to the sand (which on closer inspection was not warm and pristine, but blisteringly hot and full of sharp rocks and debris) and dug inside the cooler for one of the beers beneath the sodas. "And this shoulda been an easy one. Those old 'beach party' films are so cookie-cutter, my little bro could pull one off, and he's, like, twelve. And we're grad students, we major in this shit." Hiss of a beer can opening. "Ah, well, fuck it."

Annie, pinching the bridge of her nose as if her head hurt, said to no one in particular: "Do you have any idea how many times I watched *Beach Blanket Bingo* to prepare for this?"

"Probably not as many times as I watched *Bikini Beach* and *Muscle Beach Party*," said Bob. He got a beer, passed one to Lynda. "I even watched them simultaneously, once, one on the TV and one on my laptop, set up side by side. It was Professor Iceberg's idea."

"Speaking of Professor Iceberg, just imagine his detached rage when he learns that we flubbed this assignment."

"We *could* start over," said Lynda, taking her phone from her bikini top, "I'm sure I can find the original song online somewhere."

"Nope, too late, already started drinking," said Paul. "Time to party for real, not for fake."

"Whatever," Lynda said, looking up from her phone, "my data's not working anyway."

"Yeah," said Ben, also on his phone, "I'm not getting any kind of signal at all. Weird."

"Honestly," Paul went on, "what the hell kind of research *is* this, you know? Go out and pretend we're in some dumb niche genre of 1960s film? What're we supposed to learn from that?"

"Paul," said Annie, "do you *ever* pay attention in class?"

"Look," Paul said, "what got me into Media Studies freshman year was that I heard there was a class on professional wrestling. I got to write a term paper on 'Macho Man' Randy Savage. Good class. Since then, though—I don't know."

"Okay. But so *why* did you go on to grad school for it?"

"You kidding? I didn't wanna have to get a *job*."

"For the love of God," said Laurie—silent till now, standing with arms crossed as she gazed out over the tremendous ocean; "won't somebody *turn off that damn music!?*"

The dubstep version of "California Sun" had continued to play in the background. Ben hopped over to the radio and reached for the volume knob as if to turn it down—but then cranked it up instead, giving Laurie a devilish look. He walked over to her, grabbing two beers on the way, and held one out to her. "Come on, don't tell me you don't like dubstep," he said, as the others all started to wobble their heads to the music, swigging their beers to the beat.

Laurie took the beer. "It interests me academically, but that's about it."

"Maybe you should try to, like, *feel* more," and he made these eyes at her, sad and hopeful, with a blossoming grin beneath—like there was something between them, him and her, or could be, and that thing was what she should be trying to *feel*. "Like, listen to your heart."

She was, actually. She'd been listening to it since the moment their project had failed and she'd glanced out over the ocean. And her heart's message was simple.

Fear.

"Do you see that?" she asked Ben. "Out there. On the water."

He squinted. Some hundred yards from shore, a whitish mass floated on the mellow waves, hard to see through the shimmer of reflected sun. With focus Ben could just make out its composition: what looked like ropy tangles of slick pale tubing. Like a rug of udon noodles.

"Just some trash," he said.

"But a minute ago I saw..."

He waited. "You saw...?"

"Part of it—moved."

They looked at each other. They sipped their beers.

Bob and Annie darted past, him chasing her, both laughing. Ben stopped them with a shout and spoke through a growing smile: "Guys, Laurie here has a great idea. We fucked up *Bikini Beach*—but we could still do *Jaws*. Look!" Acting like a bad actor acting terrified. "Out there! On the water!"

And they all turned and squinted together.

At nothing.

"It's gone," Laurie said. Edging closer to the water, peering harder. "Where'd it go?"

Bob was grinning like his face was broken. "Yeah, *Jaws*. Or *Humanoids from the Deep*. Horror from the ancient ocean. I like it." He pointed at Laurie, whose gaze remained sutured to the spot out on the water where the strange thing had been. "And you're the Girl Who Knows. We'll not take heed of your premonitory waves of dread, and later pay for that heedlessness with our lives."

Paul and Lynda had walked up to listen, and now Lynda added, "After lots of promiscuous sex, of course," and winked at Paul beside her, who answered with a wiggle of his eyebrows. He tilted back his head to drain his beer, threw the can behind him, and said, "Hey—who's up for a swim?"

"*Great* idea," said Bob, looking right at Laurie.

And Bob, Annie, Paul, and Lynda dashed off into the water, splashing and hollering as they ran, the white-flecked azure of the sea rising ever higher around them until finally they leaned forward into it and stretched out to swim—straight toward the place where Laurie had seen the blob of pale ropes, or whatever it had been... blubbery strands all splayed like fingers, heaped like spaghetti, and *one of them had lifted and a wave went through it*—like the wriggle of an eel, that nacreous length had lashed at the air for one grotesque second... its tip like the sickly tail of a rat, it had seemed to point at her...

But it was gone now.

"Maybe you were right," she said to Ben, who stood next to her still, watching the others paddle out into the sparkling vastness. "Just some trash."

"Yeah. Hey, you ever seen *Creepshow?*"

"Of course."

"This whole 'creepy thing in the water' thing kind of reminds me of that one story from it. You know, the one where there's the creepy thing in the water."

"I think you're thinking of *Creepshow 2.*"

"No..."

"Yes. The segment with that monster that's like an oil slick or something? Anyway, I don't want to talk about movies right now."

"Sorry. I can't seem to help myself." He took a dramatic gulp of beer. "You remember Professor Iceberg's lecture about the viral nature of media images? He compared it to one of those freaky parasites you hear about with the unbelievable life cycles. Like the lancet fluke, that lives in cows, who poop out its eggs, which get eaten by a snail, who coughs out wads of the young, which get eaten by an ant, who has its nervous system taken over by the flukes, which causes the ant to climb a blade of grass at night and wait at the top to be eaten by a cow—who becomes the new host, and the cycle repeats. Or something like that. And that kind of bizarre parasitic life cycle, it's the same thing with media images, only their cycle is this: they enter a human through the eyes and ears, gestate in the mind and heart, and then hatch and hijack the nervous system, causing their host to spew them back into the environment by a certain action of the vocal apparatus, or sometimes by the orchestrated discharge of hand movements. So I guess you could say I'm full of parasites. I really can't help myself when I want to paint these one thousand and one references into every area of discourse. I'm infected by film and internet, the printing press. I'm a zombified vector of—"

Laurie hurriedly drained her beer, tossed the can down, and ran forward into the great wet reach of the ocean. Her heart still murmured its chant of fear, hollering to her head that this was a *bad* idea—but she just *had* to get away from Ben and his affectatious regurgitation of Professor Iceberg's lecture, all delivered at her with that same flirty look he'd been using earlier, that seemed this time to say how she ought to be seeing him in an amended light, based on how *smart* he unexpectedly was—brainy, just the way she liked 'em—when actually she recalled the lecture and knew that he had been repeating lines of it verbatim, obviously memorized from his notes without significant understanding... with only the calculated aim to impress...

Between that and the ocean horror, well—she'd take her chances in the water.

Maybe it really had been nothing, anyway. Her imagination. Too much stress lately. She'd been studying so hard.

***

Ben had followed her into the water, of course, but the task of staying afloat kept him from blathering too much, and once they reached the others it was easier to shield herself from his attentions. Whenever he swam near her, she'd find something to say to Annie; and Bob and Paul occupied him the other half of the time with their tomfoolery. Everyone had fun for a while pretending they were in some horrible movie about the aquatic menace that Laurie had seen—everyone but Laurie, that is, who still couldn't shake the buzz of dread from her brain, and who found herself scanning the water every fifteen seconds for any trace of something wrong. She barely heard Lynda addressing her and Ben with, "Did you guys, like, *see* it? The sunken car? For real, on the swim out, an *actual* convertible, in the water. Its top down and everything, not even that old looking. About forty feet back that way," and she barely heard herself answering, "No," she hadn't—hadn't what?—already losing track of the topic, too distracted, because she'd finally detected her trace of something *wrong*...

The boys were gone.

A second ago they'd been behind her, splashing and shouting. Then: silence.

She spun, checking all around. They weren't anywhere. No bubbles or choppiness on the blue's undulating skin to indicate where they might have just dove under. No dark blots where they might've been lurking close to the surface. Three grown men, erased sharply from the scene.

Annie and Lynda noticed now too. Made confused, dubious faces.

Annie opened her mouth to say something, probably call the guys assholes for trying to scare them, since it was clear that that was what was going on, only it *wasn't* working...

...but Laurie didn't get to hear what she actually said: because to Laurie it *wasn't* clear that that was what was going on; and she *was* scared; and her body leapt ahead of her mind in deciding what to do, which was to plunge down into the water—driving in deep, with eyes open and searching, frantic to locate her friends... if it wasn't already too late...

She had never seen such clear water—like mountain air made liquid—yet the panic flooding her brain seeped even into her vision, so that the clarity twisted into murk. Several yards from her, a cluster of shapes hung swaying near the sandy bottom, some twenty feet down. She clawed her way toward the sunken shapes, their features—arms, legs, hair—resolving as she focused on them and closed the space between them and her.

It was Bob, Paul, and Ben. Grappling with something on the bottom, their backs were to her, only Ben's head turned slightly, so that she saw one wide, staring eye. She tried to make out what they were fighting with—something on the seafloor they were groping at: what looked like smooth white rocks, big and round... almost like the domes of skulls half buried in the sand...

She thrashed on through the water toward her friends, unable to think of how she could actually help them, but driven by the sense that she *had* to.

Ben's one eye locked on her.

He spun.

Bob and Paul spun too.

She'd gotten to within five feet of them, and now, as they whirled around to face her, her view of the horror was clear and close. Each had some elongated blob, green and coarse, emerging from the groin area. Wrapped around these green terrors, their hands jerked urgently, as if trying to yank the long blobs in two. Laurie could only stare on, shocked brain scrabbling to decode the situation.

A small dark hole opened at the end of one of the green shafts.

And from the hole came spewing a mass of slick pale ropes—blubbery strands unspooling into the water... like an eruption of udon noodles...

Laurie screamed, bubbles exploding from her wrenched mouth.

The ropey horror gushing toward her—it was the stuff she'd seen on the water earlier; the weird thing she'd been afraid of instantly, and hadn't *stopped* being afraid of, even after she'd started to pretend that she knew better—that it had been nothing, really.

Just some trash.

Holes opened on the other two green stalks, and the same eruption of white tubes came spitting out of them—whipping through the water toward Laurie's face, from which the bubble-blowing scream seemed interminable...

...until she saw the guys' faces.

They were laughing. Grinning so huge it had to hurt.

Her scream continued on a second, then snapped off as she suddenly understood. The elongated green things were sea cucumbers. The guys were holding them at their crotches like simulated penises, pretending to masturbate with them, with the erupting white ropes meant to imitate semen spurted forth at the cusp of orgasm. What they'd been doing with their backs to her was grappling with the creatures, pulling them up from where they clung to the skull-like rocks. Waiting for her to get close before they sprang their lewd prank.

She recognized it instantly, of course, as a scene from *Jackass: The Movie*, which she had had to watch once as part of a class on reality television. In the film, some of the troupe learn an interesting fact about sea cucumbers: that they have a defense mechanism whereby they eject their internal organs to ward off predators. This discharge occurs as a spurt of white tubules. So, a gush of whitish substance from the tip of something phallic—naturally the *Jackass* cast had felt compelled to enact the scene that Laurie had just witnessed recreated...

The motion slow underwater, she swung her open hand at the nearest of the grinning, imbecilic faces—Ben's, it turned out—landing a soundless but solid blow that she hoped would hurt on multiple levels. Then, chest aching from the oxygen loss incurred through screaming, she kicked up desperately toward the surface. Shot gasping into the air. Blind for a moment as she batted the water from her eyes. Deaf as the stressed blood still thrummed in her ears.

The first thing she heard, when she could again, was Bob, Paul, and Ben all cackling behind her as they surfaced. The first thing she saw was Annie and Lynda smiling as the guys related the little joke they'd pulled. The prank they'd plagiarized.

A prank. Just a prank.

No monster.

She'd been crawling with fright, then crashing with it, at what ultimately was nothing. A natural phenomenon—obscure and somewhat gross, but natural nonetheless, and no harm to her.

So why was she still terrified?

***

Night fell. They set up tents on the beach and built a fire. Annie and Paul smoked pot from a bong. Bob found a used condom in the sand and snatched it up with a twig and flung it into the fire, and everyone ran back from the smoldering biohazard in jubilant disgust. The guys talked on and on about the stunt they'd performed with the sea cucumbers— "holothurians," Bob kept calling them, impersonating some dweeby biologist—while Lynda berated them for emulating something as insipid as *Jackass*, to which Paul countered that their source had been the movie and not the show, and that film was an inherently more dignified format than television, such that *Jackass: The Movie* was art, even if *Jackass*, the series, was just embarrassing trash. Annie immediately disagreed about the distinction between movies and TV, citing it as a bourgeois notion.

Laurie withdrew to her tent without a word and zipped herself inside.

Five, ten minutes later, a hand knocked at the flap—stupidly, as if at a solid door—and Ben's drunken voice whispered her name.

Not unzipping the flap, "What do you want?" she intoned.

He unzipped it himself, stuck his face in along the open side. "You seem upset. Do you wanna, like, talk about it? Or something? Maybe you should try to have some fun. You still could, if you tried. We could have some together—you know?"

She sat up in the dark and said, "Listen to me very carefully, Ben: I'm not going to have sex with you." She said, "This is not the kind of movie you think it is."

And she pushed past him out the flap of the tent and stalked off down the beach.

She didn't bother making sure she wasn't followed. If he tried, he'd be sorry. She walked away far from the fire's light and her friends' guffawing. Sat on a huge length of driftwood, stared out over the terrible immensity of the sea. Glimmers of moonlight on its darkness. The incessant hiss of its deep churnings. Inconceivable events out there; life and death inexhaustible. Out there.

She stood. Clear now what must be done if she wished for any peace that night. It was the fear at her core that was damming her up, thwarting the flows of rest, calm, insight, fun. And that fear, while maybe not coming from just one place, did have one place that epitomized it. One deep and thunderous place. And she could strike at it there.

She took off what she had on and strode naked into the low waves. The water rose up her open body, tingling at her vulnerable matter, and she lay forward into it and took up a rhythm of determined strokes that carried her far from shore in little time. Stopping, she hung in place, treading the dark and alien water—an animal speck upon its nighttime profundity, bare beneath the implacable moon.

"See?" she muttered to herself. "Nothing to be afraid of."

Turning slowly in the water, she chuckled and grinned at the trial of it all. The foolish dread in a system of no control. "You're okay," she said. And she was.

Until she turned further and saw the thing on the water.

A slam of adrenaline spiked through her, her heart stuttered off beat in a way that overrode all time-sense itself. Floating a short yard from her face, the throng of slender tubules, dull white in the gloom, seemed to stare at her. Several long green bodies bobbed among the mass, also seeming to stare. She stared back. She and the startling things bobbed together.

Sea cucumbers.

She took a breath. These had to be the sea cucumbers that the guys had molested earlier. Likely they'd been too rough with the delicate creatures, and the things had died soon after, floating up to the surface with their ejaculated viscera still hanging out.

Killed for a joke. And not even an original one.

"Assholes," she said, and started to turn. Ready to swim back. She'd gotten what she needed. The dread hadn't left her, really, but she'd collared it somehow, made it pliant to her higher mind. Good enough. She'd go get some sleep, and then it'd be even better than good enough.

Just when she was almost turned away from it, the tangle of pale ropes moved.

A quivery bouquet of them rose up off the water. The bundle of slick tubing stood poised for a second, framed against the huge black sky. A wriggle went through it, and it reared back like a cobra. It shook, making a sound like wet tongues writhing. Rising higher and higher...

Laurie, who thought she had been afraid before, understood that she'd never known true fear till now. Understood, on a level underlying her obliterated mind, that true fear was as a god in its enormity next to her.

It was the last thing she ever would understood.

For in that next instant the mop of horrid tubules whipped forward and engulfed her face. The slippery tendrils coursed around her skull, wrapping about her head like a hundred fingers, or parodies of fingers, digits cartoonishly stretched into boneless noodles. Her body tried to scream but there was no air for the scream to ride out on as the tendrils closed in a solid sheet across her terror-gaped mouth. For a final second she could still peer out through the heap of attacking strands—saw the moon, space, ocean; saw the long green bodies of the sea cucumbers arching upright on the water, the tendrils around her head leading back to them—those ejected strands now rewinding into their points of origin, into the apertures that clapped obscenely open-shut-open as the sea cucumbers reeled their viscera in... pulling themselves along toward Laurie... flopping jerkily in their strange labor...

Not dead. Not dead.

Then the sight fell black as the tendrils invaded her eyes.

The squirming threads punched through her corneas. They crowded in through her pupils, to the interior of each eyeball. They found the optic nerve.

Climbed it to the brain.

While the snaking fingers that entered each ear drilled their way there too.

***

Ben lay drunk-spinning in his sleeping bag, his little tent dark around him, and listened to the sex from Paul and Lynda's tent. Or was it Bob and Annie's? Probably was happening in both. Could he try either tent with the idea of a threesome? Yeah, and get punched. He wished his phone would get a signal so he could use his data to watch porn. He kept trying to masturbate but the booze in him had his dick going soft. Porn would help. He didn't know why none of their phones were working. It was this place. This beach was fucking weird.

Speaking of weird—that bitch Laurie had something really wrong with her. They could've been getting it on right now. Bob was with Annie, Paul was with Lynda—that left just him and Laurie. Like, it was an obvious arrangement. They only had so much time on this earth.

A hand knocked at the flap.

He started to sit up, and the flap was already opening.

She climbed in. He could see her face despite the dark, but the surprise of what was happening kept him from recognizing her at first. She was nude, flesh glistening from a swim and her soaked hair dripping. Her nipples stuck out like acorns, hard from the cool water drying on them.

"Laurie...?"

She didn't answer. She crawled next to him, found the zipper on his sleeping bag, and opened it and slid in on top of him. His dick was already out from trying to masturbate, and before he knew it he was inside of her. His erection problems forgotten.

"Like, wow... Laurie..."

His mind tried to question this sudden turn, but he stopped it. Here was just proof that he'd been right all along. This was meant to happen.

She kissed him. Felt odd, like her mouth was a bit puffed, tongue coarse and swollen. Whatever. Making out wasn't his primary concern. But there was something else weird, too, that he couldn't quite identify. Then it came to him: she'd had her eyes closed this entire time. They were closed now, in what he assumed must be ecstasy, as she rode on top of him—but so had they been shut when first she crept into his tent, and at every moment since.

"Hey," he said. "Look at me."

Her lids snapped open.

And where her eyes should have been, there yawned two ragged cavities of red-black ruin.

Her hands gripped his head on both sides, pinning it. She opened her mouth and her tongue slid out, and he saw why it had felt so funny.

It was a sea cucumber. Rooted in her mouth, in place of a tongue. Dangling out through her lips, it wagged like a bloated tail.

He kept thinking that he should be screaming. But he couldn't seem to do it. A puckered orifice twitched open at the end of Laurie's replacement tongue; he stared into it; it stared back; and a burst of white cords bloomed from it at pyrotechnic speed—filling his vision in a hideous flash, then blotting it out completely as the cords enveloped his face.

Laurie's fingers, buried in Ben's hair, split along their tips, and more sea cucumbers thrust their way out from inside her digits. Smaller ones, like babies. They spat forth networks of thread that roiled over Ben's temples... groping toward his ears...

Their entry was like that of burning millipedes. His eardrums ruptured with a bludgeoning pop, and the feel of the tendrils burrowing in through the bony coils beyond was like broken glass rolling on ulcerous gums. Some part of him realized he was finally screaming, and felt surprised at the way it had simply kicked in without him, after all that failure to will it. None of his shrieks could escape, though, from behind the mask of repulsive tubules. He lay there beneath Laurie, the two of them still seemingly locked in erotic congress, and shrieked only to himself, trapped in this last and most intimate kiss as his eyes and ears poured thick rivulets of blood against the intruding organs of that ultimate inhumanity; he lay there bequeathing his brain to the outer thing claiming it.

By the time he was no longer him, the whole thing just felt good.

***

143

Lynda moaned under Paul, then said, "What the...?" as a motion at the tent's flap drew her gaze: a slow opening of the zipper, with a man's silhouette cast on the flap by the embers of their bonfire outside. At her sudden change Paul whipped his head around to see what she was looking at—just in time to watch Ben's upper body poke through the flap.

The idiot was wearing sunglasses. "Threesome?" he said.

Unbelievable. Fucking unbelievable.

Paul was going to punch the creep.

In his anger he didn't notice the strangeness of Ben's voice... the muffled, waterlogged vibrato of it... didn't notice the wormy things erupting from Ben's fingertips... too focused on the urge to knock that jackass flat...

It was a blow he never got to deliver.

Ben stuck out his tongue. Splayed his fingers.

And then all Paul knew was the swarming white fibers, and the screaming: his own, and Lynda's, and that from the tent next to theirs, where Bob and Annie lay entangled with Laurie—whose advances they had on the contrary accepted, adventurously... the three of them atremble in a shrieking, bleeding embrace: an adventure even greater than imagined.

No need to muzzle the screams now. No one who might hear and get away.

Besides, it was quiet again soon enough.

***

The yellow Jeep Wrangler shot down the beach toward the water's silvered edge. The six teenagers sat grinning in their seats as the vehicle hurtled into the waves, which crashed up over it but did not stop it. On the radio, "California Sun" was playing—the original, not a remix, though no one had done a thing to the file. As if the song had done it itself. It accompanied them as they drove on, the water rising over their Jeep, which somehow continued to operate, even under five, ten, fifteen feet of water. They sped along the sandy bottom, passing the other submerged vehicles, of which the convertible they'd seen on their swim that day was but one example. They stopped and got out and screwed their bodies down through the silt until only their heads were showing—their heads, which with time's decay would come to resemble smooth white rocks. Within their brains the larvae droned, growing—even now pushing at the stitch-points of their skulls, working at sprouting free... to

144

wait anchored and patient again, swaying in the current... twisting, shimmying... under a cold California moon.

A PRAYER FOR THE SURFER BOYS

David James Keaton

I thought it would be funny to walk the beach with a door under my arm. I'd wait for a surfer to harass me, maybe record it all on my phone or something, and this would out these punks for what they really were, a bunch of entitled trust-fund babies that should be way too old for this kinda shit. Way too old to claim a section of beach as their own and needle any and all comers to make outsiders never want to surf or swim there again. Way too old to be posting pictures of themselves on Facebook messing with the wildlife. Certainly too old to be dressed like sharks while doing all this.

"We'll burn you every single wave," the first shark muttered, ten minutes after I hit the beach, shuffling past but aiming his surfboard at my face like a weapon.

"Nice day, isn't it!" I shouted, stabbing the base of my door into the sand and leaning on it to catch my breath. It wasn't the heaviest door in the world but it wasn't easy to trudge up and down the seashore with it. But the door was essential for my joke. My brother gave it to me, scrap from his side job building houses for Habitat for Humanity, where they were tearing down an old apartment building so they could hammer it right back up again. This beautiful door didn't match the newer, cheaper doors they were installing, so it wouldn't be missed. It was old-school, too. Rich mahogany, speakeasy style, with a knocker, and a big, gold doorknob like a brass hamburger. The previous owner disfigured it a bit by drilling a peephole, but the rest was cherry.

"The day will be a lot nicer when you're gone!" another shark said without looking over. The shark trailing him spit at my feet. Now, when I say "shark," I mean the online rumors were true, and these were grown-ass men in black wetsuits with big dorsal fins jutting out of the middle of their backs. I'm not sure if wetsuits came like that, if it was some next-level San Jose Sharks hockey gear, or if their long-suffering mothers sewed them on before packing their lunches. But I hoped to get close enough to touch one before the day was out. Everything was going as planned so far. The sharks were fucking with me right on schedule. But I was a little confused by the sense of rivalry. They were scoffing at me like I was going to surf with them. Even though I was carrying a god-goddamn door.

Another surfer stomped past, flipping a foot full of sand my way, followed by a half-hearted raspberry. They seemed to be losing interest, so I tried another tactic.

"Hey! Here's a joke for you," I said, and he whirled around, almost catching me in the chest with the skeg off his board. "What's the difference between a pizza and a surfer?"

He just blinked.

"A surfer can't feed a family of five." No reaction.

"Unless they're sharks!" I added. Still nada, but there were plenty more walking fish hybrids shadowing him, so, inspired, I stepped back behind my excellent door and rested my ear on the wood.

"Okay, I got one! Knock knock," I said, rapping the gold ring as I worked to keep it balanced in the sand. "Who's there!" I answered for myself. "To…" I said.

"To who?" came a voice on the other side of my door. A shark had taken the bait.

"To *whom,*" I corrected, and the shark yanked the door open and rightfully punched me in the face.

***

Like most people, I'd first heard the claims of "localism" after the internet-famous incident involving my brother. The term referred to the escalating turf wars where locals vandalized your vehicle, whipped sand dollars at your head, or simply threatened to kick your ass for even setting foot on their precious beaches. At the time, my brother was down here in Palos Verdes working environmental cleanup for the city. He was a good guy, but a sucker for seedy beach-front life, fascinated by the Biblical nature of the homeless near the ocean, all those sandals mixed with surf, a plight I accused him of never acknowledging in the cities. Even though the surfers fought so hard for the area, they didn't think twice about leaving bottles and half-smoked roaches everywhere. My brother told me that in surfer slang, "pollution" referred to interlopers trying to drop in on their waves. Always ready to give people the benefit of the doubt, he wondered if they just didn't understand the concept of pollution after they hijacked the word.

The day of the drama, he'd been following up a report of a beached shortfin Mako struggling in the surf, and he found the adolescent shark quickly, as well as the circle of a dozen or so aged surfers holding it up for selfies as its gills flexed in vain. They were jackassing and chasing each other around with it like a football when my brother walked up, and he could already see it was moments from expiring and long past saving. He calmly explained that interfering with protected fish or wildlife like this Mako was against the law in California, when one of them tried to snap the shark at him like a wet towel in a locker room, effectively turning the poor creature's stomach and intestinal track inside out. My brother reeled in shock from this. Years of volunteer work had steeled his resolve at the sight of roadkill and oil spills along the coastline, but he was bad with confrontation, and combined with such a random act of cruelty, as well as the glistening purple ropes of innards vaulting over those needle teeth like spring-loaded snakes from a jar of nuts, it was just too much for him, and he collapsed. A random beachcomber called my brother an ambulance, but he was lying there getting sunburned for a while, and, of course, his encounter with the surfers ended up on YouTube, where it quickly went viral. This is where I saw it, like everybody else, backtracking to my computer after catching his name on a local news report. Reporters identified the gang as the "Bay Boys," though news cameras circled a nearby beer-strewn, concrete-and-stone fort tagged "Warlords," a name they apparently couldn't get to stick. On the internet, everyone knew about the Bay Boys, and I even read about an El Segundo cop involved in a lawsuit to oust them, but none of the cases went anywhere. Most police actually sanctioned their shenanigans, and any tourists who complained were told, "Sorry, plenty of beach elsewhere." Palos Verdes Estates cops, where their intimidation was by far the worst, even openly encouraged the Bay Boys, letting them off speeding tickets and other traffic infractions, according to some of the more coherent YouTube comments on my brother's video, a place that turned into a support group of sorts where more and more people shared stories of their own run-ins, including dozens of members of the Aloha Point Surf Club, who were forced to disband after 20 years because of the abuse. They were the ones who first described seeing their fins.

I guessed it was probably in the local fuzz's best interests to keep the beaches thinned out. The Bay Boys were idiots, but law enforcement probably figured they were the lesser of two evils compared to a thousand vacationers and a rise in both types of "pollution." So, with the cops secretly behind them, and confidence now flowing as fast as their cheap Saint Archers beer, the Bay Boys broke zoning laws building their clubhouse from earthquake rubble and driftwood. Then they broke laws against good taste by apparently slapping fins on their wetsuits soon after that. More videos cropped up in the following weeks, including drone footage orbiting the Bay Boys clubhouse, right up until the tiny helicopter was shotgunned out of the sky. One clip showed brawls in waist deep water and faces being held under for way too long. I couldn't believe what I was seeing, as a fist fight in the surf looked dangerously close to attempted murder.

I tried to egg my brother into joining the class-action suit when it was all peaking in the news, but he was having none of it. He was a good Christian, turning the other cheek and all that shit. And he was off to his next mission, helping some other strangers or stranded beasts in some noble way. I wasn't that into selfless acts so much, but this incident was driving me nuts, giving me some bad ideas, so when I stopped by to pretend I was helping him rip down the public housing, it was easy to scrounge the lumber pile. The next day I pulled on my jorts, threw my formidable door in the back of my pick-up, and headed down to the water cause some problems. My dog was in the window watching me go, head cocked, back leg scratching a chronic infestation around his ear. He seemed particularly confused, not just by his lack of name or discernible breed, but by this walking door. And though this probably doesn't make as much sense out loud to dogs or humans, bringing a door to go surfing just felt like an obnoxious juxtaposition, like showing up to a wedding and dribbling a basketball down the aisle. I wanted it to be clear that I was there to cause problems, and hopefully this maximized the chances of someone documenting my own online sequel.

I didn't tell my brother any of this. He was a good guy and hated confrontation, remember, but those qualities didn't run in the family.

***

"Landshark," a voice whispered, and I squinted at the rainbow halo of ocean droplets orbiting the shadow looming over me. I was laid out on top of my door, knocker ring resting on my head like a crown, still reeling from the punch. Another shark high-fived the perpetrator, then they both ran toward the water as I sat up on my elbows and rubbed my bloody nose on my knuckle.

I sat on my door and soaked up the rays for a bit, waiting for my next move. Truth was, I didn't really have a next move. I'd forgotten to record the run-in on my phone, which I'd left in my truck, and I hadn't thought too much past my plan of walking a beach with a door under my arm like an asshole and trying to coax surfers to harass me. But with me even sitting with my toes anchored in the sand and showing no incentive to head toward the water and steal their coveted waves, the Bay Boys still couldn't help themselves, and dozens more shark-fin-sporting bros I hadn't noticed rose up from the surf and high-stepped it back up the beach to give me shit.

"You lost or something, Stu?"

"Nope."

"Wrong place for you, guy!"

"I thought this beach was for everybody," I shrugged, shading my eyes for a better look.

"Naw, man," one shark smiled through his white handlebar moustache, tucking his gray hair behind his ear as he stepped up closer. "That's where they lied to you. People around here hassle people, or even work your car."

"Really."

"Oh, yeah, and if you take it to court, that shit costs, what? Ten grand at least. Pain in the ass!" he laughed. "I sure don't want to go through that again. I mean, I'll waste so much money after kicking someone's ass. But I'm stupid like that, you know?"

"Right. So, are you the Aloha Point Surf Club?" I asked, knowing they were his nemeses.

"Fuck no! We fucked them up."

"Good," I said, and laid back on my door again, arms behind my head. The wizened surfer stared down at me a second, then extended a hand.

"The name's Noah," he said as I shook it, flinching at the sand between his fingers. "You wanna come stand in the soup for a tick? Now, you're a Jake, so I can't let you in the real water, even for an ankle-buster, but you might get a treat seeing one of the boys tombstone it on a cruncher."

I wasn't sure what any of that meant, but I was all about this "tombstoning," since it sounded fatal. I stood up and started to brush off my knocker and blow sand out of the peephole.

"Naw, leave the door, Jake."

"Hey, how'd you know my name wasn't Jake," I grinned, and Noah laughed back, clapping me on the shoulder.

***

Standing in the surf boil and watching the Bay Boys bob around trying to line up a good wave, I cupped some water and sloshed a mouthful of salt, then spit to get the sun-baked blood off my teeth. I'd assumed that showing up to the beach with a goddamn door under my arm would be so ridiculous it would neuter the Bay Boys' bluster, as I was clearly not competition. This was a new wrinkle, as I never expected I'd be so lucky as to get befriended by someone from their ranks. I decided to play out my hand, eager for things to escalate any way they could. Because if there was one thing I was good at, it was betraying a friendship, especial-especially one only an hour old.

I stood on the ocean for a long time. When the sun started sinking and it got harder to see their fins on the horizon zigzagging through their tubes, Noah invited me back to the clubhouse where they were stoking a fire. Their famous headquarters was tucked around the other side of a jetty, as shitty up close as it was online, barely a lean-to really, but the merman shadows dancing around the flames made it seem much more sinister. With the sun down, the name "Warlords" almost didn't seem ridiculous. Almost. I sat down on a milk crate next to Noah, and he nodded, clearly impressed with his scene. I noticed scattered piles of what appeared to be spent shotgun shells, and I stiffened. I jokingly asked what dead President mask was trendy for bank robberies that year, and two sharks stood up and left.

"Hey, can I touch that?" I finally asked after a couple more beers, pointing to the dorsal fin on Noah's back. One of the bigger sharks with black still streaking his beard stopped cracking driftwood for the fire and looked at Noah, skeptical.

"Why not," Noah said after a second, and I gave his fin a good squeeze.

Maybe it was the cheap beer, but my heart was hammering, because it wasn't the texture I expected. I thought maybe it would feel like plastic, or rubber, but this was leathery, spiny, like snakeskin boots if they had a pulse, like petting it the wrong way might be dangerous. I tried to bend the tip of the fin, and Noah's shoulders suddenly hitched as he jerked away.

"Sorry, man," I said, wiping my hands on my trunks.

"Careful, brother. It's real."

It's real?

"What do you mean 'real?'"

Noah shared a glance with the bearded shark, who smiled and went back to cracking wood. Noah looked me up and down, then sighed.

"Yeah, man, they're real! Real, live shark fins," he said, basking in my confusion. He leaned in to whisper. "See, a cop we know sniped a box of these off a truck during a drunk stop. Gave them to us as tribute. These fins were headed for some high-end soup in San Fran Chinatown. Cures boners, I don't know."

I looked at his fin, black but sparkling in the firelight, studying the seam where it seemed to push through the thick skin of his suit, and I didn't know which possibility was more horrifying. That they wore poached fins like trophies after still-living and sheared sharks were chucked overboard to starve by criminals pandering in superstition, or the suddenly more reasonable prospect that they had fins growing from their backs.

Either way, I decided more drinking was the best option.

***

Things I learned that night include...

The clubhouse wasn't littered with shotgun shells after all. Those were spent poppers, a.k.a. "anal" nitrates, a recreational inhalant, popular in the disco era, for enhancing sexual experience and facilitating anal intercourse by relaxing the sphincter muscles. And at first glance, it seemed the Bay Boys must love poppers, but not for the reasons I would have guessed. They loved them because hemorrhoids were the secret scourge of surfboarders. Sitting so long on those boards, or hunkering down on sandbars to take a shit, these were problems. And they weren't spring chickens, of course, so this lifestyle wreaked havoc on their butts. Noah confessed his crew was once enlisted in a dubious scientific study, an upstart professor's blatant attempt to gain notoriety equal to the Stanford Prison Experiment, though his study was the much-less-infamous Stanford Prolapse Experiment, which, if you watched the films, appeared to be nothing but 25 college students straddling surfboards in the Stanford biology department parking lot. Noah then confessed that the combination of swollen anal nerves and a desert climate like California resulted in an even more extreme condition very rarely discussed outside their circle, when his predecessor awoke one morning with an engorged sand flea nursing blood directly from his anus. Noah swore they saluted the flea's tenacity and bore it no ill will, but a squatting over the bonfire to burn it off was the only real cure. Sadly, this resulted in "Warlord's" retirement forever. They made me drink a toast to the man, nodding respect toward his spray-painted memorial, and I finally noticed the apostrophe.

"Not to de-mystify the sport or anything..." Noah smiled, and I fought the urge to make a joke about insects crawling up a ramp into Noah's ass, two by two.

That night I learned all about water fleas, too, how they had a record 31,000 genes jam-packed into their DNA, making them the most adaptable thing on the planet, and that a "broceanographer" like Noah found beaches with the fewest fleas, but the most waves, and that the only way someone like Noah lost status as the reigning king of the Bay Boys was if "Neptune sent him packing." Neptune did this by "stamping their passport," which translated as any evidence of a bite mark on their boards or their bodies. Any visible proof of a shark attack and they started at the bottom of the hierarchy all over again, civilian status. Con-Contrary to popular opinion, a shark bite on a surf board was not a badge of honor. It was bad luck, Noah cautioned. Worse than that. He said just one bite and no one would catch a wave on that break for a decade.

***

I paced myself and tried to hang, but they out-drank me easily. They were staying up all night, too. Remember, these were ancient trust-fund toddlers, and without real jobs, their waking hours weren't just reversed, they were perpetual. They'd be riding the waves again at dawn. They called this "going home."

I went down to the water alone, and walked through the cold salt and foam. The shoreline was like a skillet the morning after grilling surf and turf, and I sloshed another palmful around my mouth and spit. I didn't avoid swallowing because of the dangers of dehydration. I avoided swallowing because the dreams of that skillet were making me ravenous.

Then I saw the Mako, upside down and circled by birds, long streamers of viscera flaring from its mouth, like a cartoonist had sketched it singing a song. I gathered the shark up under my arm and took it with me into the water. I was pretty drunk, but I wanted my own fins. I was convinced I could truly infiltrate the gang with a fin on my back, and we swam together as I gingerly rolled up the guts and put the outsides back in. I'd read on the internet that sharks sometimes ejected their stomachs out of their mouths when hooked, so except for a few pieces the seagulls had snatched, it looked good as new. That's the amazing thing about a dead shark. There was never an urge to brush a hand over its eyeballs so it rested in piece. Alive or dead, those eyes would always remain the same.

You wouldn't think swimming with a dead shark would be easy, but it's actually the most natural thing in the world. So natural I began to wonder if we were made to be together. Our upper arms and pectoral muscles hugged perfectly under their pectoral fin, like we were part of the same puzzle, and the two of us cut through the water as intuitive as a motorcycle and sidecar.

I looked back to their fading bonfire and through the drunken haze, and remembered my mission of getting payback for my brother. I thought maybe faking a shark attack might be the easiest thing ever. All you'd need is a shark, really, and I had that. Okay, I might need a shark and... maybe a bear trap? A bear trap stuffed into those jaws and the crucial part of this fish would be back in perfect working order. It almost felt wrong to supplement the muscle power of a shark with a mechanical trap, not to mention the troubling Dr. Moreau mash-up between the wa-water and the woods I was now contemplating, but I decided that was probably just overthinking shit.

It would teach Noah a lesson. It would teach them all a lesson. Just one snap and one stamp on their bodies, or their surrogate bodies, and that's all it would take. They'd be banished from this spot.

I rolled my body to swim on my back awhile, pulling the dead shark onto my belly, its dorsal fin dividing waves that filled my mouth and nose. My fin was small for now, and it was on my chest instead of my back, but I wore it proudly. I knew it would grow.

***

Tipsy, I stumbled up to my truck, threw my shark and my door into the back, and drove to my brother's house. I knew he'd be up. Though he worked for a living, unlike us, he didn't keep normal hours either, mostly due to his film obsessions. My brother might have hated confrontations, but he sure loved movies about confrontations, especially in the middle of the night. And Peckinpah's nasty fable *Straw Dogs* was one of his favorites. In fact, he loved that one so much that in order to honor its most important character, he went out and got himself a bear trap and nailed it over his fireplace. I knew he was all about this movie because it was at its heart a cautionary tale about a timid guy rising up, but he swore he just liked the love story. Yeah, right. It's crazy, but of all of the religious people I've known, the vast majority watched the most fucked up films.

Years back, I helped him set the spring and hang the thing, and we christened it Chekov's Trap, and my brother vowed that if he died before it went off, he had wasted his life.

When I got to his house, I told him I was the answer to his prayers, but it still took a little convincing.

"Why would I give you this?"

"Because I'll put it to good use, I promise."

"Doing what?"

"Getting back at some assholes."

"Who did what?"

I sighed, looked up, looked down, and finally just unloaded it all.

"I want to use your bear trap to kinda reanimate a dead shark's mouth and then maybe chomp it on those surfer punks who thought it was funny to turn an animal inside out and then piss on you while you were unconscious and immortalize that moment forever on the world wide web."

Ten minutes later I was walking to my car with a bear trap under my arm.

"You could come with me, Jake," I said, knowing full well my brother would never do this. I respected his pacifism, but I'd always had more backbone than him. And this was not a metaphor either. My last MRI revealed I was prone to ruptured discs because of the extra space around my spinal cord, which meant manual labor was a problem, even though that was all I could find on the West Coast, even with my nine years of college with an undeclared major. It was the ultimate paradox that I didn't have the back for the only kind of work I'd ever be qualified to do. It sorta made sense in California though, where a word like "sick" meant at least three different things, just like Jake.

"Forget it, Jake. It's Surfer Town!" my brother laughed, as I started my truck and backed out. I assumed this was a movie reference and gave him a consolation honk. Weirdo.

***

I was still drunk and shouldn't have been driving, but I got there quick, and I figured I could just drop Noah's name to the Palos Verdes police if I got pulled over. But the streets were empty. The streets were ours. I parked in the lot on the cliff and trekked down to the beach carrying a door, a dead shark, and a bear trap. Like people do.

The dawn broke right when I got back to the clubhouse. It was empty, the Bay Boys back in the water lining up for their waves. In the morning sun, I saw the sand was littered with shotgun shells after all, and I smiled at the extreme level of bullshit Noah could sling. In the warmth of that sunrise, I looked to the skyline and thought I could almost believe in a god. Almost. I was never a religious man like my brother, but he did teach me all the prayers.

There were prayers of veneration, prayers of supplication, prayers of worship, prayers of consecration, prayers of intercession, and prayers of imprecation. That last one was my favorite. It was when you prayed for God to mess up your enemies. Well, more like judgment for the wicked, but it was the only one I still used, and I used that prayer so much it was pretty much the only voice in my head. And on a beach at dawn I was afraid everyone could hear that voice, so I plugged my ears just in case, forced the trap deep into the slack jaws to lock teeth upon teeth upon teeth, then I prayed that something in the ocean would fuck them up good

Shark-on-shark action, please. Amen.

155

I couldn't be the only one praying like this, and I wondered if maybe this was why surfers got bit so often. Could I be the only one singing this psalm?

My brother would have been upset. He once scolded me that using a prayer of imprecation on a human foe was out of context, unjustifiable, just plain wrong. I would have told him, "Don't worry, bro. These dudes were sharks."

I laid my own shark and its new smile out onto my door and straddled it, walking us into the ocean, then I kicked straight towards the shoal of black fins in the distance.

***

Something was wrong. The Bay Boys were arguing, fighting for the same waves, and at least three of them had just been axed, the lip of one wave catching them in the grill and chucking them backwards, head over fins. The chaos had them paddling in all directions, and I locked eyes with Noah, who did a duck dive under a surge to lose the crowd and buttonhook back towards me.

"Are you kidding, Jake?" he said when he got close. "The hell is that?"

I answered the first question, but only in spirit.

"You like my log?

"You'll get your ass chopped out here, Jake. Take your 747 and get the fuck out."

"You mean my funboard?" I asked, willfully obtuse. I'd remembered a lot of lingo from the fire the night before. For example, I knew "Noah" was slang for "shark," which was the closest surfer slang came to Cockney slang (Noah equals Noah's Ark, which rhymes with shark). This made sense. Cockney rhyming slang originated as a way to code conversations from law enforcement, and to actually say "shark" on the water was an invitation for trouble. "Sharky" also described a lot of chop, but in California, it also described a lot of sharks. This was likely the strangest and most direct bit of jargon ever conceived, as it circled right on back to its origin, sort of like someone handing you a "piece of cake" that was really easy to bake. Or someone pretending to have no food to share then literally spilling a can of beans on the floor. Something like that. I was still a little drunk. How about riding shotgun with a shotgun? A weapon I was still expecting to see a Bay Boy wield.

"This right here?" I told him, knocking wood between my legs and ignoring the dead shark. "This is a goddamn door. Like right off a house."

"Okay."

He shook his head in disgust and paddled away, starting to line up again for a run. He was wearing a pink-and-black "shortie" today, a sleeveless wetsuit for the hottest days, but his fin was still there. And in the small of his back, under this fin, I noticed a second bulge. Possibly a weapon.

"Drop in on me with that fuckin' door, and you're dead!" he yelled out the side of his mouth. "And that's not slang, Jake. Out here, dead means dead. You'll never stand up on our watch."

I nodded and stroked my shark, careful to keep my hand out of its spring-loaded maw. The bear trap gave it a gleaming, wicked grin, but it didn't look too unusual. I had a feeling a bear trap would look reasonable in any shark's mouth.

I stayed where it was glassy, did some push-ups on my board to keep my back pain at bay, and I watched the Bay Boys continue to have trouble. Missing wave after wave, pleading for better waves that never came. They continued to mutter their crazy shit like, "That grom won't rip switchfoot in the slot unless you cutback, waxhead," and I closed my eyes to soak up their otherworldly chatter, imagining my door sliding along the surface of an icy moonscape. Then the waves separated Noah from the pack and brought him close again, and I put my plan into motion. But my attempt to stamp his passport was a disaster.

Noah was on his knees when he veered close to my door, and I carefully pulled my shark's new iron jaw wide and locked the pin. I got down on my belly, paddling toward Noah. I was off his radar, and his back was turned so I could stare at the fin, lining up for the perfect bite. I slid my shark out in front of me and into the water, aiming for a hard snap on his squaretail. Then I saw his hand reach around his back and pull the gun from the long split in his shortie as he spun a leg over his board to face me. He took aim, and fired.

Thank Christ it's a toy, I had time to realize.

Not quite a toy though. Not a real gun, but a flare gun, and still pretty dangerous. It nailed my shark right in the mouth, and the bear trap snapped shut, jets of sparks roaring up through its eyes and nostril. Noah smiled like someone who'd shot hundreds of dead sharks looking to nip his board, then he tucked his yellow gun back into his wet suit and kicked away like I was nothing.

I sat with my burning shark, watching the orange fire gush from its gills. The lining of its mouth began to smoke and cook, the water in its snout popping like popcorn, and it smelled delicious. I was contemplating my own bite when I felt the bump under my feet.

It was big. Big in the way only something that slides silently under you is big. Big in the way only something that can kill you with cruel indifference is big. I looked to the Bay Boys, and saw them clustered tight. They were looking around, looking down, and it seemed like they were being herded. I'd seen something like this in videos, when the amateurs clashed with the locals, when gangs formed a sorta prayer circle in the ocean to frustrate anyone paddling for a wave. But this was different, more like the ocean was working to keep the surfers stacked up, like the water itself was functioning in concert with an unseen predator, rounding up prey into a squirming nucleus ripe for easy pickings.

I pointed my toes and felt the same huge something still gliding under my feet with no end any time soon. I was excited to be corralled with the rest. My prayer had been for the sharks, and now I was one, too.

Then the prow of the thing ascended in front of me, breaching directly behind Noah, water raining from its summit, and at first I thought it was a whale. But it was transparent, or translucent. Under the surface, I had no doubt it was invisible, but in that moment it was barely perceptible in the sunlight, which revealed armored plates like glass and prisms of color refracted in its massive head. My brain was still mapping the beast onto more familiar forms when a mountain of ocean rolled toward me then smoothed out as it dove. Noah was gone.

The air was silent, no sea breeze, and not a single Bay Boy to be found. Then two huge, lucent fins suddenly broke on either side of me, rotated high in the sky, until one crashed down dangerously close, narrowly missing a devastating slap over my door. I pulled my feet on board and closed my eyes, clutching my dead shark and its burning smile for warmth.

Then I remembered my peephole. It seemed like a good compromise. I cupped my hands around it and took a look.

There was an eyeball looking back. One lone eye, emotionless but intent. It was the size of a tractor tire, insect-like, buried in a living, crystalline structure. Two pairs of segmented antennae branched from the eye, which reached out to hold my door fast. They traced the length and shape of it, then pierced the waves near my legs to brush the metal hinges. I made myself small as the antennae crawled up and tickled the shark, tentatively tapping the heat of the flare still rumbling in its mouth. They jerked, then retreated back into the water. Peering down through my tiny fish-eye lens, I saw the giant sink low enough to finally chart its edges, and I realized how mind-splitting enormous the creature really was.

The huge, segmented carapace spasmed and curled to pick up momentum for a dive, as the alien mandibles in its crown spun their hardware like watch parts. The mouth wiggled and thrummed like a factory, terrifying tendrils and bristles drumming like fingers, fanning then coming back together like the shuffle of an invisible deck of cards, and I realized it was working men through the strange machinery of its body. It was every Bay Boy being swallowed, then corralled through the maze of its body, and this helped me to diagram the rest of it and finally recognized the species, or at least its tiny descendents. I often pulled its offspring from the eyes of my dog whenever they abandoned the easy blood meals of his belly to crawl through the long forest of his fur and finally rest to drink the tears off his corneas. When I would catch one, then hold those tiny intruders up to a light, I would only have a moment to study their downturned lobster-like heads and marvel at how much they resembled a denizen of the sea. I understood now that flea collars were the castle wall and the last line of defense, as they must all dream of this prehistoric past and of one day climbing that collar to find their way home and baptize in the holy saltwater of a canine eye.

I stared through my door, the reflections of the sunlight sketching the tail end of the great insectoid form line by line, a body as big and detailed as a crop circle. I imagined these huge creatures were always in our oceans, invisible away from the sun until they fed, and I decided the surfers, too, would become transparent as they digested, only perceived as real until they were eaten, like anything else really.

The two great fins like crystal airplane wings rose high again, touching their tips in prayer, then knocked on my door one last time, upending my perch. Then they pulsed down, their wake almost flipping me over again. And through my peephole I saw the huge creature descend, saw Noah struggling in the labyrinth of his invisible prison. The fins beat once more, and it was gone.

I looked around the still water, and saw the fleet of unmanned surfboards, directionless and dancing. Tombstoning. One trembled violently, then flipped twice until it was still, and I knew it was the last of the Bay Boys, foot finally cut free to surf a glass throat forever.

Alone, I caught a wave on my door. I stood up high. It was everything they said it was.

***

I was arrested in the parking lot. The news would later report I had the smoking "gums" in my hand, the steel-toothed grin of a dead Mako flickering like a Jack-o'-lantern, which cops had to wrestle away. I couldn't explain what happened to the Bay Boys even if I wanted to, or why I had seven of their surfboards stacked in the back of my pick-up. Someone placed a hand on my wet head to guide me in the police car, and I blacked out for a second when my forehead bumped the roof. But while I was gone, I travelled back to the moment I was surfing my first tube, when I was in the "green room," as they called it, sometimes known as the Pope's Bedroom, sometimes referred to as the Astronaut's Garden, that emerald oasis inside a wave, somewhere a tourist had no business being, standing up strong while the ocean rolled around me to keep me safe until the tail of the great beast descended into the endless dark beneath my door.

**

I knock on my door sometimes, and it drives everybody nuts. I knock on the plastic when my brother comes to visit, too, but he always plays along. He mocks the new streaks of gray in my hair, which I thought at first were the result of locking eyes with an ancient aquatic mystery, but it was just citric acid from a power drink a surfer had chucked in my face at the bonfire that had prematurely frosted my tips. He doesn't believe my story, but, of course, he forgives me.

"Knock knock."

"Who's there?"

"Will you remember me in a year?"

"Yes."

"Will you remember me in a month?"

"Yes."

"Will you remember me in a week?"

"Yes."

"Knock knock."

"Who's there?" he croaked.

"See, you forgot me already," I said. And it would be okay when he did.

One night, I dreamed of plucking an engorged flea from the dusty lunar crater of my navel and flicking it through the bars of my cell, where it bounced across the concrete floor like a marble. In the morning, when we filed out for breakfast, I stepped over the comet streak of blood it had suckled from the scar tissue of an umbilical cord I'd always assumed long dead.

I do push-ups in prison, to get ready for the ocean again someday, to hopefully drink from that eye. Sit-ups are more difficult though. The knob of bone in the middle of my spine continues to grow, and it's painful to roll it against the concrete floor. It aches even when I sleep on my stomach, as it longs for water, a surface that yields, a flexible world that allows a body to grow unhindered in any direction. My back hurts, but this pain is wonderful, too, and the guards get mad when I slice holes in all my shirts. I explain that, in every sense of the word, I am sick.

CATFISH GODS

Weston Ochse

Trey sat on the community dock staring out across the green August water of Chicamaugua Reservoir. His tanned legs swung in tune to the waves. His fingers gripped the rough gray wood as thoughts of mortality tripped through his thirteen-year-old mind.

His grandfather had died six months ago and there were times when the heat and the bickering of his family and the memory of the loss became so much that he needed to be alone. Times like that he'd sit and remember every word the old man had spoken. Remember every action. Every smile.

All grandfathers are special, but Trey felt his was even more so. It was as if the man's mere presence could calm the world. It was as if he was a God and when Gods die, one never forgets.

The dock was where Trey went when he needed to remember and think. Other than his bed, it was the one place he spent most of his time. His first fight, his first bass, the first time he slid his trembling fingers along the curve of a breast as he massaged oil into the soft skin of an older high school girl—all had taken place on the dock. Called the Community Dock, it had been abandoned by the city years before he moved in. Although the access was grown over with tall weeds, a path had been pounded into the red Tennessee clay by a faithful herd of children who now called it their own. The dock was a sacred place where parents never tread.

There was one month a year when nobody could swim in the lake and this was the month. It made the interminably hot days long and filled with a hundred attempts to ease the constant boredom. The only good thing was that the mosquitoes had all been killed when the TVA men lowered the water level by several feet, leaving the eggs to dry and die along the muddy beaches of the Tennessee lake. The side effect, of course, was that long weeds grew up from the lake bottom as the sun, for the first time since winter, finally managed to plumb the depths, arousing the lake's deadly kudzu cousin. The weeds were as thick as a wrist and halted fishing, boating, and now swimming since they found Billy Picket drowned last year. They said the weed had wrapped around him a dozen times as if the leafy arms had reached out and snagged him, but that was just something the grownups said to scare the kids away.

At least he was pretty sure it was.

So even with the lull in swimming, and the death of his grandfather, and the possibility of cthulhu weeds searching for sustenance, Trey's thirteen-year-old mind identified his freedom and the golden sunset against the green water as a rare time he would remember when he was old and the lessons of school and the minutiae of life were long forgotten.

***

The next day dawned ugly as the light of the summer sun was dulled by the dishwater sky. The waves of the slate gray lake seemed to reach up as if they could liberate the light.

Trey struggled out of bed and plodded into the kitchen. The coldness of the sky did nothing to alleviate the humidity, sweat immediately forming as a second skin. He poured himself a tall orange juice and held the glass against his face.

As he drank, he walked to the floor-to-ceiling window and eyed the driveway. Only the old Ford was left. His parents had driven to Jacob Mountain for a Sunday gathering—*part business, part fun*, they'd said. He'd been invited, but had pretended to be sick and promised to stay in bed until they returned. At thirteen, his parents had lengthened his leash and today was the first day they had ever let him free.

Trey smiled. He and Greg had planned it well. Today was their fishing day and they were going to try the loading dock across the inlet at the old TNT plant which was rumored to be the deepest place in the entire lake -- with the exception of the dam itself, of course. Every week, tarp shrouded barges could be seen being loaded with the Army's secret stuff. If all the tales were even half true, then there were fish down there as large as automobiles.

Trey had dressed and was getting the gear together in the garage when Greg swung around the corner of the driveway toting his favorite rod and an oversized tackle box.

"What's up, Trey? You ready for a little fishing? Ready to catch the big one?"

Trey nodded. Greg was three years younger, but a good friend nonetheless. When it came to fishing, age didn't matter anyway. As long as you were patient and followed a few basic rules, it was God's will that sent the fish your way. At least that's what his grandfather used to say.

"Go ahead and take the poles down to the dock. I'm gonna get the battery out of the car."

"Are you sure we ain't gonna get into trouble about this?" asked Greg, his blue eyes worried under his shag of red hair.

"Naw. They'll never even find out. They ain't supposed to be back until after dark anyway and we'll be done long before that."

"What if we actually catch one of them beasts?"

It was Old Man Hassle that called them *beasts* and Greg was at the age to believe everything the old caretaker said. Trey was pretty certain they wouldn't see any catfish that big, but twenty-five or thirty pounders were fairly common.

"Shit. If we bring one in, I'll just tell the folks I was feeling better. I'll tell them you and me went fishing from the dock. They won't be real happy, but Dad will be so impressed with the fish, he'll bring mom around."

Greg grinned from ear to ear, the dream of a huge fish and his best friend's intelligence was going to make this a day to remember.

***

They slid the yellow canoe from under the community dock and Trey pressed his sneaker against the footpad that was the trolling motor's accelerator. He'd taken it from the downstairs storeroom, its very presence among old boxes and broken tools creating the idea to fish by the TNT dock. The dock was too far to paddle, so the small motor was what made the trip possible.

The motor had been a gift from his grandfather to his father and had yet to be used. Trey felt a sadness in that and saw his use of the old motor as a way to be closer to his grandfather. In his heart, he knew the old man wouldn't mind. He could almost see him now, standing in heaven, a martini grasped in his large hands staring down and wishing his grandson luck.

The weather had worsened. Brackish two-foot swells made the going slow and difficult in the small boat. Greg sat in the prow gripping the seat with both hands. When Trey guided them around the larger clumps of weeds, both of them were wary of getting them caught in the motor. Occasionally, they'd pass a fish held just under the water in the unrelenting grip of the weed, eyes milky and rotten.

The air was heavy with humidity, their shirts and shorts already sopping with sweat. The scent of honeysuckle drifted from the shore on the wind, mixing with the smell of rotting fish and the heady scent of the weeds. Breathing was hard during any August in Tennessee, but upon the lake's surface it was almost impossible. Both boys alternately held their breath against the foul smells of deadness and the sweetness of the surrounding forest.

They'd both grown up on the lake, their summers filled with days where shoes and shirts were left indoors as they tried to become one with the sun and the water. When they weren't fishing or mowing lawns for some extra money, they were swimming around the community dock. Their favorite sport was underwater tag, spending more time holding their breath under than they did playing above.

During those long games, Trey often imagined he knew how a fish felt, chased and cornered by a fisherman. He could hold his breath for over two minutes and would slither in and around the old wooden pilings, propelling himself from one end of the dock to the other in his efforts to escape the touch of his friends. The only greater feeling was when he shot to the surface for that breath of air that he needed for another dive.

Often, when his mother and father were fighting and he found himself down on the dock, crying and wishing to be someone else, he would pray to the Gods of the Fishes. He would beg to be released from his human bonds and become one with the water -- a true fish. Their lives were simple and he envied the pleasure of the water, imagining himself too smart for the hook, plumbing the depths and coasting with the current, forever in search of nothing in particular except the freedom from everything it takes to be human.

Trey had often thought that of all the fishes to choose from he'd wish to become a catfish. Their lives were spent on the bottom, gliding and discovering the cast-off treasures of their human hunters. They moved with the slow stately purposefulness of kings. They lived long lives and grew to be immense. He remembered the picture he saw in the Guinness Book of World Records, the jaw of the fish large enough to swallow a small boy.

And then there were Old Man Hassle's stories. Trey wasn't the only one who talked about it -- everyone had heard the rumors -- but it was the old caretaker of the community dock who spoke of it more than anyone else.

The lake was only about fifty years old and wasn't the sort of place to hold things ancient and mysterious. Still, divers would descend every few months to check the dam's integrity, searching for any cracks or holes in the millions of tons of concrete that could threaten the greater part of Chattanooga sitting just down river as a magnificent southern gem. During the years, old wrecks of cars and trains had been dumped along the base to add to the width. These rusting fortifications were deadly to the divers, some becoming caught in the tangles of twisted metal as they inspected and pretended to be fishes. Even so, there was no end to divers who wanted to delve the lakes deepest depths. The pay was supposedly the highest of all, and the list was long.

And that same list moved quickly as the divers went down, came back up and swore never to enter the lake again. It was the catfish that sent them scurrying back to the surface, arriving screaming and babbling incoherently. They spoke of catfish as big as Ford LTDs and Lincoln Towncars that swam up to stare at them as they inspected the aging concrete. They swore the fish looked at them like they had big questions they wanted answered, only the divers didn't understand what they could be.

People said it was all the old cars that bad been dumped down in the lake's depths that provided them with their source of measurement and it was this single thing that made people believe the stories. It was also what had kept people coming from everywhere in attempts to catch the mythical beasts.

Trey and Greg crossed the barrier from the haven of the green weed and shallower water, to the black mysteriousness of the deeper water. They breathed a sigh of relief to be safe from Billy Picket's fate. Greg turned in his seat and began preparing his rod, attaching a number six hook and opening a can of corn with an old P-38.

As they moved to the fishing hole, they found themselves in the shadow of the immense dock where the barges were loaded. They stared at the pilings, easily three times larger than any telephone pole and covered with a black coating of tar that kept the water from rotting the important timber. The dock itself rose at least a hundred feet above them, a thousand stray wisps of fishing line from the large tires bolted to the side evidence of bad casts and impossible snags.

Trey cut the motor.

They drifted for a moment and then stilled.

The dock was protected from the wind by a small peninsula of trees, creating calm water where even the brown bubbles of pollution remained immovable. As Greg dropped his line in the water, Trey turned and tightened the clamps on the motor. It would be his death if it fell over the side. Like the battery between his feet, the motor was *off limits*. As long as it didn't break or sink, however, he felt sure that his father would never find out he'd used it.

Mere moments later the smaller boy stood up and screamed in delight as he reeled in a rather pathetic bluegill.

"Greg. Sit down. Are you stupid? You're gonna dump the boat," said Trey as he gripped both sides, attempting to steady the rocking.

"But I got one. I got one," said the younger boy, smiling happily.

"Shit, man. You got bait. After a few more of those, then we'll really start fishing."

Greg sat down and frowned a little as he removed the hook from the brittle lips of the flapping fish. Like all kids with scars on their hands, he was careful to avoid the sharp spines along the small fish's back. He tossed it into the middle of the boat where it wiggled wretchedly.

"You know what Old Man Hassle said, don't you?" asked Greg, casting a line again.

"That old coot says a lot of things. I wouldn't believe too much of what he says. My daddy says he's an old drunk, anyway," replied Trey, also tossing in a line.

It was Old Man Hassle that had given Trey the idea to try the old Army Docks for catfish, but he wouldn't let his younger friend know exactly how much he really liked the old man.

"Yeah. My mom says the same thing, but still, he's been around forever." Greg cursed as he missed the strike of a fish. He brought the empty hook into the boat, slid on a kernel of corn and tossed it back over the side.

"So what does he say?" asked Trey, pretty sure he knew the answer already.

"He said the biggest of all the catfish live down there," said Greg, pointing into the blackness. "He said this is the place where they lay their eggs. Where they grow new ones."

Trey had heard about the big ones, but the egg story was a new one.

"Old Man Hassle says it's the catfish that make the weeds grow," continued the smaller boy. "Like a fence to keep other fish out. And people, too."

"That's plain stupid. How could fish make the weeds grow?" Trey asked. It was science, biology rather that made it occur. His biology teacher called it photosynthesis. It was the sun, reaching down to the lake floor, making long forgotten seeds blossom and bloom. "I think the old coot was drunk when he told you that. Anyway, it's the TVA men killing the mosquitoes. As far as the eggs go, they can grow anywhere. This isn't the only place."

"No. Really, Trey. Think about it." Greg's words began to pile on each her. "It makes sense. Old Man Hassle says they're gods. Catfish Gods. He says they have the power to stop people from catching them if they want. It's the bad ones that we catch. Not the good ones. We could never catch the good ones even if we knew how, says Old Man Hassle."

"It makes no sense at all. It's stupid, Greg. How can a fish be a God?" Trey shook his head. "Why would you want to catch them, then? Catch a God? Impossible."

Greg was still out of breath from his speech, but it didn't stop him from frowning. He was silent for a moment, then nodded. "Yeah, it is pretty stupid."

Trey could tell that his logic had sunk in. The littler boy looked up to him, and more often than not, would do anything to impress him.

***

It took half an hour before they'd brought in enough bluegill and crappie for bait. That was the fun about catfish. You never had to buy bait for them. Trey had learned long ago, it was the guts that they preferred over anything else. Disgusting as it was, at least it kept the girls from fishing for them. Once you got used to the tiny intestines, kidneys, bloody brine and fish poop and learned how to hold your breath, it wasn't a problem.

Last year, after he'd heard of the guts, right before the weeds took over, he had been in the same canoe fishing along the muddy flats just off shore from the houses. He had his trout rig and was drifting guts from a large hook, the bait held down by a large sinker, bumping along the bottom. It was his first time using the guts, and he wouldn't have done it except he was fresh out of worms and had snagged all the lures he had stolen from his dad's tacklebox on sunken stumps and trash. He really wasn't expecting to catch anything, just enjoying the wind off the water and the sun, hoping for a tan that would carry him through the winter. When the fish first hit, he thought he'd caught another snag. But when the *snag* began to pull the boat out deep, he knew it was an incredible fish.

It took him an hour of alternately paddling and pulling; always sure to keep tension on his four-pound test at all times, before he finally reached the shore. It took another ten minutes for him to haul in the biggest fish he had ever caught. To that day his father hardly believed that his own son had brought in a twenty-five pound catfish on such microscopic line.

That had been his first catfish and catching it made him feel more than human. Soon, he found himself on the docks, late at night fishing with trot lines laced with multiple hooks. He would sneak out, having left his rod and gear under his window before bedtime, and make his way through the darkness to the dock. He rarely caught anything and would wake up near dawn when the chill of the new sun made it too uncomfortable to remain near the water. His mother would pester him about sleeping in, finally waking him around noon, and criticizing him for his laziness. Trey never gave away the truths of his nights, however. They were too special, communing with the sky and the water, thinking of all his grandfather had taught him about fishing and life. He enjoyed the peace and feeling of being separated from everything, yet still connected to the universe. As he held the lines, he pretended he was floating in the sky, the water a reflection of the universe.

Trey had to gut all the fish while Greg stared away, pretending to ignore the pop of released flesh and the blood that seeped into the bottom of the boat, making the water a disarming pink. Finished, Trey placed the corpses in a white plastic bag and piled the guts in a small bucket.

"Alright," he said smiling. "You can look now. I'm done."

"What? I was just staring at the water. Looking for some fish."

Trey smiled wider. He'd leave his friend alone and not mention the fact that there was no way his friend could see fish in the dark brackish water.

"Help yourself," he said gesturing at the pile that was already drawing green-bottomed flies. "It's time to catch one of your Gods."

Greg glared for a moment, wondering if it was an insult or a joke, then grabbed a length of purple intestine and placed it on the new rig. They were using a triple swivel with a sinker offset from the large hook so the bait could drift a few tantalizing inches from the muddy bottom.

When they'd let out enough line, they both leaned back and stared at the lazy brackish sky. On occasion, they would follow a particular cloud, watching as it changed shapes until finally disappearing into the kudzu covered forest that was their horizon.

Finally, Greg's pole doubled over sending him standing as he tried to control the dancing rod. The canoe rocked madly. Trey struggled to still it by shifting his weight. Greg screamed at the top of his lungs as he began to reel furiously.

"Slow down. Slow down, Greg. You're going to break the line," said Trey. "Slow and steady. Slow and steady." His grandfather had taught him that. Hell, he'd taught him everything he knew about fishing except what his dad had taught him about creek fishing. Too many people got too excited and lost their catch. Fishing was a tough thing.

Greg ignored him, his pole making a right angle towards the water. His reeling slowed, less from his effort than the fish's far below. It began to pull the small boat and Trey spun and toggled the trolling motor on. He maneuvered the boat to provide a steady pull against the tug of the captured fish.

It had to be a catfish.

And a big one.

The excitement was contagious, and soon Trey found himself shouting and encouraging Greg. He prayed that the line or the rod wouldn't snap. He prayed that his friend wouldn't get jerked in, forgetting to let go and drown in the murky depths. Trey couldn't help but remember the words of Old Man Hassle, imagining that his young friend had a God on the end of his line. He prayed to the fishes themselves, begging them to let these two boys catch one.

Just as suddenly as he'd felt the hit, there'd come a wretched snap as the line gave away to the combined pressures of the fish and the reverse pull of the boat. Greg fell back hard, hitting his head against the metal rim of the canoe. Trey stopped the engine immediately and managed to catch the rod before it fell into the lake.

Greg sat up slowly, tears flowing from his eyes.

"Are you okay, Greg?" asked Trey, the wake of the fight still sending ripples across the water.

"Yeah. Yeah. Fuck me," the little boy said, wiping his cheeks with the front of his T-shirt. "I just hurt my head is all."

Trey watched him rubbing the growing bump and knew that it was a deeper pain. He'd almost caught the big one. He'd had it and it was gone.

But that's what made fishing special and so unique. You always tried for that bigger fish, every moment a chance. When you lost it, it was forever lost and you had to start over, not where you left off. When you finally caught it, the glory was so fleeting that it was no time at all before you went looking for an even larger one.

"Shit. That was a big one too. Damn big," said Trey.

"Yeah. Damn big," repeated Greg, still staring at the water.

"I wonder if it has any brothers?" asked Trey. "I still got my line in the water. You better fix yours."

Greg spent a few moments staring longingly at the lake, then hurried to refit his line.

Trey returned to his own line and argued with himself over the need to check the bait. It was an important argument, one where many experienced fishermen made mistakes. If you pulled it up as the fish was contemplating the catch, your chance was forever lost. If you left it in the water with an empty hook, you were wasting the day. It was a tough choice, but Trey decided to leave his hook alone.

He'd chosen wisely. It was right after they finished their egg salad sandwiches when Trey's rod buckled.

Trey was caught off guard and he almost lost the Ugly Stick as it slipped and banged against the edge of the boat. It wasn't until the last moment that he managed to grip it, already half in the water.

Trey jerked the rod out of the water, partly to set the hook and partly because he couldn't help himself as he stumbled back, knocking Greg over in the process. Somehow, he managed to stand and felt the thrumming of the taught line.

He immediately knew it was the largest catfish he had ever latched onto.

Trey squatted by the motor and struggled to turn it on. It gave a hum, but when he glanced over the edge, he saw the blades turning excruciatingly slowly, evidence of a dying battery. He glanced over his shoulder and eyed the community dock, half a mile away. With only one paddle, it would take forever to reach.

Trey decided against the motor and screamed for Greg to reel in his own line. Momentarily annoyed, Greg soon complied and pulled his line in. The two changed places. All the while, the canoe was being pulled inexorably towards the pilings. It was mere moments before the front of the boat hit the sticky wood and with his free hand, Trey grabbed hold. It was better than being drug out into the lake, or even the weeds. What he prayed for, however, was that the fish wouldn't wrap the line around the great pole that speared the floor far far beneath him.

Luckily, he didn't have his usual trout rig, but the heavy-duty rig he'd been given last Christmas and it wasn't called the Ugly Stick for nothing. The line was twenty-pound test and could handle upwards of a hundred pounds if used skillfully. The tip of the rod continued to dance and jump as he could feel a long hulk, struggling far below to get free.

Then suddenly the line went slack. Trey stopped reeling and cried out, tears filling his eyes, just as they had filled Greg's before. Then with an insight drawn from experience he realized the fish could be attempting to surface. Wiping his eyes, he redoubled his fight, reeling the line in furious and quick. He couldn't match the speed of the fish, however, and when the beast surfaced, Greg screamed.

Its gaping maw, at least two feet across, snapped at the air on the left side of the boat as it rose out of the water. The head of the great fish slammed into the water with a huge splash, soaking the boys and the boat as it disappeared silently back into the murk.

Then something rammed them from beneath sending Greg flying into the water and Trey flailing to the bottom of the canoe. A tail smacked the lake surface several times on the right side of the canoe.

Then chaos returned to order as the fish disappeared and the urgency of the moment subsided.

Greg, treading water, began to alternately scream and gurgle as he panicked, trying to kick the fish and swim back to the boat, simultaneously.

"Trey. Trey. Gggg-help me!"

Trey picked himself slowly up from the cramped floor of the canoe, now covered in fish guts and soaked with the bloody mixture from his earlier cutting. The rod forgotten, he grabbed the paddle and held it towards his struggling friend. Within seconds Greg was back in the boat, hyperventilating and crying.

"Jesus fucking Christ. Did you see the size of that thing?"

"Did I *see* it? It almost *ate* me!" screamed back Greg.

Trey was about to tell him how stupid that was, then stopped. It *had* been the biggest fish he'd ever seen. Too many times he'd swum in the deep water, the *Jaws* soundtrack playing in his mind. Even though no one had ever heard of a person being eaten in a freshwater lake by a shark or a fish, and even though no one had ever been chewed up by a catfish, he couldn't help but wonder.

Trey glanced around and saw that his rod was gone. It was surely on the bottom of the lake being drug around by his own Moby Dick. He maneuvered Greg into the seat and noticed the young boy was beginning to shiver uncontrollably. Trey jerked off his shirt and replaced Greg's with his dry one. He ordered his friend to remove his shoes and massaged his feet to get them warm. Then he worked at the boy's arms and shoulders until he could see the blood return.

All the while, the both of them were crying, their chance at greatness, twice removed.

"I wanna go home," said Greg, trying hard to stop crying. "I don't want to fish anymore."

"Okay. Okay," said Trey, wanting to stay and try again. The lure of all fishermen who had just lost the big one was upon him, but he had lost his rod. There was only Greg's and there was an unwritten rule never to fish with anyone else's pole. His grandfather had said that *if you caught something on someone else's rig, it wouldn't really be your own.* The great fish, if it could be re-caught, would belong to Greg and that just wouldn't do.

Trey gazed at the sky. A storm was moving in. Hard gray clouds pushed aside the lighter gray. They probably had only fifteen minutes before it hit -- just long enough for Greg to dry off before he became soaked again. It would take twice that to make it back across the inlet to the community dock. Trey eyed the immense TNT dock and thought about taking shelter beneath it for a time. He had no idea how long the storm would last however, and Greg really needed to get home and into dry clothes.

"Shit," said Trey, accepting his fate.

It was then that he saw his fishing pole about five feet under the water and wrapped around one of the pilings. The Ugly Stick had snapped in two and the line appeared to be all that was holding it in place.

"Look! There's my pole," he said pointing into the water.

Greg turned slowly to where Trey pointed, then sat straight when he saw the unmistakable lines of the rod. "Maybe you can save the reel."

"Sure," said Trey. Perhaps he'd found a small happiness in the tragedy. He'd thought it lost forever. No telling what his father would say or do to him when he discovered that it was missing. As he drew closer, he noticed the tip. It thrashed once, twice, then a series of hard jerks, creating bubbles that rose to the surface. "Holy Freaking Cow. Look at that! The fish. It's still on. The fish is still on the line!"

Instead of being thrilled, Greg got a worried look on his face. "Don't go in there. Don't go into the water." Greg shook his head hard and stared into the bottom of the boat. "It just too big. Too damn big."

Trey watched his friend for a second and then glanced back at the fishing pole. He let his eyes drift along the piling and for the first time, noticed there were bars jutting out from the sides. Like those on telephone poles, they'd been previously camouflaged by bits of seaweed and moss and fishing line.

It was indeed a huge fish, but *Jaws* could never happen here. All Trey had to do was climb down, cut the line and then get his reel back. His dad was going to wonder where it was anyway, considering it was a Christmas present and Trey's favorite gift. If they went to the mountains next week, he would never be able to explain it away.

"Naw. It's okay. The fish is gone. I know that. I'm just going to get the pole and the reel. My father would kill me if I lost the whole rig. Anyway, if he finds out it's missing, my parents will find out what we're doing today. And my parents will tell your parents and then we'll be grounded from the lake all summer."

At the threat of grounding, Greg brought his head up sharply. The lake was their life. Trey watched as the emotions sifted through intelligence, expressions dancing on his friend's face.

Finally, Greg sighed and nodded his head slowly. "Okay, but hurry up," he said. "And be careful."

Hurry up and be careful, thought Trey. Those were two things that shouldn't go together. He wasn't going to hurry, but he would certainly be careful.

Trey paddled the canoe back up to the piling, the shadow of the dock placing them in darkness. The smell of decay was strongest here. He noticed the eddies of black oil and multicolored gasoline-slick mixed with trash and the brown bubbles of pollution. If the lake was Heaven, this was Hell. Trey leaned past Greg and used the short length of rope attached to the front of the boat to tie it firmly into place. He removed his tennis shoes and placed them on the seat. He stood and stared at the nasty water, not wanting to enter, but needing to get the reel.

"Alright. Watch me, man. Everything is gonna be okay. I'm just going to get the rod and I'll be right back." Trey put a hand on Greg's shoulder. "Stay cool."

With that, ed a foot on the metal edge of the canoe and pushed off. The water embraced him as he, feet first, sliced deeply from warm to cool water. He pushed himself back to the surface and side-armed his way over to the piling. Counting to three by thousands, hyperventilating until his lungs were full, he descended pulling himself down using the slippery spikes. The rod was deeper than he'd originally thought, probably fifteen feet.

Through the murky water, he saw the rod and the line wrapped around the piling six or seven times. It was the heaviness of the line that had saved his reel. The tugging had stopped, but he doubted the fish was entirely gone. Maybe he still had a chance to catch it. He really didn't need to cut the line. He could deceive the fish. After all, he was human and he had the superior brain. Trey depressed the reel and let out about five feet of slack. Careful not to tug on the line still attached to the fish, he began to unwind the rod from the piling. He was almost finished when he paused and returned to the surface.

"What the hell are you doing, Trey? I thought you were gonna cut the line."

Trey breathed heavily across the water and grinned. "I got everything under control. When I come back up, I'm gonna hand you the rod. Hold onto it tight until I get back into the boat."

"Don't do it, Trey," begged Greg, his eyes beginning to tear up again. "It's too big. It's gonna eat you. I'm telling you, the fish is too big."

Trey laughed. "It's not gonna eat me, Greg. Don't get your panties in a wad. I got everything under control." He reached up and punched his friend in the arm. "Hey! Trust me."

By the look in the smaller boy's eyes, Tret could tell trust was being smothered by fear. Trey cocked his head, winked hard, then, after another count of three, descended back down along the piling.

In no time, he managed to free the rod and line from the piling. He was about to ascend to the surface when he was jerked impossibly hard. Trey surged through the water plunging deeper and deeper. He'd gone fifty feet by the time he thought to let go of the rod. Even after he released it, the incredible momentum continued as he was propelled to-towards the bottom.

The pressure on his head was becoming incredible. He felt like a knife was being thrust into the center of his brain. Thankfully, some tinge of sanity within his mind kept him from screaming and releasing the precious air he needed to survive.

Finally, his descent slowed. The bottom was somewhere near, hidden by shadows below. Trey glanced upwards and like a lighter darkness, glimpsed the faraway surface. Or what he thought was the surface. He was too deep. Deeper than he had ever been before.

Trying hard not to panic, he began to ascend as slowly as possible because of the immense pressure being exerted upon his body. He achieved only a few feet before he felt his ascent halt. Something gripped each ankle painfully.

Trey stared down and watched in horror as weeds wrapped around his ankle. In the almost darkness, he watched as two more moved for him like tentacles from some multi-limbed beast, encircling his wrists and pulling his arms out hard. Many more waved below, as if beckoning him deeper. The decaying corpses of a hundred fish stared back at him, as did the skulls of animals, picked clean and gleaming.

Trey thrashed, attempting to free himself from the living weed, realizing he was quickly running out of air. As his air depleted, instead of his vision dimming, he saw the water brightening. Although he was very deep, he could now see through the water like it was near the surface and clear.

A presence came into his vision, rising gradually from the depths beneath him. The only movements were the minute openings and closings of the mouth and the almost intelligent waving of its long whiskers. When the catfish was even with Trey's head and staring straight into his eyes, it opened its mouth wide revealing rows of bony teeth and pulsating gills.

Trey slammed his eyes shut. He jerked at his bonds. He refused to see what was about to eat him and felt the warmth of urine seep from his cold shriveled penis. When the first of the whiskers brushed against his face, he screamed, releasing all of his air, condemning him to death.

He finally even lost enough strength to scream and his body reflexively went to suck in the brackish water of the lake, filling his lungs with what he could never breath. But it didn't happen that way. Trey felt a warmth along his face and neck. It flowed into his chest. A calmness filled him, stilling his panic and his need to breathe. Slowly, Trey opened his eyes to stare into the bottomless eyes of the catfish's. His fear had left him and he watched as the whiskers, dozens of them, caressed his skin. The mouth opened and closed and he couldn't help but admire the synchronization of the gills.

Trey hung in the water, held fast by the weeds, staring into the huge maw of a fish that he had wanted to catch. The need to breathe had departed him and he wondered if he had drowned. He wondered if he was dead.

Perhaps.

The voice was in his head and filled him with the fullness of love. It was the same feeling as when Shelby had told him she loved him for the first time. Every part of his body had been consumed by the heavy electric feeling of happiness. If this was death, he wanted more of it.

Love is a wonderful thing. It is life.

Yes it is, he felt himself thinking. *It transcends death. Makes life good living,* as his grandfather had said.

He realized, without panic and as if it was utterly sane, that the fish was speaking to him.

Am I dead? he asked.

Perhaps, came the same reply.

How am I breathing?

You are not.

Then I am dead. Although he said it, the thought held no terror for him.

Perhaps.

Why do you keep saying that? Why do you keep saying perhaps?

The choice is yours.

The answer confused Trey. Maybe the fish was mad for his attempts to catch him. Even with the love pervading his body, he laughed at the insanity of the concept. How could a fish be mad? How could it have feelings? Still--

Are you angry?

No. It is the way of the world.

To hunt you, to kill you? That doesn't make you mad.

It is the way.

Then what is the choice you speak of?

Would you die for me?

For you?

Trey was sure he didn't understand the question. Die for a fish? For a catfish? Why should he give his life up for a -- but then it wasn't just a fish, was it? Could a fish do this? Trey remembered what Greg had said about the Catfish Gods. It was stupid, but he was alive, not breathing. Only a God could make that happen. He didn't know what to say. Trey thought of Billy Picket. Had he been asked the question? Had he an-answered wrong?

I don't understand.

Would you die for me?

Trey stared hard at the fish hovering in the water before him, caressing tender whiskers along his cheeks. It was easily a hundred pounds. Maybe double that. Its eyes were bottomless black pools that held a strange warmth. He could not deny the majesty of the beast. It was magnificent. It would be perfect above the mantle of any fireplace, eclipsing the largest swordfish. It would make a bass of any size appear to be a pathetic wannabe minnow.

Trey knew his answer was important, but he knew, as well, that the fish understood his every thought.

Why should I die for you? I don't understand. He stole himself for death, but pleaded desperately for an answer.

Because I would die for you.

The answer surprised him. A fish like this, powerful, magical -- a Catfish God -- would die for him? Truly, he was nothing special. Sure, Trey felt himself important, but in the greater universe, he was nothing. What would make this catfish die for him? He knew his mother would die for him. He knew his father would as well. And his grandfather, the old man wouldn't hesitate. Till this day, as he was kneeling before the casket, Trey had never told anyone that he had begged God to take him instead --to let his grandfather live again. If he died now -- if he was to perish down in the depths of Chickamauga Reservoir -- maybe then he could see his grandfather again. Maybe he could make him some more martinis as the old man lorded over the world. Maybe he would see him smile.

Trey stared deep into the eyes of the fish, alien, but also curiously human, searching for the answer. There, among the blackness, he saw the same look that Shelby, his mother, his father, his grandfather, even Greg, on occasion, had given him.

Instead of drowning, instead of feeling the quick burning warmth of a lungful of watery death, he felt the warmth of love. Unconditional and pure, it was there for him, just for being alive. Would grandfather want him to die for him? He pictured the old man's tall John Wayne features and knew the answer.

Yes. I would die for you.

Then you understand. Go in peace and live long.

The firm grip of the weeds suddenly released him and Trey felt himself floating towards the surface. He watched the imperious figure of the Catfish God until it had become one with the shadowy depths. It wasn't until his head bobbed to the surface that his body contracted and jackknifed. He automatically relented and allowed his body to breathe in the sweetness of the putrid, yet life-giving air of the dock.

"Trey. Trey. Trey," came the jubilant shouts.

Glancing up, he saw Greg, cheeks puffy and hair matted as if the storm had come and gone. His eyes were as red as his hair and his voice held the hoarseness of a widow.

"Trey. I thought you were dead," said the boy, tears renewing their slalom through his freckles. "It's been hours."

"Hours?" asked Trey absently as he levered himself into the boat. He examined the sky and saw that the sun was setting.

"I couldn't leave. I thought you were dead. I didn't know what to have to tell people. I didn't want to--"

Trey stared at his friend openly with a fondness that hadn't been there before. Greg noticed it and his eyes widened. Then his face went serious and he wiped his cheeks.

"I thought you were dead. How?"

Trey shook his head. "I have no idea, man. All I know right now is that I love you for waiting."

"Yech," Greg said, poking his tongue between his lips but still smiling. "You gay or something?"

Trey looked off toward the community dock and began to paddle. "Naw, just happy to be here."

His grandpa used to say that.

"What are you going to tell your parents about your fishing pole?" Greg asked.

"I'll think of something." *Maybe give them a fish story. Maybe tell them about a God. Or maybe even, he'd just let them know how much he loved them, and how sorry he was for not being where he was supposed to have been.* Whatever he said, it was all going to be all right.

COLD GRAVE

Gabino Iglesias

The sky was dark despite it being noon. Winter was rearing its ugly head and it looked like it had woken up with an attitude. There was an uncomfortable chill in the air that made you zip up your jacket the second you stepped outside and then sweat a little when you walked indoors. Roberto's stomach growled, signaling lunchtime, but the man driving the truck didn't look like he was considering taking a break any time soon. The man's name was Vitali, and he looked like something made out of rock. He'd been training Roberto for two days now, uttering maybe a hundred words in the process. He had a thick Russian accent that seemed perfect for the job he'd been doing for thirty years. Roberto was grateful he got all the instructions he needed from Mark, the chubby man with the bad combover who made him sign the paperwork for the gig, because most of what Vitali had been saying was either confusing or simply unintelligible.

The radio was on. Two guys argued about the dangers of letting Muslims into the country. Roberto thought about the last time a Muslim started some shit in his neighborhood and came up blank. The truck's heater was on, but it was losing the battle against the sharp wind sneaking though every opening in the old vehicle's rusty frame. Hart Island is only about a mile long and a quarter of a mile wide, so water can bee seen regardless of where you're standing, and being surrounded by it provides the cold wind with extra teeth. Roberto looked out at the water and then at some tall Bronx buildings in the distance. The truck and his stomach complained again, this time in unison.

The cold made Roberto think about his daughter, Andrea. Low temperatures were not good for her lungs. The doctor said cold air constricts her bronchi. Living somewhere warmer would do her good, but they can't afford to move. This new job was great because it would allow them to apply for a better apartment with better heating. Mark also mentioned something about the health insurance and apparently the co-pay would be lower, which meant they'd be able to afford better medicine instead of the generic garbage they'd been giving Andrea since she started needing respiratory therapies. On top of all that, Roberto planned to hustle and save until they could get the hell outta New York.

"Now we pick up the shipment," said Vitali. It was a statement. Roberto knew it required no reply, so he remained quiet. Outside the window, Roberto saw large trenches on the ground like dark wounds and hundreds of corpses in bare wooden caskets already laid out. Vitali told them the trenches were dug by Rikers Island inmates. He also said he was not supposed to interact with them when they came to the island. They even dug special holes for severed body parts, according to Vitali, but those were beyond the trees and couldn't be seen from the dirty road they were on. Roberto knew this gig his drug dealing cousin got him was going to take some getting used to, but the money he'd be making on the side was all the incentive he needed to work hard at adapting. Hell, for Andrea, he'd dig those damn trenches with his teeth.

The truck shuddered to a stop in front of a dilapidated red brick building with gaping holes where the windows used to be. Vitali pulled the key from the ignition, opened his door, and stepped into the cold air in a single fluid motion that didn't look quite natural for such an old man. Roberto took a deep breath and joined him outside. They took a few steps and stood in front of the water on a small pier on the west side of the island. There was a van waiting on a gravel road that led to the crumbling edifice. Roberto spotted several tiny white angel statues along the rotting pathway around a nondescript garage building about twenty feet from the van.

"Any minute they will be here," Vitali said without looking at his watch.

Roberto stared out at the water and thought about Sundays spent fishing with his father and the wild stories the old men his father knew always told. Fishing out body parts, fetuses, fish with two heads or four eyes or strange rhythms coming from their gaping mouths. The stories went on and on. Some he laughed at, but some he had listened to in silence and then they'd come back to him to haunt his dreams at night. What he was doing in Hart Island was something that could just as well be one of those crazy old fisherman stories.

Vitali stood there, next to Roberto, unmoving, like something planted long ago that had turned unshakeable. A few seconds later, a small ferry chugged its way out of the fog that still clung to the water despite the time of day and approached the island. In a couple of minutes, it reached the pier, slowed down, and started turning sideways. The name of the city was painted in yellow and blue letters on the side of the ferry. A tall, heavyset black man wearing a blue hoodie appeared starboard and threw Roberto and Vitali a rope.

With the boat gently bobbing up and down against the pier, the big man with the hoodie and a smaller, bearded guy with blue eyes jumped off the ferry.

"Hey, V," said the shorter guy. "We have fourteen boxes for you today. Want them here or near the van?"

"Near the van is okay, Michael."

Vitali didn't introduce Roberto and the two men didn't ask about him. They turned around and jumped back into the ferry. A few minutes later, they came out with the first box and hauled it onto the pier using a yellow cart with a hydraulic lift. On the first trip to the van, the big man looked at Roberto and gave him an almost imperceptible nod.

Roberto looked at the unpainted pine boxes and wondered about their contents. He was thankful there weren't any small boxes being unloaded. He didn't think he could have managed a dead kid on top of everything else going on in his head. There were almost a million bodies on this small stretch of land. Roberto tried to imagine them under his feet. He thought about the boxes full of random limbs and the shorter trenches dug to bury kids. He tried hard to toughen himself up, to become the man he needed to be to do what he had to do at some fast-approaching moment of the day.

The two men finished stacking the fourteen pine boxes near the back of the van and made their way back to the ferry.

"That's it for now, V," said Michael. "I don't think we'll need to make another trip today. We'll be here at the same time tomorrow. This the guy taking over for you?"

Vitali moved his head down once, slowly. He didn't say anything. Michael nodded a few times and told the big man to untie them. Without another word, the two men disappeared into the inside of the ferry, turned it around, and headed back to the mainland.

When the ferry was no longer visible, Vitali turned to Roberto.

"Now you will meet a ghost. He name is Giorgio. He's the man who brings us the packages. He waits in his boat for the city men to do their thing and then comes to do his. We get rid of those first. Then we come back and take care of the boxes."

It was the longest thing the Russian had said since they'd been together. Then the sound of a motor came from the water and Vitali pointed toward the approaching boat.

"That is the ghost."

The small boat pulled up to the pier. A small man with a baseball cap pulled low on his forehead jumped out and tied the vessel to the same post Vitali had previously used.

"Hey, Vitali, this the new guy?"

"Yes."

The man approached Roberto with his hand out. Roberto took it and looked at the chunk of face under the hat. The skin was almost translucent. The white and pink tone of his flesh reminded Roberto of the huge salamanders he used to see at night on his grandmother's balcony on those summers he spent in Puerto Rico.

"I'm Roberto."

"I'm Giorgio. Mark said you're gonna be feeding the fishes now that Vitali is retiring, that right?"

"Yes, sir."

"No need to call me, sir, man. Both of us are here to get our hands dirty, aren't we?"

For a moment, the comment threw Roberto off. What did the man know? Then he remembered what was ahead for them and relaxed.

"Anyway, I have two packages for you, gentlemen. Let's get to it."

Giorgio jumped back into his boat. Roberto watched as he removed the cover under which the motor should have been. Instead of the boat's motor, however, there were two black plastic tarps. Their general shape gave away the contents.

"Don't know how much Vitali has told you, Roberto. The old goombah ain't much of a talker. The thing about these tarps is that you have to use them all the way to the water and then remove them. Always keep a blade with you to make things easier. You can hose them down near the water and give them back to me next time I come over or stash them somewhere once they're clean, but you have to drop the bodies into the water without them. Also, don't keep shit. Even if the bodies are wearing something or still have a wallet on them, which will probably never happen. You get them, you push them into the water exactly where Vitali's going to show you and that's it. That's the way we do things to keep everything clean, capisce?"

Roberto nodded. Now that he had two corpses in front of him, the next step once again freaked him out. He thought of Andrea. The bonus for the little extra dumping he was going to do would get him an extra three grand at the end of the day. The money was too good to pass up. He thought about moving to Florida or California. Somewhere where you could actually take a dip in the ocean and not die from some horrible flesh-eating disease two days later. He thought about warm air and how that would let his daughter laugh without her happiness quickly devolving into a coughing fit.

"Hey, come down here and give me a hand with these."

Giorgio's voice cut through Roberto's thoughts. He jumped onboard and leaned down to grab the first body. Giorgio told him to swing it into the pier and, once they had both on land, to quickly stash them in the back of the van.

"On days where I'm making a delivery, the security guys will get a call and stay home. They get a bit of extra moolah for playing sick, you know what I mean? First you'll get the folks from the city and then me, but you take care of my packages first. Always. Once you take care of that, come back for the city's dead. The rest of the day is yours until you go home. Always ride the city's boat in and out. The guys captaining those small boats change all the damn time, so not a damn word about this to anyone unless I tell you to, capisce? Oh, and bring a book or a cell phone or something, man. It gets fucking boring out here most of the time."

Giorgio untied his boat as he spoke. Then he looked at Vitali.

"Happy retirement, V. Can't say it's been a pleasure, but it ain't been half bad, right?"

For the first time since he'd met him, Roberto watched Vitali's mouth curl up into something resembling a smile.

"You are a cold son of a bitch, Giorgio. Good luck to you, my friend."

Giorgio offered a humorous salute to the men standing on the pier and turned his boat around.

Vitali walked to the van and opened the back door.

"Put the packages in there."

Roberto was going to ask him for a hand, but then realized he'd be doing this by himself every day.

Roberto pushed and pulled the bodies into the black plastic that covered the back of the van, closed the door, and jumped in. The exertion had made him start to breathe hard. He could see his breath dance in front of his face for a second before vanishing into the cold air around him.

Vitali drove north on the dirt road. A small forest appeared in front of them. Roberto noticed there were no trenches on the side of the dirt road now. He wanted to ask Vitali if it was because they were saving this space for later or because it was already packed with boxes.

They drove through the dark trees, the van jumping from one pool of shadows to the next, the tires quietly making a thin cloud of dust and dirt behind them.

Finally, the trees opened up to a small patch of grass in front of the water. A wooden pier that seemed to have been built a hundred years ago went about fifteen feet into the cold, churning water.

"This is the place," Vitali said.

Both men left the van and walked to the back of it. Vitali opened the door and used both hands to pull a body to the edge of the van. Then he bent his knees, hugged the body toward him, pressed his shoulder into it, and stood up, the tarp perfectly placed atop his right shoulder.

Roberto tried to do the same thing and almost fell on his face. Luckily, the old man hadn't been watching. By the time Roberto had the second body perched on his shoulder, Vitali was already stepping onto the pier.

Roberto walked a bit faster to catch up. He managed to get behind the old man and only dropped the body he was carrying a few seconds after Vitali.

In silence, Vitali pulled a box cutter from his right pocket and sliced the ropes that were holding the tarp in place. He then used his boot to roll the body a bit, revealing the body.

Roberto looked down at the dead man. He was a chubby guy with a head full of black curls and a goatee. His face was swollen. There was a black, slightly puckered hole above his right eye. His tongue was halfway out of his mouth. He wore a light blue shirt that was stained with blood and dark jeans. He didn't have on any shoes or socks.

"Take him to the edge and push him into the water. Keep your eyes on him. The bodies leave no trace because these are special fish," said Vitali.

Roberto did as he was told. The corpse hit the water with a splash and the chubby man's arms became animated by the moving water. The body moved away from the pier for a few seconds and then something yanked it down a bit. Roberto kneeled to get a better look at the fish. The animals doing the dirty work had to be something like saltwater piranhas or medium-sized sharks if they managed to make entire bodies disappear so quickly.

Two large, grey figures moved around the body. The backs of the fish were much wider than Roberto had expected. Videos of goliath groupers he'd seen online came to mind. Then something grey shot out of the water and landed on the corpse's chest. It looked like a toddler's hand, except it was grey. A second later, a second hand joined the first. Roberto watched, astonished, as something resembling a human face broke the surface and looked at him. The thing had teeth that would put a shark to shame and a small, squat nose. There was no hair on the head of the fish, but it otherwise looked human. The head and neck gave way to a broad back and then the thick, grey body Roberto had already seen. There were four things around the body now, slowly biting into it while pulling it down into the dark water.

"They are always hungry," Vitali said.

Roberto turned. The old man was standing right behind him.

"What…what are they?"

"I don't know what they are, only what they do. And I also know why you're here."

"What?" Roberto asked, afraid his voice was going to give him away.

"Look at them go!" Vitali said.

Roberto turned. Then he felt both of Vitali's hands land on his upper back like a couple of small runaway trains. Momentum took over and Roberto flew forward, splashing into the cold water.

The coldness reached into Roberto's lungs and crushed them. His head broke the surface. He tried to inhale, but his body wasn't responding.

"I took care of my predecessor. I'm sure no one remembered to tell Mark that. Too bad for you."

Roberto was close to the pier. He wanted to move toward it, he was moving his arms and kicking his legs, but he wasn't moving. He felt tiny hands, hands the size of Andrea's, pulling at his jacket, trying to bring him down.

He tried to scream, but the lack of air in his lungs turned his attempt into a pitiful grunt. Then he felt pressure on his right calf. It was followed by a pain unlike anything he had ever felt. Teeth scraped against bone. Roberto pushed down on the water and finally got a lungful of air. The scream that escaped his throat morphed into something subdued as he was yanked underwater. He looked down and grabbed one of the tiny hands that was pulling at his jacket. He pulled on it with all his strength. Then one of the creatures bit him between his right shoulder and neck. The dark water around him became even darker as strong, tiny grey hands pulled him further down.

JOHN DORY

D.G. Sutter

In the light of the dawn, the small wooden boat drifted over the sand bars ensconced by tall aqua sea grass. Low tide hit your nostrils the minute you left the woods. The mix of salt air and clam flats was all too familiar for people who had grown up in Ipswich, but to those who were out-of-towners the scent could be perceived as foul, off-putting, almost enough to drive one away from the shore and into the sanctity of a warm home with a bowl of chowder.

The surf was calm and there was barely any movement on the river. Halfway to the neck, the dory passed by Ed Murphy's lobster boat, and both captains exhausted themselves with waves in passing.

"How'a'ya?" Roy yelled over the hum of diesel engines, his words nearly drowned out by the swishing of the brackish water.

The dory bounced out of the way of the crusted out lobster boat, covered with slime and chum, and Roy pulled hard starboard to steer off the dunes. The river was all his to drift, plenty of leeway and loads of open space to play. Being your own boss had its perks on occasion. Roy cut the engine and let the tide take him downstream, enjoying the sun rise on the first morning out of the warm season.

He opened the small cooler and popped a Budweiser for the beginning of the day. The bubbles teased his tongue and refreshed his palette. His calloused fingers fumbled for his lighter and Marlboros. The first drag and sip went so well together, almost better than coffee.

The pinks and greens splayed out over the edge of town and ocean opened up ahead. Small waves lapped at the shore, carrying with them masses of red seaweed and foam that was not the kind you wanted on top of a hot beverage. It would be a tough day out on the flats having to weed through all of that junk.

Roy pulled the dory ashore. He stood and stepped into his mudders, grabbed his rake, and planted his feet in the soft sand. He started on his way, treading lightly, eyes carefully searching for the subsequent bubbles to pop through to the surface. Within an hour, he had several bags down, sorting through steamers, littles, counts, and top necks. After years of doing the job, he no longer thought of these things as food, but nuisances.

As the day wore on, the tides dragged in and vanished the accessibility of the potential areas to dig clams. Roy stuck to the shore, plucking through weed and ropes on his way. He hit a patch of quahogs and filled a bushel fast, then another, and two more. On the fifth, he dug a broken shell and happened upon an odd sight.

Set deep in the shell of tan and white was a beating red and orange body. Roy, unafraid, reached into the crevice and squeezed it between two fingers. It was soft and oozed liquid that was like water, but slick as oil. He teased it between two fingers, finding no identifying characteristics or truly distinguishable features—other than the tiny dimples set into the exterior. Roy pushed it inside and closed the shell.

He put it in his pocket and finished gathering the bushel. None of the others had such a sad looking and lazy hinge. They remained closed and airtight, alive. Roy thought of what was in his pocket as he packed the gear into his truck's cab, how he'd never seen something like it in all his life, especially inside of another mollusk. It seemed almost parasitic.

His fingers stung where he'd touched the creature. Roy dipped his two fingers in the gentle sea and let whatever oil was collected there drift casually back to where it'd come. The residual effect persisted and needled and stuck with Roy as unnatural, something that had great potential for horrific damage.

When he got back into town, Roy dipped into Pratty's C.A.V. to score a few drinks. The bartender, a short squat guy with a beard, named Oscar—poured him a few fingers of Turkey Hill in the glass at the edge of the bar, where Roy always sat.

Roy took a seat next to Tom Stoughton. Tom nodded and raised his own snifter. "Good day out there?"

Roy took the ball cap from his head and placed it on the oaken bar. "Hell of a day."

Tom eyeballed the hat sitting before him. "Christ, do you ever wash that thing?"

Roy chuckled. "Not since before the war."

"I only hauled a few hundred yellowtails and a couple boxes of blackbacks. Fuckin' Irish herring boats killed the ledges."

"You say Irish like you ain't one."

"Eh, shut up ya Wop bastard."

Oscar poured Tom another snifter, which he picked up with liver-spotted fingers. Tom laid a twenty down on the counter. That would keep them going a few rounds.

"You hear about Loopy?" Tom asked.

"Nope, what about?"

"Got his leg caught on a rope last night, diving, out fixing his hull in the early mornin'..."

Roy gulped at the Turkey Hill and slammed the glass so that Oscar's attention would be upon him. The bar hand filled the glass in silence and went back to watching the Sox game.

"Holy hell," Roy said. "What about the boat?"

"Found sittin' in the harbor."

"*Who* found him?"

"Coast Guard, trolling Ten Pound Island. Said he was half-eaten, blue in the face."

"Not how I wanna go. That's brutal."

"You dreamin' about it?" Tom asked, nudging him with an elbow.

"I'm gonna tie dynamite to my chest and walk to the end of the pier...let the seagulls gobble me down and shit me out all over Glouces-ter."

"That's fuckin' romantic, Roy. I can see it now. The mayor would have a ball with that one."

They drink together.

"On my terms, ya know."

Tom tilts his head to indicate that he understands.

"You guys see this," Oscar interrupts. "They're trying to make Pedey the new captain. I never much liked him. Overrated."

"Pud," Roy says, "He's the best second baseman in the American League. Four MVPs, been on the team longest. Who the hell would you pick?"

Oscar waves him off. "Mookie."

Roy turns to Tom. "You hearin' this garbage? Mookie?"

"Every day o'my life."

"We need a better place to hang out." Roy rings his hands under the bar.

They sit in silence, drinking, for a few moments. Oscar refills their glasses yet another time and paces behind the bar as more talk of New England sports gets underway on NESN.

Roy takes the clam out of his pocket and places it on the counter. He pushes it to his old friend. "Ever see something like this?"

Tom rolls the clam shell in his hand. "It's a littleneck clam, of course I have.You know I always thought it funny...a good clam smells like a bad fart."

Roy laughs out loud. "You're damn right. What about what's inside there, though? Ever seen something like that?"

Tom sighs and cracks it apart, pulls out the red and orange sponge. Black appendages had started to grow out of the body; they slithered like worms and grazed Tom's hand, making him drop it on the floor of the bar.

"What is it?" Tom asks.

"Zactly what I'm asking you."

Roy held out his two fingers with which he had touched the entity. The skin was starting to curl off like lead paint, beneath it was gangrenous.

"You better wash your hands," he said, patting Tom's back and throwing a twenty on the bar. "Say 'hi' to your sister and mother for me."

***

The following morning, Roy woke with a gasp. He felt tightness in his chest. The dreams from the night before plagued his perceptions—waves rolling over his head, sharks devouring him whole. He hobbled out of bed and made a quick coffee to drown the thoughts and perk him up, though the fear of a heart attack was heavy at hand.

As he reached for the sugar, Roy noticed the spots on his arms, much like barnacles. Where there should have been flesh, the skin dipped into short canyons. Black dots had formed in each of the dozen or so pockets that spotted his forearm. A sinking tightened his gut. He felt untimely sick. They reminded him of the sores that covered swordfish who had infections. You could pull out worms two feet long, lumps of cancer big as bowling balls.

He poured some rubbing alcohol on the odd spots and set about to his truck. If they weren't cleared up by mid-day, he would head to Addison Gilbert Hospital. Otherwise, there was no sense in losing a day's worth of fishing being holed up the ER, staring at *The Price is Right* and a room full of slobs.

Rather than driving all the way to Essex to set out, Roy made for Wingaersheek Beach. It was closer in proximity to the hospital, if the need arose, and also closer to home if the entirety of the situation was overwhelming. The tides were rough, possibly from an impending storm, and as the saying goes: 'Red skies at night, sailors' delight; red skies by morning, sailors take warning'. It would be a short day as the beet red dawn spoke.

He made sure to wash his arm well in the saltwater as he dredged; it was a great cure for ailments or to disinfect. The weeds there were no less of a hindrance by comparison. Roy was ankle deep in tide, hell some of it red tide, drowning his steps and interrupting true progress. The clams might not be good with all the hogwash.

Along the Eastern bank, he finally struck clams as the tide waned a bit more. Each and every one was full of the red and orange organisms. He threw them in anger above the waves, past foam and the fish below. Roy waded out of the flat unfulfilled. He would alert the town of a possible contamination of red tide, which could in turn force an area closure in the fishery and set him back several days.

On the dory, Roy started to peel free his gear and saw the collection of bodies sucked onto the rubber of his boots. He quickly kicked them off and pushed the skins down past his feet. They were crawling over his legs and he could feel them crawling under his pants.

These were matured further than the sponges. Foot long black appendages slithered out of the orange bodies; the tips were stuck into the skin of his leg. The surface of his skin burned. Roy frantically swatted at the creatures—stepping high, kicking, and trying to break them loose. His foot slapped the small dory's gunnels and Roy flipped overboard, literally head over heels.

The undertow took him out in seconds. The breath sucked out of his lungs. He opened his eyes, but only darkness and brown murk could be seen between thousands and thousands of orange parasites. He managed to kick with his feet and rise to the surface. His boat was a mile back towards shore, bobbing and lonely. A rogue wave struck him from behind, and in his befuddled state he never saw it coming. When he again opened his eyes and gained some form of composure, the parasites were climbing onto his face, sliding the black arms or tongues under his eyelids, into his nostrils. The scream he let out formed a cascade of bubbles that rose over his head and clouded any view of the red sky above.

***

Tom fell asleep in his recliner that night. He left a pile of butts in the ashtray and a plate of spaghetti on the end table. The television blurted out late night ads of made-for-TV products.

His mouth hung open and a line of drool pasted his shirt and dribbled down to his bicep. The snores of drunkenness filled the small apartment that he rented above the downtown drag. From the dip in his arm, came a slender black feeler. It dug, and dug, unbeknownst to Tom, until the fresh orange body was freed of his skin.

It crawled silently up the shirt of the fisherman until it was just below his ear hole. It felt with the tendril, and finding the space adequate, managed to squeeze inside and disappear.

Tom awoke with a jolt. He slapped at his ear.

Mumbling, Tom said something about spiders and cabbage and passed out in the afterglow of a razor sharp blade that could cut a tomato three different ways.

IT CAME FROM THE SEA

C.V. Hunt

"I don't know about this," I said.

Teresa dropped my hand. Her shoulders slumped in a defeated manner. She turned to face me. Her expression was hard to read through her sunglasses but I could feel her disappointment. I readied myself for the bout of pleading.

"You promised," she said.

"I know. I know. I just . . ." I eyed the boats tied to the dock. They bobbed in the water lackadaisically. A gull cried out somewhere in the distance. "I don't know anything about boats and the sea is so endless . . . like the universe. You know, scientists don't even know everything that's in the ocean. It freaks me out."

"Jessie. Honey." Her disappointment dissolved. She rubbed my arm to comfort me. "I know what I'm doing. We won't stray far from the bay. I promise. We'll stay close enough for you to see land. Would that make you feel better?"

I made an uneasy sound. Teresa closed the gap between us and set her backpack on the ground. The sunlight made her blond hair shine. She leaned in to kiss me and wrapped her arms around my waist. She tasted like cherry ChapStick and smelled like sunscreen. We both wore shorts and tank tops over swimsuits and her skin against mine felt warmed by the sun. Warmth and lust flooded through me.

Teresa broke the kiss first. She said, "This is something I want to share with you. You promised you'd come with me when we met." She gave a small laugh. "I mean, we've met each other's parents. I think it's about time you met the sea." She half turned and waved down the dock. "I only sail half as much since you moved in. I feel like I should sell the damn thing."

I whined. "No. Don't do that. I don't want you to give up something because of me."

She took my hand and pouted. "Please try. I love you."

"I love you too," I responded automatically. I took a deep breath and let it out slowly, hoping it would calm my nerves. "All right . . . I hope I don't get sea sick."

"Did you take the Dramamine?"

"Yes."

"You'll be fine." She lifted her backpack, slung it over one arm, and pulled on my hand. "Come on."

A sun-weathered man stood on the bow of his boat watching us with an intense curiosity as Teresa dragged me down the dock.

She stopped in front of a thirty-foot sailboat. Teresa jumped aboard first and then helped me. The boat bobbed unpredictably and walking was disorienting. She showed me around the deck, pointed at things, and rattled off the proper names for items I knew I would never remember. She made sure to show me the lifejackets and the emergency flares and explained how to use them because she knew it would put my mind at ease. Lastly she took me below the deck to the cozy living quarters.

I was able to get around without stooping in the cabin but Teresa was taller and had to slightly bow. The boat had a tiny kitchen, a table with a bench, and a queen-size bed. The rocking of the boat was more disorienting below deck. Teresa emptied her backpack of the groceries and put the items in their respective places.

I flopped onto the bed and beckoned Teresa to join me.

"Oh no." She grabbed my arm and tried to pull me up. "The sea first."

"You're no fun."

I followed her back up the three steep stairs. I took a seat at the back of the boat. I didn't want to be an obstacle as she ran about to release the boat from the dock. She stopped by the wheel, inserted a key, and pressed some buttons. The motor started.

"I thought this was a sailboat," I said.

"It is. The motor makes it easier to maneuver out of the bay." She turned the wheel and the boat began to back away from the dock.

The boat didn't seem to bounce as much once it was in motion. As she steered through the bay I took the opportunity to enjoy the scenery. I avoided looking over the edge at the water and tried to put my fears aside. Once we were out of the bay the swells grew higher. The bounce of the boat became more jarring. I gripped a rail near my seat, terrified of being pitched over the side.

A boat passed us, a larger wave sweeping up to our boat. I thought, *This is it. I'm going to die.* Teresa stood at the wheel with her legs firmly planted. The muscles in her calves constricted as she balanced herself against the motion.

"This is scary!" I called over the noise of the motor and ocean.

Teresa looked at me over her shoulder. "It'll get better in a couple of minutes!"

"I hope so!"

A few more minutes into the open ocean and the swells calmed. Teresa slowed the boat and shut off the engine. She bustled around the deck, tying and untying ropes until the sails were lifted and in the correct position. I was amazed at how fast we traveled with only the aid of the wind. Once Teresa was satisfied with our position she lowered the sails and dropped the anchor. The shore was visible in the distance as she'd promised. I timidly gave in to the fear of the unknown and peered over the edge of the boat. I was shocked to find the water incredibly clear. I had imagined an endless void of blackness.

Teresa disappeared below deck and reappeared a few seconds later with two cans of beer. We stripped down to our swimsuits and sunned ourselves. Once Teresa finished her beer she decided to take a quick dip in the water to cool down.

I chose to watch her and thought it might set my mind at ease to see someone enter the water and exit unscathed. I stood at the ladder as she began to descend.

"Come on. It'll be fine." She grabbed my ankle playfully.

"I'm not ready." I held my hand to shield my eyes from the sun and tried to see if there were any fish near us. "I'm afraid if I felt a fish brush against me I'd panic and drown."

"All right. But you don't know what you're missing."

She bent down, grabbed a handful of water, and splashed me. She turned abruptly and dove into the water. She reappeared shortly, playfully splashed me, and disappeared below the surface. She continued this routine and I didn't mind the cooling effect of the water on my sun-warmed skin. I grew comfortable with the scenario, my fear of the sea abating some.

Teresa disappeared below the surface again but something was off this time. She was under longer than the previous times. The fear reared its ugly head and my heart skipped a beat as the microseconds collected and worry poisoned my thoughts. I called her name even though I was sure she wouldn't be able to hear me under water. Panic coursed through my veins. I dropped to my knees by the ladder. I searched the water for her.

Suddenly she resurfaced a foot from the ladder, gasping for air, panic stricken. She latched onto a rung of the ladder and pulled herself up. I moved out of the way so she could climb aboard.

Still gasping for air, she shouted, "Something attacked me!"

"What?" My body vibrated with adrenaline.

Teresa dropped to her knees on the deck, fighting to regain her breath. She gripped her lower stomach and bent forward.

I knelt beside her and put my hand on her back. "Are you okay? What was it?"

"I don't know," she panted. "I thought I saw something but then an . . . eel attacked me."

"There're eels here?"

"I didn't think the water was shallow enough. I guess I was wrong. I don't know. It sorta looked like an eel or a snake or something. It was thinner than an eel. It was after my . . ."

Teresa sat back and looked at her crotch. A little blood ran down her thigh and mixed with the water on her body before dripping onto the deck.

"Oh my god!" I said. "We have to get you to a hospital!"

She stood and made her way to the living quarters below deck. I followed her in a state of panic. Her demeanor changed rapidly. Now stoic and calm, she entered the tiny bathroom and shut the door.

I stood outside the door and said, "I think we should go back."

I heard a cabinet open and close, followed by the unmistakable sound of tearing plastic.

"Teresa?"

"Give me a second."

"Are you hurt?"

"I started my period."

"Are you sure? It's a week early."

"What do you mean am I sure? I know what a period is."

Her retort stung. I took a step back from the door. She sounded angry and we'd never fought. The toilet flushed. I heard running water and the rattle of pills being shaken from a bottle. She opened the door, appearing peaked and tired.

"I'm sorry," I said, trying to dismantle an argument before it started. "I was worried."

She gave me a half smile. "It's okay." She popped the pills into her mouth and dry swallowed them. "I think I'm going to lie down for a few minutes." She rubbed her lower belly.

She always had cramps the first day of her cycle. I knew she wouldn't want to do anything until the aspirin did its job. I nodded and agreed to join her. She dried her hair with a towel, removed her swimsuit, and pulled on a pair of underwear before slipping into bed. I removed my suit and lay naked beside her. Sunlight shone on us from a skylight above the bed. I snuggled up to her. The rocking boat made it difficult for me to sleep but I eventually nodded off.

I woke an hour later to the sounds of cooking. I slipped out of bed. Teresa, wearing a T-shirt and shorts, was preparing hamburgers on a single electric burner.

She said, "Food's almost done."

"What time is it?" I dug through my bag and pulled some clothes on.

"Eight o'clock." She flipped the burgers.

I retrieved condiments from the mini fridge and sat at the table. Two paper plates sat on the counter. Each plate held a bun. Only one bun had a slice of tomato and lettuce on it. Teresa scooped up the burgers and sat them on the buns. She brought both plates to the table and sat the one with tomato and lettuce in front of me.

"Thank you," I said.

Teresa put the top bun on her burger, lifted it, and took a bite. I added ketchup and mustard to mine.

I said, "You don't want anything on yours?"

She spoke around a full mouth. "No."

I took a bite and realized mine was rare. I wasn't a fan of rare burgers. I preferred medium-well. Teresa swallowed and took another bite. A mixture of blood and grease splattered on her plate. I'd never known Teresa to eat a burger any other way than well-done. She'd previously given me a hard time, saying medium-well was barbaric.

I said, "You're eating a rare burger?"

She shrugged and continued chewing. Her demeanor was guarded and something felt wrong. I wrote it off to her starting her period even though she wasn't one to suffer irritability or mood swings during her cycle. I knew I would be agitated if I'd planned a getaway for the two of us and my period decided to come early and became an obstacle for intimacy. We finished our dinner in silence.

After dinner we sat on the deck and watched the sunset. Teresa was distant and avoidant of conversation. She stared at the water and I took the opportunity to read while there was still daylight. A few boats passed in the distance, exiting and entering the bay. When the sun slipped over the horizon the lights on the shore became more prominent. Teresa illuminated the outside of the boat so other boats were aware of our presence. The boat's lights were blue and cast eerie shadows. We drank a few more beers and I watched the other boats maneuver in the night to take my mind off the pitch-black and endless appearance of the sea. Eventually we retired for the night. I hoped a good night's sleep would improve Teresa's mood.

***

Teresa woke me from a dreamless sleep. The blue lights barely filtered through the skylight. It took me a few sleepy and alcohol-fueled seconds to realize where I was and what was happening.

Teresa was spooning me. We'd gone to bed in our underwear and the skin of her bare breasts was cool against my back. Her chilly hand wandered into my underwear. She began to work her finger in and out of my vagina.

"Teresa?" I said.

"Hmm."

She removed her finger from inside me and began to rub my clit. The heat of my arousal cleared the sleep and lingering alcohol from my mind. She kissed the back of my neck and licked my shoulder. Her tongue was as cool as her touch. Goosebumps rose on my skin.

I whispered, "Your period . . ."

An orgasm began to build within me. I arched my back and pressed my buttocks into her crotch. She ground her pubis into me. My breathing became loud and the heat of my growing orgasm caused me to break out in a thin layer of sweat.

Teresa whispered, "It was a false alarm." Her words were hoarse and slurred.

The term 'false alarm' meant she had spotted but didn't actually start her period. I thought there was a lot of blood for it to be a false alarm but put it out of my mind.

I gave myself over to the orgasm and bucked with each wave of pleasure as Teresa continued to coax my clit. She made an agreeable sound and delivered more kisses to my neck and shoulder. Once my orgasm had subsided I rolled over to face her.

The faint blue light cast dark shadows and made everything barely visible. Teresa's lips appeared dark. I tried to deliver a kiss but she placed her hands on my shoulders and applied a gentle downward pressure, letting me know what she wanted. I kissed her collarbone and trailed my lips to one of her taut nipples. Her skin was clammy and I wondered if she was running a fever or if it was the effect of the night ocean air. I sucked and licked her nipple while gently pinching the other. Her skin tasted salty. She cooed and tried to grind her pubis into me before grabbing my hair and guiding me farther down her body. I removed her panties and she spread her legs to reveal her shaved but stubbly pussy. She smelled like the ocean. I slipped my hands under her thighs, grabbed her hips, and began to lick her clit. She moaned and held the back of my head while I worked. I slipped two fingers inside of her wet vagina and began to coax her G-spot while I licked her clit. She removed her hand from the back of my head and I looked up at her to see her pinching her own nipples and staring at me with an angry expression. Her look gave me pause. My fingers hit an obstruction inside of her, followed by a sharp prick to the fingertips.

I yelped, withdrew my hand from inside her, and shot up to a kneeling position. I examined my fingers in the scant light. They glistened with Teresa's juices. A darker liquid ran down my hand from the tips of my two wounded fingers.

Teresa sat up without a word. I slipped out of bed and checked my hip on the corner of the kitchen table before fumbling with the light switch by the kitchenette. I squinted against the sudden brightness. I examined my fingers over the sink. Two crescent shaped slits marked either side of each finger. It appeared they'd been pinched by something with enough force to make a clean cut in the skin.

Teresa had slipped out of bed and now stood with her feet planted far from each other at the foot of the bed, fifteen feet from me.

"Something cut me," I said.

I turned my attention to Teresa. In my confused state, it took a few seconds to register her condition. Her skin was a sickly shade of gray and her eyes had become milky. Her lips were crimson and blood dripped down her chin. A black protuberance as long as her torso extended from her vagina. Blood ran down her thighs and a serpent-like thing swayed listlessly back and forth from her vagina. The thing stopped moving and fixed its white eyes on me.

"Teresa?" I whimpered. I gripped the counter and began to shake.

She took a clumsy step. Her voice was thick and didn't belong to her. More blood leaked from her mouth when she spoke. "It's okay." Her tongue was black and pointed and covered in blood. "It doesn't hurt." The creature protruding from her vagina inclined its head toward me and I knew the tip of its tail was acting as her tongue. She took another step toward me.

I fumbled on the counter for something to protect myself with and found nothing. Teresa took another slow step toward me and I wrenched open a kitchen drawer. The drawer came free from the cabinet, sending cooking utensils clattering onto the floor. I spotted a butcher knife and crouched to snatch it up. I stayed on my haunches and pointed the knife at Teresa who'd crossed half the distance between us. She stopped. The creature regarded me with curiosity.

My voice quivered and broke. "Stay away from me!" Tears threatened to spill from my eyes.

I stood and began to reach for the radio mounted on the wall beside the sink. I didn't know how to use it but I had to try. Even a squawk of help would draw attention.

The serpent slid from within Teresa's lifeless body and she crumbled to the floor before I could manage to call for help. A sob of grief escaped me but there was no time. The serpent quickly crossed the distance between us and encircled my leg. I caught it behind its head with my free hand and stopped it six inches from my crotch. I was thankful I had on underwear but knew the material wouldn't stop it if it got loose. Teresa's swimsuit hadn't stopped it. The thing flailed its head back and forth, snapping its jaws and trying to bite me. It was cold and slimy with Teresa's blood. Up close I could see its gills.

I struggled to keep a hold on the creature and cut it with the butcher knife. It kept squirming and repositioning itself around my leg. I sliced wildly, missed it, and cut my thigh. I screamed in frustration and my grip slipped an inch. The end of the creature was coiled around my ankle and the tip of its tail lay on the ground between my feet. Its underbelly was exposed toward the tip of its tail and I could see a slit in its skin. I assumed it was either its anus or sex. The creature slipped more, gaining ground. Another inch and the thing would be able to twist and bite my wrist. In a last desperate attempt I lifted my free leg and brought my heel down as hard as I could on the spot I thought might be vulnerable.

Pain shot up my calf from the impact. The creature screeched, backed out of my hold effortlessly, and let go of my leg. It flopped around wildly on the floor. I didn't wait for it to regain itself.

I ran up the steps for the door, almost fell when I pulled it inward, and slammed it behind me. I peered through the window on the top half of the door and didn't see the creature. My hand lay on the horizontal lever handle and I felt it move. I gripped the handle and pulled the door while trying to see what was happening on the other side. The creature had coiled itself around the handle and was trying to use its weight to open the door.

I held the door handle and began to search the immediate area for a solution. The lighting was terrible. I spotted a dark coil a few feet away, shrieked, and started kicking in its direction, thinking it was another one of the snake-things and it had slithered out of the sea. It took a few seconds for me to realize the motionless coil was a rope.

At a loss, I checked back through the window to find the creature staring at me through the glass. I knew I had to either kill it or get off the boat. For the moment, I had it trapped. If I could keep it contained long enough maybe I could figure out how to steer the boat back to the shore.

I held the doorknob and extended my leg toward the rope. Using my foot I managed to get hold of the rope, pull it toward me, and find the end. I tied the rope around the door handle, held it taut, and started to back away.

The creature reared back and slammed its head into the window. With enough force, the glass would break. I knew my time was limited.

I kept the rope taut and ran toward the side railing. The boat swayed with the ocean. I slipped, my momentum almost launching me over the side. There were smears of something dark on the deck and I knew the self-inflicted knife wound needed staunching soon.

I secured the rope to the rail. The creature banged rhythmically against the glass as I worked. When I was done with the rope I stumbled over to the wheel.

Panic had taken hold of me and my hands shook uncontrollably. I tried to calm myself and think. I knew I had to lift the anchor first. I ran toward the front of the boat and tried to remember what Teresa had done. She had tied a length of rope around the chain to the anchor and attached it to the boat. I struggled with the knots and heard a familiar sound in the distance.

A set of lights bounced rhythmically along the water in the direction of the bay. By the sound of its engine I could tell it was a speed boat. I immediately stopped what I was doing and turned to run toward the wheel. I slipped from the blood on my foot, fell, and hit my chin on the deck. My teeth slammed against each other and sparks of pain illuminated my vision. I forced myself to get up. I couldn't stop because if I did I would end up dead like Teresa. My heart ached, knowing she was gone.

I held the railing and rushed back to the wheel. It dawned on me that the sound of the creature banging its head on the window had ceased. There were smears of blood on the intact window. The thing had probably knocked itself unconscious.

I threw open the bench seat near the wheel and retrieved the orange flare gun box. I tried to remember how Teresa said it worked. The contents of the box spilled onto the deck when I opened it up upside down.

The other boat was picking up speed and would pass in less than a minute. I grabbed the comically fat gun and one of the shells rolled around on the deck. I tried to force the gun open. While fumbling with it I pulled the hammer. The gun opened.

A loud clack drew my attention to the cabin door. The thing had reappeared and was now hammering the window with a butter knife it held in its mouth.

I said, "You've got to be fucking kidding me."

Clack! The tip of the knife put a crack in the window.

Time was up. I had to get off the boat.

I rammed the flare in the gun and snapped it shut. I lifted the gun into the air and pulled the trigger. The flare shot into the night sky, sputtering and flashing. Something deep inside me screamed triumphantly but a rational part said it didn't matter. The boat wouldn't make it. I was going to die. Maybe that was better. I would be with Teresa. I only wished the death wouldn't hurt.

Clack!

The sound of the boat's motor dropped an octave as it slowed and changed course. The vehicle made a beeline toward me. I watched the other boat as the smack of metal on glass continued behind me. The boat was fast but oddly felt as if it were moving in slow motion.

There was nothing I could do but wait to see who made it first. Through the panic of impending death some of my senses came back. I was still holding the flare gun. I flipped the hammer, dumped the spent shell, and dropped to the deck in search of another. I found one rolling back and forth by the wheel and reloaded.

The engine from the approaching boat stopped and it continued to drift toward me.

Another clack produced the sound of breaking glass. The creature had chipped a small hole in the glass at the bottom of the window frame but it wasn't big enough for it to pass through.

"Ahoy!" someone shouted in the distance. "Is everything okay?"

The other boat drifted fifty feet away and was only half the size of Teresa's. The lighting on their craft was yellow and bright. A portly man gripped the railing. A short chubby woman stood beside him. They were both clad in matching windbreakers. I reflexively covered my naked breasts with one arm.

The creature hit the glass again.

I shouted, "I'm being attacked by an animal!" I sobbed. "It killed my girlfriend! Please get me off this boat!"

The man leapt toward the wheel of his boat.

The woman shouted, "Are you a good swimmer?"

Tears sprang from my eyes as the fear of the ocean came crashing back. "I don't want to get in the water! That's where it came from!"

The other boat's engine roared to life and the craft began to close the distance. Another piece of glass fell and shattered. I turned to spot the creature dropping the knife. It cautiously started through the hole it had created. I screamed, pointed the flare gun at the creature, and pulled the trigger. The flare embedded into the door a foot below the window. The creature recoiled from the flare and screeched.

The boat lurched beneath my feet, followed by a crunching noise. I grabbed the railing to keep from falling.

"Bill!" the woman shouted. "You'll sink us both!"

Our boats were touching.

The creature was making its way out and around the flare. I threw the gun at the creature and scrambled over and onto the other boat. The woman had made her way to me. She helped me down onto the deck.

"Go! Go! Go!" I shouted. "Before it gets on your boat!"

"Bill!" the woman shouted.

The boat roared and shot forward. The woman and I fell to the deck. The sound of the two boats scraping against each other briefly filled the night and I thought we might sink.

The sound stopped and we were speeding away.

I sat up and leaned against a bench. The woman beside me did the same, pulling off her windbreaker and wrapping it around me. I began to sob uncontrollably. The boat's speed stabilized enough for us to stand.

The woman said, "We'll get you back to land."

I nodded at her. I searched for the sailboat in the distance and spotted the ghostly blue light. But there was something else about the boat. A large shadow, barely perceptible against the night sky, hung over the boat. The woman followed my gaze. I blinked and tried to decipher what I was seeing. A large serpentine entity protruded from the ocean. Its head hovered a hundred feet above the boat.

"What is that?" the woman said. She yelled at the man, "Look at that!" She pointed at the boat. "What is it?"

The man pulled a lever by the wheel and his boat slowed. He squinted into the night at the other craft. The shadow suddenly darted downward and crashed across the middle of Teresa's boat. The craft buckled and split. The man killed the engine of his boat and the three of us watched as Teresa, the boat that was her second love, and whatever had taken her life, bobbed and twisted and slowly sank into the sea.

ROOM OF WATER

Kathryn E. McGee

Brooke stroked the creatures embedded in the iron frame of the bathroom mirror. They had large eyes and wide-open mouths. Their bodies were amorphous, punctuated by fins and gills. She rubbed her hand over the creatures, around the frame a few times.

Feeling a sting, she pulled away from the mirror. Blood pooled at the tip of her pinky finger. She'd been bitten. That was the first thing she thought—*bitten*. But that couldn't be right. She must have caught her skin on a sharp piece of metal. She put her wound to her mouth and sucked.

The sting persisted.

She held her hand under the sink, flushing it with cool water. Then she dried her wound, wrapped it in a bandage, and applied pressure. She sat down on the edge of the large bathtub and rested, pushing against the painful spot. Her eyes glazed over while she pressed her fingertip, pressed it harder.

Footsteps.

She heard footsteps outside the door and peered out into the master bedroom. The door to the bedroom was closed, but she could tell—could sense—that Colin was approaching from the hallway.

Brooke prepared the greeting she would give her husband when he walked into the room. *Hey, honey.* That's what she would say. Colin would respond with a brief, "Hello," and go on about his business. It would be a normal exchange, a typical moment together, except this time she'd have something more to offer.

What do you think of the new mirror?

When she had seen the mirror at the antique store earlier that day, she'd known it was right—the perfect fit for the master bathroom. She immediately thought of how it would look above the sink, reflecting candlelight beautifully. She heard the sounds of the music she and Colin would play—maybe Sinatra or Coltrane—while together late at night, holding each other in front of the mirror while they waited for the tub to fill with warm, sudsy water. How long had it been since they'd been together this way?

The footsteps in the hallway grew louder and Colin swung the bedroom door open. Brooke leaned out to look at him from where she sat on the edge of the tub.

"Hey, honey," she said, her voice singsong, her mind still fantasizing.

Colin issued a sharp head nod and murmured, "Hello," before his eyes darted around the bedroom. "Have you seen my phone?"

"What do you think of the new bathroom mirror?" Brooke said. "Do you like it? Did I hang it straight?"

"Looks fine. What I really need is to find my phone. Patrick and Liz will be arriving soon. They might need help parking or something. They might need me."

"It's on the nightstand, on your side of the bed."

"That's right." He plucked his phone from the table.

Brooke walked into the bedroom. "You wanna have a glass of wine before they get here?" This was something they used to do, a sort of ritual. When they'd hang out with friends, they'd always reserve time before or after to be together—just the two of them.

"Nah, not really feeling it," he said. "I'll wait for everyone to get here before I start boozing. Don't need the extra carbs, you know?" He patted his ever-expanding belly.

Brooke's eyes left his stomach and found the framed photo of them on the dresser nearby. In the photo they were on vacation in Mexico, back when carbs hadn't mattered, when there hadn't been any sense of stress or worry. She could still feel his hands gripping her beneath the crashing ocean waves, his fingertips stroking her back when she lay on the sand, his fingertips roaming endlessly when they were back in the hotel room in the bathtub together and later again under the sheets. Touching her, always touching her.

You're so beautiful.

That's what he would say.

With his phone in hand, Colin left the room.

Brooke stood there alone and realized she needed to get changed for dinner. She considered what to wear. She and Colin were supposed to be making food together and she was late getting ready, but felt little concern about the time. The truth was she dreaded the night ahead. The people coming over were Colin's friends, not hers. They were at least ten years younger, in their late twenties or early thirties. Colin had met them through work and thought the world of them. They were nice people. Brooke had simply never been able to connect; she found it disorienting to spend an evening pretending that she did.

The doorbell rang.

"I'll get it!" Colin shouted from somewhere outside the bedroom. Brooke heard the front door opening. She breathed in sharply, then reminded herself to take breaths that were even and slow. "Hey, guys!" Colin's voice rang out. "Come on in. How are you doing? What can I getcha to drink? Let me pour you all a glass of wine to start!"

Brooke grabbed a top and a fresh pair of jeans, draping her clothes over the bathtub while she dressed. Feeling drawn to the bathroom mirror again, she changed quickly and stood in front of the glass. Despite her wounded pinky, she fingered the small molded faces and fishtail bodies in the frame, appreciating the way they felt, appreciating their artistry. They made her think of going away somewhere nice on vacation, back to the ocean.

"Brooke, hurry up!" Colin called from outside the door. "Everyone is waiting."

"I'm just changing," she said.

I'll be right there.

That's what she meant to say next.

But the words didn't come.

The creatures in the frame had started to move, small eyes and mouths opening slowly and closing again, repeating this motion in rhythm, the mouths reaching for her and lightly suctioning her skin. The feeling was relaxing, soothing, and even when the bandage on her pinky finger loosened and fell off, she didn't stop—*couldn't stop*—touching the frame.

"Brooke!" Colin's voice broke her concentration.

She pulled her hand away, suddenly aware of the cold tiles on the bathroom floor, of a chill in the air. What had she been doing? What had she been *feeling*? Nothing, nothing had happened. What she'd thought had occurred had been in her mind; there was no other explanation. The creatures in the frame could *not* have just come alive.

She gripped the countertop and closed her eyes. After a few moments she dressed and made her way across the blue woven rug in the bedroom, down the hallway, and into the kitchen. There they were: Liz and Patrick. Patrick and Liz. Brooke felt an intense pulse of pain in her wounded pinky finger—a pulse that shot through her entire body. She tried to smile.

"Hey, guys!" she said, ignoring the pain. Liz and Patrick gave her enthusiastic greetings complete with big hugs, though she'd rather not have touched them. "Who wants a cocktail?" she heard herself ask.

She retrieved the pitcher she'd prepared earlier, and poured four crystal goblets full, adding ice cubes shaped like hearts. Everyone seemed grateful. Even Colin. He put his hands on her shoulders, looked her in the eye and said, "You are *wonderful!*"

He never said this sort of thing when they were alone anymore—only when others were around. She had once asked him why he behaved this way. He had looked at her with a furrowed brow as if she were being deliberately absurd. She'd felt stupid for asking.

Brooke smiled wide before addressing his friends. "What have you guys been up to recently?" Sometimes the sound of her own voice in social situations impressed her. How had she gotten it together so quickly? Just a minute ago, she'd been a wreck—and no one knew.

"Well," Patrick said, "We just got back from visiting my family up north. Stayed there a couple of weeks, if you can believe *that,* and now we're just—"

Patrick's words trailed off. He was talking, talking, talking, but Brooke couldn't hear what he was saying. Her eyes and ears had tuned in almost immediately to another conversation.

Colin had moved with Liz toward the refrigerator. He had taken the young woman a few feet away as if for private talk. Liz was explaining something while pulling a strand of her long auburn hair in front of her face, looking up at Collin through black eyelashes that contrasted sharply with her smooth ivory skin. She wore rose-colored blush and had painted her lips red.

Brooke saw Colin take a strand of Liz's hair and tuck it gently behind her right ear. The hair fell loose and he tucked it behind her ear again. Liz laughed playfully and touched both of Colin's shoulders.

Touch is just a way to show intimacy.

That's what Colin would say.

Brooke couldn't help but watch Liz's hands as they remained, inexplicably, on Colin's shoulders. She couldn't help but watch as Colin touched Liz's forearm, cradling it gently with his right hand while he spoke to her.

Why was he doing this?

Brooke could barely recall the last time he had touched her with such familiarity. Then she remembered Mexico, being under the blanket of the sea, and tried to tell herself he still loved her, that he still *wanted* her. She thought of water rushing around them and the warmth of the summer sun.

Liz giggled and spread her arms wide. She caught Colin up in a hug.

"It's just been way too long," she said. "Way to freakin' long since we've seen you. You know you are one of my *very* favorite people."

Colin tapped Liz on the tip of the nose. "And you are one of mine."

Liz slurped her cocktail. "Delicious." She looked at Brooke and beamed. "Thanks for the *delicious* drink."

"So what are you making for dinner?" Patrick asked Brooke, jumping in as if nothing at all were wrong. Had he been talking this whole time? Had she been talking? Food. She was serving food soon. But what was she serving? She stared at Patrick, her brain suddenly empty. She needed to say something, to say *anything*. Her mind was clouded by what Liz had said.

You know you are one of my very *favorite people.*

Patrick looked at her expectantly.

Her pinky finger throbbed. Her head spun. She tried to find words but could only think of Colin brushing the hair back behind Liz's ear—over and over again. Why couldn't she release her brain from this repeated thought? Why couldn't she speak? The throbbing in her hand turned to knife-stabbing pain. She gagged. Her pinky finger hurt badly, so badly.

The lights in the kitchen flickered.

"What is going on here?" Colin craned his neck to look at the overhead fixture.

The lights flickered again.

With the pain in her finger now dizzying, nearly blinding, Brooke was suddenly overwhelmed with nausea. She had to get out of the room. She dropped the glass she'd been holding, vaguely aware of the sound of the crystal shattering on the kitchen floor as she ran down the hallway to her bedroom.

She shut the door and locked it, then retreated into the bathroom and locked that door as well. Sitting on the edge of the tub, she focused on her breathing—like she'd learned in yoga class. Her nausea went away. Her pain dulled. The desire she'd felt to leave the kitchen was replaced by a desire for something else. She stood up and stared into the mirror. All she wanted to do was reach out and touch it again. Touch the mirror. Touch the mirror.

"Brooke?" She heard Colin calling after her. His voice was distant, locked behind the bathroom and bedroom doors. "Are you okay?"

No, she wanted to say. *Come in here, hold me, help me feel better.*

She couldn't bring herself to speak.

She touched the mirror.

One of the petite faces extended out from the frame. A slender grey body stretched toward her, far enough to reach her pinky. It took her bleeding wound into its open mouth and sucked on her gently. The pain in her finger melted away. Her thoughts went with it.

"Brooke?" Colin called for her. He kept saying her name, asking where she had she gone. Distant and faraway, his voice was drowned out by the sound of the creature sucking on her skin. Then his voice broke through, disrupting her concentration. She heard people laughing, Liz laughing, wine glasses clinking, clattering, *crashing.*

You know you are one of my very *favorite people.*

She pulled her hand away. What had she been doing? Was she going crazy? She searched her eyes in the mirror, saw the lines in her face—the ones that hadn't been there when she'd first met Colin and now framed her eyes and mouth, raked slices into her forehead. She could still picture Liz with her flawless ivory skin, looking up at Colin and beaming. She hated that she'd stayed with Colin for so long—for *decades.*

She hated the way her face looked.

A ceramic candleholder that had been a wedding present sat on the counter nearby and she grabbed it, wielding it overhead. Before she could stop herself, she'd smashed it against the beautiful new mirror. The glass broke and a web of cracks radiated outward. Water began to leak from the cracks and dribble onto the tile floor.

Water?

Brooke stared at the slow trickle, mesmerized. She touched it to see if it was real. It was. So were the sounds the creatures made. The creatures in the frame had begun to moan and cry, their small bodies struggling as if trying to break free of the frame.

What was going on? Had she slipped and hit her head? Was she dreaming?

The trickle grew into a stream and cool water rushed out of the mirror into the bathroom, soaking the bathmat, soaking the floor around her, soaking everything. The water level quickly rose until it poured over the lip of the tub, filling the basin, rose even higher until it was waist deep in the room. The bath towels, trash can, soap dish, and other small items came loose from the floor and countertop, floating around her.

Get out or you'll drown, she thought.

I'm drowning already.

The creatures in the frame writhed, their small bodies finally separating from the frame and turning cerulean blue, with pink and violet streaks at the tip of each fin. Their movements revealed shiny underbellies with rows of suction cups that vibrated and glistened.

One-by-one the creatures dove into the water.

Brooke backed away, stepping carefully into the tub, wading into the furthest corner of the room.

The creatures swam to her. They found the raw end of her pinky finger where they all gathered, suckling her juices and growing larger. She felt suddenly calm, strangely comforted by the feeling of their caress, which made all of the pain in her hand, in her *mind*, release.

She felt herself slipping.

Imagining she was lying back in the tub, her neck supported by the porcelain lip, she closed her eyes…

Colin's voice broke through.

"Brooke? Are you coming back to the party? I picked the bedroom lock, but the bathroom lock is sticking. Let me in."

"I'm not coming back," she said and felt a great sense of relief. Colin didn't reply. Had he heard her? Did it matter?

What mattered were the creatures, sucking harder, piercing more openings in the smooth skin of her stomach and pads of her feet. It felt good. It felt so good to be touched. To be touched *like that* again.

The vibrating suction cups latched onto her new openings. Tingling sensations came and went and then came deeply, filling her entire body, making her every muscle spasm, sending pleasure rushing through and all around her until she could barely breathe.

The water level rose to the height of Brooke's chin.

She focused on the humming sounds, the crashing sounds, the rhythm of the water. She didn't worry about the rising tide or the cold temperature, growing colder with every minute, nor did she worry about her muscles weakening. The creatures sucked harder, vibrated harder, while the faint, faraway sounds of Colin's voice were lost amidst sprays of water and drifting pillows of seaweed.

More creatures gathered, soothing her beneath the water, draining her, and she grew tired. There wasn't much left, not much energy left. Her vision faded and her body grew heavy. She floated until the water rose above her neck and the ceiling of her bathroom disappeared, revealing the orange and yellow glow of sunrise. A man's voice, impossibly beautiful, crooned from a distant place while cool water rushed into her ears and the suckling creatures doubled in size, pulling her under the glassy surface of the sea.

WHERE THE RIVER BENDS

Nate Southard

Something moved in the river. Under the silver disc of the moon, Ray saw the thing break the water's surface. Pale and mottled, shot through with gray veins, it slithered like a snake, but he knew he saw only part of its immense body. Somewhere further upriver, one of them bellowed, a sound somewhere between a roar and the lowing of a gigantic cow.

"You saw one, right?" he asked. "Like, all of one?"

"Not really," Charlie said. "Most of one, I guess. Or at least more than I'd ever seen before."

Ray gave his friend a quick glance, then watched the thing's tail arc out of the river with a splash before disappearing again.

"What was it?" he asked.

"Big. Bigger than anything I've ever seen.

"About six months back. They were still trying to move tugs up and down the river then. Remember how they were saying were searching for a way to get them all out of the water, that they could save the water supply? Just kill all the monsters? Those were the days."

He tried not to think about it, but he recalled the newscasts and the whispers on street corners and in diner booths. Over months, wonder had turned into worry. Into fear and then a sad kind of surrender. Not for the first time, he checked his watch and wondered how close Angie and the others might be.

"It tore a barge and tug apart," Charlie said. "I'm not even sure I saw half of it, but what I did see wrapped around that tug like a boa constrictor. It didn't drag it under, just crushed it. From on the bank--not even down close like this, but at the top of the hill--I could hear all of it cracking and breaking, and I could hear the guys inside screaming."

"Did they jump?"

"Would you?"

"Maybe then. Not now."

"Of course. No point now." Charlie tossed back his head. *"It's the end--"*

"Dude, seriously. You sing that, and I'll knock you on your ass."

"Fine. You sure you want to stand that close?"

Ray looked at the toes of his boots, a good yard from the river's lapping currents. Probably enough distance. Sure. "It's cool," he said.

Charlie stood with his hands in his pockets a moment. "They're having a dance at the high school tonight."

"Really?"

"Yeah. Might as well give the teenagers something to do, right? Act like nothing's different. There's a fallout shelter underneath. They can retreat there before everything hits."

"I guess that makes sense." Ray kicked a stone into the river. The tiny splash calmed him some, but the several larger splashes that followed wiped away the calm. "How long do they have?"

"They?" Charlie asked. "How long do any of us have?"

"Right."

"Less than an hour, probably. New York and Washington are gone. The rest of it's just a matter of catching up."

"Can't believe they're nuking everything."

"Hey, if it kills those things…."

"Right."

For the first time, Ray felt a sharp flutter of nerves in his stomach. Angie had said she was on her way, that she had to pick up Davey and Tara but that she'd be there soon. She hadn't shown yet, though. Looking over his shoulder, he saw his footprints in the mud, winding from the shore through the trees. He hoped she remembered the spot, but she'd only been out once or twice. Maybe she could follow his tracks.

Breathing deep, he told himself it would be fine. Angie would arrive soon, and he wouldn't have to spend his last hour searching frantically for her. A part of him felt guilty. Why hadn't he been with her all day?

"She'll be here," Charlie said. "They all will."

"Hope so." He watched the river's waters. It still flowed along lazily, its black surface unaware the world was ending. For an instant, he wondered if he should be scared, but he laughed off the idea. What was the point of fear, anymore? One more hour, at most, and it wouldn't matter. None of it.

"You think we're doing the right thing?" he asked.

Charlie shrugged. He shook the beer can in his hand and then tossed it when he realized it was empty. "Compared to what? Wait a year? Two? What if it doesn't kill those things? What if it does but there's nothing worth coming back to? I don't like the odds, man. Might as well call it a good run and check out."

"Yeah," Ray said. "You're probably right?"

"Probably?"

"Think that's the best I can do right now."

"Hey!"

Ray turned to find Angie leading the others through the trees. She wore a wool cap and scarf, as though preparing for a long, cold winter, and he couldn't help but laugh at the visual. When she saw his smile, she blew him a kiss. Then, she handed off the twin six-packs in her hands to Charlie.

"You found beer?" he asked.

"I'm resourceful. If there are good times to be found, I will find them."

He threw his arms around her. "I was afraid you wouldn't find us."

"Not a chance. Kiss me."

He pressed his lips to hers, and he felt the heat of tears in his eyes. One hour. Less than that, probably. So many years with the world point guns at each other, arguing over race and religion and politics and money, no one daring to shoot first. Then something bigger than all of it had arrived, and everyone had decided to start firing at once.

"Want a beer?" Angie asked.

Blinking away the water in his eyes, he gave her a smile. "Several."

***

As Ray neared the end of his second beer--warm, but still strangely tasty--he felt the start of a buzz. His last buzz, he knew. Might as well try to savor it some.

He stood at the river's shore, his arm around Angie's waist as they watched the water navigate the bend before them. "I used to come down her to watch tug boats," he said. "Me and my dad."

"You miss him," she said, and her arms tightened around him. He'd mentioned his father a lot over the past few years, and he'd hoped, as everything came to an end, he could maybe forget the man for a while. But the old man crept into his mind, standing in the corner, arms crossed and a smile warming his face.

"Yeah, but...y'know. Other things going on."

"You can say that again."

He gave her a grin. "I'd rather not."

"Hey!" Davey said. "Got an update."

Ray turned, but he wasn't sure he wanted to hear. What did an update really matter? They were down to minutes, maybe. Certainly no more than twenty. His stomach churned, and it wasn't because of the alcohol. The world was ending, taking him--taking all of them--with it.

How many people had died knowing they only had minutes left to live? What would be left for those who made it? Anything?

"You got online?" Charlie asked.

"It's spotty, but yeah." He read off his phone while Tara and Charlie peered over his shoulder. "Dallas, Chicago, Denver. They've been hit. Looks like…Vegas, too."

"Is there even water in Vegas? It's the desert."

Gotta be thorough, I guess."

"Aw, man. I was gonna check out the Luxor this summer."

"Rooms'll be cheap."

Something tugged at Ray's chest. He gave Angie another squeeze and then kissed her forehead. "Hey, guys. Let's do a toast, real quick."

Charlie shot his hand up so fast, beer sprayed into the sky. "To the end of the world!"

"Maybe something a little more serious?" Angie said.

"What's more serious than that?"

Ray stepped toward his friends, he and Angie closing a circle with them. "I'll think of something."

"Better hurry," Tara said.

"Right."

For a moment, he closed his eyes. He tried to gather everything he felt into a tight knot, something he could manage and describe. When he opened his eyes, he found everyone looking at him, waiting. Again, Angie hugged him.

"None of us…." The words died on his tongue, and he took another second to breathe new life into them.

"This…none of us expected it. We didn't think something like this would ever happen. How could we, right? But we're here. It's out last night together. Out last few minutes, even." He gestured at the ashes surrounding them. "It's already started, but it's going to end soon. I'm not happy about it, and I know none of you are. But I'm glad we're all here. I'm glad we're doing this together. If they have to blow up the world to save it, there's no one else I'd rather be with when they light the fuse. Cheers."

Cans touched with a flat, percussive sound, and Ray knocked back the last of his beer. In the darkness, something groaned. Again, he heard something break through the water's surface. Once he kissed Angie's lips, he gave the group a smile.

"Let's go swimming."

"You're not serious," Davey said. For the first time, he looked a little scared.

"Not even a little."

Tara stared past him, watching the rippling blackness with frightened eyes. She took half a step back from the river. "It's the whole reason--"

"I know. We all know that. And now...minutes? What's the point?"

"Screw it," Angie said. "I'm in. Let's go." She kicked off her shoes one at a time, peeled off her shirt.

Ray followed. The buzz running through his system was electric pleasure, a crackling numbness that pulled his lips into a smile and drug laughter up from his belly. As he climbed out of his jeans, he made sure he didn't look at the river. Already, he could hear the water churning somewhere beyond their laughter. The things under the surface knew they were coming. And those things were happy. And probably hungry.

"Are you sure?" Angie asked. They stepped to the river's edge.

Cold water lapped at his toes. His hand found Angie's, their fingers intertwining. He gave her hand a squeeze. "Yeah. Let's swim."

"Whoo!" Davey let out a second joyous cry as he charged into the water, his splashing loud and celebratory. Charlie and Tara followed. Together, they released a chorus into a sky.

Ray and Angie entered more slowly. One step at a time, the walked into the river. He felt the waves lap at his ankles. Then, his calves. More than once, his fingers tightened reflexively. Before them, the river churned.

"Do you think it'll hurt?" Angie asked.

"It all hurts," he said. "At least we get to pick."

"Good point." Beneath their feet, rocks gave way to soft soil, sloped down as they found themselves waist-deep in the river.

"Oh, shit," Davey said. He tread water a dozen yards in front of them. "I can feel them. Sliding past my legs."

He disappeared in a sudden rush, yanked below the surface before he could draw breath to scream. The surface rippled a little and then fell still.

Tara managed a scream. Then, her breath came in a series of sharp burst. "Here it comes," she said. "Here it--"

Something yanked her under.

Angie released his hand and started treading water. Ray followed. "Look at me," he said. "Nowhere else."

"I'll try."

Something rumbled in the distance. A bright light bloomed over the horizon.

"This is it," she said.

214

"I know." He peeked past her shoulder. Charlie was gone. In his place, the water slid over itself. Something pale and slick broke the surface, a large piece of something even larger. A light like fire shimmered off its surface, and then the thing dove beneath the river's plane.

Ray listened to the coming rush of fire and destruction, and he wondered if the thing in the river would take them before the wave of pure oblivion. All the world ending, a terrible race toward the finale.

Something slipped past his leg, started wrapping around it.

"I love you," he said.

Angie smiled. "I love you, too."

She disappeared under the water, and Ray took his last breath.

THE END

CHECK OUT OTHER GREAT DEEP SEA THRILLERS

PREHISTORIC BEASTS AND WHERE TO FIGHT THEM
by Hugo Navikov

IN THE DEPTHS, SOMETHING WAITS ...

Acclaimed film director Jake Bentneus pilots a custom submersible to the bottom of Challenger Deep in the Pacific, the deepest point of any ocean of Earth. But something lurks at the hot hydrothermal vents, a creature—a dinosaur—too big to exist.

Gigadon.

It not only exists, but it follows him, hungrily, back to the surface. Later, a barely living Bentneus offers a $1 billion prize to anyone who can find and kill the monster. His best bet is renowned ichthyopaleontologist Sean Muir, who had predicted adapted dinosaurs lived at the bottom of the ocean.

MEGALODON: APEX PREDATOR
by S.J. Larsson

English adventurer Sir Jeffery Mallory charters a ship for a top secret expedition to Antarctica. What starts out as a search and capture mission soon turns into a terrifying fight for survival as the crew come face to face with the fiercest ocean predator to have ever existed- Carcharodon Megalodon. Alone and with no hope of rescue the crew will need all their resources if they are to survive not only a 60 foot shark but also the harsh Antarctic conditions. Megalodon: Apex Predator is a deep-sea adventure filled with action, twists and savage prehistoric sharks.

CHECK OUT OTHER GREAT DEEP SEA THRILLERS

HELL'S TEETH
by Paul Mannering

In the cold South Pacific waters off the coast of New Zealand, a team of divers and scientists are preparing for three days in a specially designed habitat 1300 feet below the surface.

In this alien and savage world, the mysterious great white sharks gather to hunt and to breed.

When the dive team's only link to the surface is destroyed, they find themselves in a desperate battle for survival. With the air running out, and no hope of rescue, they must use their wits to survive against sharks, each other, and a terrifying nightmare of legend.

MONSTERS IN OUR WAKE
by J.H. Moncrieff

In the idyllic waters of the South Pacific lurks a dangerous and insatiable predator; a monster whose bloodlust and greed threatens the very survival of our planet...the oil industry. Thousands of miles from the nearest human settlement, deep on the ocean floor, ancient creatures have lived peacefully for millennia. But when an oil drill bursts through their lair, Nøkken attacks, damaging the drilling ship's engine and trapping the desperate crew. The longer the humans remain in Nøkken's territory, struggling to repair their ailing ship, the more confrontations occur between the two species. When the death toll rises, the crew turns on each other, and marine geologist Flora Duchovney realizes the scariest monsters aren't below the surface.

CHECK OUT OTHER GREAT DEEP SEA THRILLERS

LOCH NESS REVENGE
by Hunter Shea

Deep in the murky waters of Loch Ness, the creature known as Nessie has returned. Twins Natalie and Austin McQueen watched in horror as their parents were devoured by the world's most infamous lake monster. Two decades later, it's their turn to hunt the legend. But what lurks in the Loch is not what they expected. Nessie is devouring everything in and around the Loch, and it's not alone. Hell has come to the Scottish Highlands. In a fierce battle between man and monster, the world may never be the same. Praise for THEY RISE : "Outrageous, balls to the wall...made me yearn for 3D glasses and a tub of popcorn, extra butter!" – The Eyes of Madness "A fast-paced, gore-heavy splatter fest of sharksploitation." The Werd "A rocket paced horror story. I enjoyed the hell out of this book" Shotgun Logic Reviews.

TERROR FROM THE DEEP
by Alex Laybourne

When deep sea seismic activity cracks open a world hidden for millions of years, terrifying leviathans of the deep are unleashed to rampage off the coast of Mexico. Trapped on an island resort, MMA fighter Troy Deane leads a small group of survivors in the fight of their lives against pre-historic beasts long thought extinct. The terror from the deep has awoken, and it will take everything they have to conquer it.

CHECK OUT OTHER GREAT
DEEP SEA THRILLERS

SEA RAPTOR
by John J. Rust

From terrorist hunter to monster hunter! Jack Rastun was a decorated U.S. Army Ranger, until an unfortunate incident forced him out of the service. He is soon hired by the Foundation for Undocumented Biological Investigation and given a new mission, to search for cryptids, creatures whose existence has not been proven by mainstream science. Teaming up with the daring and beautiful wildlife photographer Karen Thatcher, they must stop a sea monster's deadly rampage along the Jersey Shore. But that's not the only danger Rastun faces. A group of murderous animal smugglers also want the creature. Rastun must utilize every skill learned from years of fighting, otherwise, his first mission for the FUBI might very well be his last.

OCEAN'S HAMMER
by D.J. Goodman

Something strange is happening in the Sea of Cortez. Whales are beaching for no apparent reason and the local hammerhead shark population, previously believed to be fished to extinction, has suddenly reappeared. Marine biologists Maria Quintero and Kevin Hoyt have come to investigate with a television producer in tow, hoping to get footage that will land them a reality TV show. The plan is to have a stand-off against a notorious illegal shark-fishing captain and then go home.

Things are not going according to plan.

There is something new in the waters of the Sea of Cortez. Something smart. Something huge. Something that has its own plans for Quintero and Hoyt.